***"I***
***Ke***

"Tha ... agic.

"I knc

"It's a suicide mission."

"I know that, too."

Angrily Linc turned his back on her. Damn! She *would* gaze up at him with that melting look, just as she had at the tavern last night. That look had made him throw caution to the wind, say "to hell with common sense" and follow her out of the bar.

Linc grudgingly admired Kerry's spirit. But it wasn't her spirit that he wanted to have warm and wanting beneath him. It was her body. He wanted to be wrapped in those shapely limbs and long, silky hair. He knew he was going to pay dearly for his ill-advised decision.

"Let's go," he said.

*Dear Reader:*

*We at Silhouette are very excited to bring you a NEW reading* **Sensation**. *Look out for the four books which will appear in our new Silhouette* **Sensation** *series every month. These stories will have the high quality you have come to expect from Silhouette, and their varied and provocative plots will encourage you to explore the wonder of falling in love – again and again!*

*Emotions run high in these drama-filled novels. Greater sensual detail and an extra edge of realism intensify the hero and heroine's relationship so that you cannot help but be caught up in their every change of mood.*

*We hope you enjoy this new* **Sensation** – *and will go on to enjoy many more.*

*We would love to hear your comments about our new line and encourage you to write to us:*


Jane Nicholls
Silhouette Books
PO Box 236
Thornton Road
Croydon
Surrey
CR9 3RU

# ERIN ST. CLAIRE

# The Devil's Own

Silhouette Sensation

*First published in Great Britain in 1988*
*by Silhouette Books, Eton House, 18–24 Paradise Road,*
*Richmond, Surrey TW9 1SR*



ISBN 0 373 57403 7

*18–8809*

*Made and printed in Great Britain*

**Other Silhouette Books by Erin St. Claire**

*Silhouette Desire*

Not Even for Love
Seduction by Design
A Kiss Remembered
Words of Silk

# *Chapter 1*

He was drunk and, consequently, just what she needed.

She studied him through the smoky, dusty haze of the *cantina*, where he sat on a bar stool, nursing his drink. The glass was chipped, its dark amber contents cloudy. He didn't seem to notice as he frequently raised it to his lips. He sat with his knees widespread, his head bent low between hunched shoulders, his elbows propped on the greasy surface of the bar.

The tavern was crowded with soldiers and the women who entertained them in rooms upstairs. Squeaky fans, rotating desultorily overhead, barely stirred the thick pall of tobacco smoke. The cloying essence of cheap perfume mixed with the stench of the unwashed bodies of men who had spent days in the jungle.

Laughter was everywhere, but the mood wasn't particularly jovial. The soldiers' eyes didn't smile. There was an aura of desperation to their merrymaking. They took their fun as they took everything else, violently.

They were young for the most part—tough, surly men who lived on a razor's edge between life and death every day. Most wore the uniform of the army of the current military regime. But whether they were locals or international mercenaries, all had that same hard look about their eyes. They were full of suspicion. Wariness shadowed every grin.

The man Kerry Bishop had her sights on was no exception. He wasn't Latin—he was American by the looks of him. Hard, well-defined biceps bulged beneath his sleeves, which had been rolled up so tightly they encircled his arms like rope. His dark hair hung long and shaggy over his shirt collar.

The portion of his jaw Kerry could see was covered with several days' growth of beard. That could be either a benefit or a handicap to her plan. A benefit because the partial beard would help disguise his face, and a handicap because few officers in the regular army would go that many days without a shave. El Presidente was a stickler for good grooming among his officers.

Well, she'd just have to chance it. Of the lot, this man was still her best bet. He not only looked the most inebriated, but the most disreputable—lean and hungry and totally without principle. Once he was sober, he would no doubt be easy to buy.

She was getting ahead of herself. She had to get him out of there first. When would the driver of that military truck, the careless one who had negligently left his keys in the ignition, return to find that the keys were gone? At any moment, he could come looking for them.

The keys now rattled in the pocket of Kerry's skirt each time she moved her legs on her journey across the room toward the man drinking alone at the bar. She dodged couples dancing to the blaring music, warded off a few clumsy passes and averted her eyes from the couples who were too carried away by passion to bother seeking privacy.

After spending almost a year in Montenegro, nothing should surprise her. The nation was in the throes of a bloody civil war, and war often reduced human beings to animals. But what she saw some of the couples doing right out in the open brought hot color to her cheeks.

Setting her jaw firmly and concentrating only on her purpose for being there, she moved closer to the man at the bar. The closer she got, the surer she became that he was exactly what she needed.

He was even more fearsome up close than he had been at a distance. He wasn't actually drinking, but angrily tossing the liquor down his throat. He wasn't tasting it. He wasn't drinking for pleasure. He wasn't there to have a good time, but to vent his anger over something. Perhaps to blot some major upset from his mind? Had someone welshed on a deal? Double-crossed him? Short-changed him?

Kerry hoped so. If he were strapped for cash he'd be much more receptive to the deal she had to offer him.

A pistol had been shoved into the waistband of his fatigue pants. There was a long, wicked machete holstered against his thigh. At his feet, surrounding the bar stool, were three canvas bags. They were so packed with the tools of his trade, that the seams of the bags were strained. Kerry shuddered to think of the destruction his private stash of weaponry was capable of. That was probably one reason why he drank alone and went unmolested. In a place like this, fights frequently broke out among the hot-blooded, trigger-happy men. But no one sought either conversation or trouble with this one who sat on the last bar stool in the row.

Unfortunately for Kerry, it was also the seat farthest from the building's only exit. There would be no slipping out a back door. She would have to transport him from the rear corner to the door. To succeed in getting him to leave with her, she would have to be her most convincing.

With that in mind, she took a deep breath, closed the remaining distance between them, and sat down on the bar stool next to his, which fortuitously was vacant. His profile was as rugged and stony as a mountain range. Not a soft, compassionate line in evidence. She tried not to think of that as she spoke to him.

"A drink, *señor*?" Her heart was pounding. Her mouth was as dry as cotton. But she conjured up an alluring smile and tentatively laid her right hand on his left one.

She was beginning to think he hadn't heard her. He just sat there, staring down into his empty glass. But, just when she was about to repeat her suggestion, he turned his head slightly and looked down at her hand where it rested on top of his.

His, Kerry noticed, was much larger than hers. It was wider by half an inch on either side, and her fingertips extended only as far as his first knuckles. He was wearing a watch. It was black, with a huge, round face and lots of dials and gadgetry. He wore no rings.

He stared at their hands for what seemed like an eternity to Kerry, before his eyes followed her arm up, slowly, to her shoulder, then up and right, to her face. A cigarette was dangling between his sullen lips. He stared at her through the curling, bluish-gray smoke.

She had practiced her smile in a mirror to make sure she was doing a fair imitation of the women who solicited in the *cantinas*. Eyes at half-mast. Lips moist and slightly parted. She knew she had to get that come-hither smile right. Everything hinged on her being convincing.

But she never got to execute that rehearsed, sultry smile. It, like most everything in her brain, vaporized when she gazed into his face for the first time. Her heavily rouged lips parted all right, but of their own accord and with no direction from her. She drew in a quick little gasp. The fluttering of her eyelashes was involuntary, not affected.

His face was a total surprise. She had expected ugliness. He was quite good-looking. She had expected unsightly traces of numerous military campaigns. He had but one scar, a tiny one above his left eyebrow. It was more interesting than unsightly. His face didn't have the harsh stamp of brutality she had anticipated, only broodiness. And his lips weren't thin and hard with insensitivity, but full and sensual.

His eyes weren't blank, as were those of most of the men who killed for hire. His eyes, even though they were fogged with alcohol, burned with internal fires that Kerry found even more unsettling than the heatless glint of indifference. Nor did he smell of sweat. His bronzed skin was glistening with a fine sheen of perspiration, but it gave off the scent of soap. He had recently washed.

Quelling her shock and trepidation—because for some strange reason, his lack of standard looks frightened her more than reassured her—she met his suspicious stare steadily. She forced herself to audition that seductive smile she'd spent hours perfecting and repeated her request as she pressed his hand.

"Beat it."

His abrupt words took her so by surprise that she actually flinched, almost falling off the slick, vinyl pad of the bar stool. He turned his head forward again and jerked his hand from beneath hers to remove the cigarette from his mouth. He ground it out in the overflowing ashtray.

Kerry was dumbfounded. Was she that unappealing? Weren't mercenaries supposed to have the appetites of animals? And wasn't that voraciousness particularly true of their sexual appetites? Fathers hid their daughters from them in dread of the unthinkable. Men protected their wives at all costs.

Now, when Kerry offered herself to one, he had ungraciously said, "Beat it," and dismissed her with a turn of his head. She must look worse than she thought. Her year in the jungle had apparently taken its toll in ways she hadn't been aware of.

True, her hair had forgotten the luxury of a hot-oil treatment. Mascara and moisturizing face cream existed for her only in another lifetime. But how attractive did a woman have to be to tempt a man with a bestial sex drive?

She weighed her options. Her plan was foolhardy at best. Success was improbable. It would be risky under the best of circumstances. It would work only if her "recruit" was cooperative. If he wasn't, it would be almost impossible to do what she had set out to do that night.

She glanced over her shoulder, wondering if she should desert this man in favor of another prospect. No. Her time was limited and rapidly running out. Whoever had left that truck parked outside could return at any moment. He might demand a shakedown of everybody in the *cantina* until the missing keys were found. Or he might have a spare set of keys. In either event, she wanted to be long gone before he returned. The truck was just as important as the man. She had to steal it, and now was the time.

Besides, she told herself, this candidate was her first and best choice. He fit all the criteria she had outlined in her mind. He was drunk, unscrupulous and obviously down on his luck.

"Please, *señor*, one drink." Pushing all caution aside, she laid her hand on his thigh near the lethal machete. He mumbled something. *"¿Qué?"* She used her whispered question as an opportunity to move closer to him.

"No time."

*"Por favor."*

He looked at her again. She made a motion that sent the scarf sliding off her head and from around her shoulders. She had previously decided to take off the scarf only as a last resort. When she had told Joe to find her a dress like the women in the taverns wore, she hadn't counted on him being so knowledgeable about such things.

From a clothesline, he had stolen the dress she now had on. It was faded. The cloth was thin from years of wear and stone washing. The red floral print was lurid and tacky. The woman who had owned the dress had been a size larger than Kerry. The ruffled shoulder straps wouldn't stay put and the bodice gaped open where it should have been filled.

She wanted to pull the dress against her chest and cover herself, but she forced herself to remain still. Rigid with shame, she let his gaze travel all the way from her exposed shoulder to her sandaled feet. He took his time. While Kerry burned with humiliation, his eyes drifted across her partially exposed breasts and down to her lap, which he studied for an indecently long time, then down her shapely, bare legs and feet to the tip of her toes.

"One drink," he said thickly.

Kerry barely kept herself from slumping with relief. She smiled flirtatiously as he called out for the querulous bartender to pour them two drinks. They watched each other while he carried over two glasses and a bottle of the potent, local liquor. The bartender poured the drinks. Kerry's mercenary, without taking his eyes off her face, fished in his pants pocket and slapped two bills onto the bar. Money in hand, the bartender shuffled off, leaving them alone.

The mercenary picked up his glass, tipped it toward Kerry in a mocking salute, and drank it all in one swallow.

She picked up her own glass. If it had been rinsed out since last being used, she would consider herself lucky. Trying not to think about that, she raised it to her lips and took a sip. The liquor tasted like industrial strength disinfectant. It took a tremendous amount of willpower not to spray it into the roughly hewn, handsome face of her mercenary. She swallowed the ghastly stuff. Her throat rebelled instantly. If she had gargled thumbtacks, it couldn't have hurt more. Tears flooded her eyes.

His eyes narrowed suspiciously, emphasizing the squint lines radiating from their outer corners. "You're not a drinker. Why'd you come over here?"

She pretended not to understand his English. Smiling, she covered his hand with her own again, and tilted her head so that her dark hair spilled across the shoulder left bare by the slipping strap. "I love you."

He merely grunted indifferently. His eyes slid closed. Panicked, Kerry thought he was about to pass out.

"We go?" she said quickly.

"Go? With you? Hell no. I told you I haven't got time even if I wanted to."

She wet her lips frantically. What was she going to do? *"Por favor."*

He focused his bleary eyes on her face, particularly on her mouth when she used her tongue to moisten her lips. His gaze moved down and remained fixedly on her breasts. Because she was so agitated and afraid that her mission would be thwarted, her breasts rose and fell rapidly beneath the tasteless dress.

Kerry didn't know whether to be glad or frightened when she saw his eyes glaze with passion. He rubbed one hand up and down his own thigh and she knew he was thinking about touching her. All his unconscious movements were indicative of his mounting arousal. That's what she had wanted, but it terrified her, too. She was playing with fire. If she didn't watch it, it could burn out of her control.

Almost before she had completed the thought, his hand shot out and grabbed her around the neck. She wasn't prepared for the sudden movement and had no time to counter it before he hauled her off the bar stool and against him.

His knees were opened. She landed against him solidly. Her breasts came only to the middle of his chest, which was as firm as it had appeared. Something hard gouged her stomach. She fervently hoped it was the butt of the pistol tucked into his waistband.

Before Kerry could get her bearings, or even gasp in astonishment, his mouth covered hers. It moved hotly and hungrily. His whiskers scraped the delicate skin around her lips, but it wasn't an entirely unpleasant sensation.

Every instinct urged her to resist him. But then her common sense asserted itself. She was supposed to be a prostitute soliciting customers. It wouldn't be in character to stave off the advances of a prospective source of income.

So she let herself become pliant.

The shock of having his tongue spear through her lips almost sent her over the edge of reason. It thrust deeply into her mouth as though searching for something. Its assault was wildly erotic. Kerry's reaction was to clutch handfuls of his shirt. His arms wrapped around her waist. He continued to kiss her, pulling her ever closer, until her back was painfully arched and she could scarcely breathe.

At last, he lifted his mouth from hers and pressed it, open, against her throat. Kerry's head fell back and her eyes rolled toward the ceiling. The lazily circling ceiling fan made her dizzier than she already was. She felt as though she were spinning in slow, diminishing circles, and that when she reached the center of this maddening vortex, she was going to explode. Yet she was powerless to extricate herself from it.

The mercenary slid his hands below her waist. One boldly fondled her bottom. The other came around and stroked the side of her breast. Kerry endured the caresses, but her breathing was quick and shallow. He muttered something so blatantly sexual, so disturbingly accurate, she wished she hadn't heard or understood him.

Nuzzling her neck in the sensitive spot just below her ear, he mumbled, "Okay, *señorita*, you've got a customer. Where to? Upstairs? Let's go."

He stood up and swayed on his feet. Kerry's equilibrium, being what it was at the moment, forced them to cling to each other until she regained her balance.

*"Mí casa."*

"Your house?" he grumbled.

*"Sí, sí,"* she said bobbing her head enthusiastically. Not giving him an opportunity to argue, she bent down and picked up one of the canvas bags at their feet. It was so heavy, it almost tore her arm from its socket. She could barely lift the bag, but managed to work the leather strap up her arm and over her shoulder.

"Jus' leave that crap and I'll—"

"No!" She bent down to pick up another of the three bags. In rapid Spanish, she began warning him about thieves and the danger of weapons getting into the hands of enemies.

"Stop that damned jibberish. I can't unnerschtand... Oh, hell. I changed my mind. No time."

"No. Back soon."

As she bent down to assist him in picking up the last of the heavy bags, she caught his eyes on the gaping front of her dress. Though she blushed beat red, she smiled at him seductively and looped her free arm through his, pressing her breasts against his upper arm the way she'd seen prostitutes do to their customers. Mutely, he fell into place beside her.

They staggered their way through the bar, which, if anything, had become even more crowded since she had come in. The mercenary drunkenly stumbled at Kerry's side. She nearly buckled beneath his weight combined with the heavy bag she was carrying over her shoulder. The other two were hooked over his shoulders, but he seemed impervious to them.

When they were almost to the door, a soldier who looked like he'd been weaned on nitroglycerin, stumbled against her and grabbed her arm. He made an obscene proposition to her in Spanish. She shook her head vehemently and splayed her hand on the mercenary's chest. The soldier looked ready to argue, but he happened to catch the fierce, possessive gleam in the mercenary's eyes and wisely changed his mind.

Kerry congratulated herself for making such a good choice. Her mercenary inspired fear in even the most fearsome. No one else accosted them on their way out of the *cantina*.

Her lungs were starved for air, and she greedily sucked it in. The tropical air was heavy and humid, but it was brisk and bracing compared to that inside the *cantina*.

Kerry was grateful for it. It cleared her head. She wished she could rest, wished she could say, "Thank God that's over." But there was still an awesome task facing her. The pickup had been easy compared to what lay ahead.

She practically dragged her staggering escort toward the military truck, which, she was grateful to see, was still parked beneath the impenetrable shadows of an almond tree. She propped the professional soldier against the side of the Japanese-made pickup while she opened the door. The truck, having once belonged to a fruit vendor, now had the government insignia stenciled over the farmer's logo.

She pushed the incoherent mercenary inside the passenger side door and closed it before he could fall out. Then, furtively glancing over her shoulder, she lifted the bags of weapons and ammunition into the bed of the pickup. At any moment she expected to hear the rat-a-tat of a machine gun and feel bullets ripping through her body. In Montenegro, they shot first and asked questions later.

She threw a tarp over the bags and climbed into the cab. Either her mercenary hadn't noticed that the truck belonged to the regular army, or he didn't care. As soon as she closed the door behind herself, he pounced on her.

He kissed her again. His desire hadn't abated. Instead, it had increased. The cooler outdoor air, which had cleared her head, seemed to have done the same for him. This wasn't the haphazard kiss of a drunk. This was the kiss of a man who knew exactly what he was doing, and knew how to do it well.

His tongue pressed insistently against her lips until they opened, then it rubbed sleekly against hers. His hands were busy. His caresses kept her gasping with shock and outrage.

*"Por favor,"* she whispered urgently, slapping his hands away and dodging his mouth.

"Whatsamatter?"

"*Mí casa*. We go."

She reached into the pocket of her skirt and produced a key. She crammed it into the ignition and started the truck, trying to ignore the nibbling he was doing on her neck and around her ear. She felt his teeth against her skin. Despite the muggy heat, her arms broke out in goose bumps.

Kerry put the truck in reverse and backed away from the tavern. The ramshackle building seemed to vibrate with raucous laughter and throbbing music. She braced herself for shouting and gunfire, but the truck moved into the street unnoticed.

Kerry was tempted to leave the headlights turned off, but decided against it. It would arouse suspicion for a military truck to drive through the city streets without its headlights on. And, it would be hazardous to drive without lights on the rutted lanes that were likely to be littered with battle debris. So she turned on the headlights. They threw light onto the war-scarred commercial buildings and shuttered housing. Even in the darkness, which was flattering, the capital city was a depressing sight.

Getting out of the city was a problem that Kerry had spent hours mulling over. No one entered or left it without having to drive through a military checkpoint. After running several reconnaissance missions, Kerry had selected the gate she would drive through now. It was one of the busiest checkpoints. Had she picked one of the less-traveled roads, the guards might be more thorough. They would more than likely stop and search a military truck driven by a woman. At the busy gate she had chosen, she would probably get no more than a cursory inspection. At least, that's what she was hoping for.

She mentally went over her plan and what she intended to say one more time.

However, it was difficult to concentrate on anything. She hadn't picked up a belligerent drunk or a funny drunk. She had picked up an amorous drunk. Between mutterings about not having much time, he planted ardent kisses on her neck and chest.

She nearly steered the truck off the road when he slipped his hand under her skirt and between her knees. There was no way she could continue to work the clutch and accelerator with her knees clamped together. She had no choice but to allow his strong fingers to curl around the lower portion of her thigh and tease the smooth underside of her knee.

She had almost adjusted to that when his hand began to reach higher. Each touch was a jolt to her system. The floor of her stomach dropped away, and she closed her eyes for a fraction of a second when he lightly squeezed a handful of her inner thigh. The skirt of her dress inched higher. Most of it was already bunched up in her lap.

*"Señor, por favor."* She tried to work her leg free of his questing hand.

He muttered something that sounded like "Need a woman," but Kerry wasn't sure. Knowing that they were only a few blocks from the crucial checkpoint, she pulled the truck over to the side of the road and let it idle.

"Please, *señor*, put this on." She reached beneath the seat where she had previously stowed the jacket and cap that she had found lying on the seat of the truck.

He didn't seem to notice her improved English or the absence of an accent, but he blinked at her stupidly. "Huh?"

She draped the military jacket over his shoulders. The jacket didn't quite accommodate their breadth, but all she needed for the guard to see was the officer's rank. The badge had been ineptly embroidered onto the sleeve, which

Kerry made certain was visible. She plopped the cap down onto the mercenary's head and adjusted it, while he just as earnestly tried to lower the shoulder straps of her dress.

"Good grief," she muttered in disgust as she pulled them back up onto her shoulders, "you're an animal." Then she remembered that she was supposed to be a whore accustomed to being manhandled. She laid her hand against his whiskered cheek and smiled in a manner that she hoped was beguiling and full of lewd promise. In melodious Spanish she told him he was a lecherous pig, but made the insult sound like a lover's enticement.

Engaging the gears of the truck again, she drove the remaining blocks to the checkpoint.

There were two cars ahead of her. The driver of the first was arguing with the guard. Good. He would welcome a military truck because there would be no hassle.

"Whas goin' on?"

The mercenary raised his head and blinked, trying to see through the dirty windshield, upon which a thousand insects had given their lives. Patting his head back into place on her shoulder, Kerry told him to leave everything to her, that they were almost there. His head lolled against her shoulder as she drove the truck up to the barricade.

The guard, no older than sixteen, sauntered toward the driver's side and shone a flashlight directly into her face. She forced herself to smile. *"Buenos noches."* She lowered her voice to a sexy, husky pitch.

*"Buenos noches,"* the guard responded suspiciously. "What's wrong with the captain?"

She clicked her tongue against the roof of her mouth. "He had too much to drink. Poor man. He's a brave soldier, but he is defeated by a bottle."

"Where are you taking him?"

"Out of the kindness of my heart, I'm driving him to my house." She winked seductively. "He asked me to nurse him through the night."

The guard grinned at her. His eyes moved over the slumping occupant of the truck. Assured that the officer was unconscious, he asked, "Why bother with him? Wouldn't you rather have a real man?" He made a crude reference to the dimensions of his manhood, which Kerry found not only unbelievable, but revolting.

Nonetheless, she simpered and lowered her lashes. "I'm sorry, but the captain has already paid me for tonight. Perhaps another time."

"Perhaps," he said cockily. "If I can afford you."

She tapped his hand flirtatiously. Making a moue of regret, she waved goodbye and put the truck into gear. The young guard commanded his partner at the checkpoint to raise the gate and she drove through it.

For several miles, Kerry tenaciously gripped the steering wheel and kept her eyes on the rearview mirror as much as she did on the winding road ahead. When it became apparent that no one was following her, she began to tremble in delayed reaction.

She had done it!

The mercenary had stayed blessedly quiet during the entire exchange with the guard. Now they were on their way and no one was even chasing them. She made a wide loop around the city and took the turnoff, which led straight into the jungle. Soon the tops of the trees interlaced over the road to form a leafy tunnel.

The road narrowed and grew bumpier with each passing mile. The mercenary's head grew heavy where it lay against her breasts. He weighted down the entire right side of her body. She tried to shove him away several times, but she couldn't budge him. Finally she gave up, concluding that having him asleep against her was better than having to fight off his aggressive love play.

She gave considerable thought to stopping before she reached the place she had sighted earlier, but talked herself out of it. The more distance she put between the mercenary and the city tonight, the more bargaining power she would have tomorrow. So she kept driving over the corrugated road with the man's head bouncing heavily against her at every chuckhole.

She became sleepy. The monotony of the headlights being mirrored off the encroaching jungle was mesmerizing. She became so drowsy that she almost missed her turn. The moment she saw the slight break in the solid wall of trees, she reacted quickly and whipped the steering wheel to the left, then pulled the truck to a stop and cut the engine.

Jungle birds, roosting in the trees overhead, loudly protested this nighttime intrusion, then resettled. The quiet darkness enclosed the small truck like a black velvet fist.

Sighing tiredly, Kerry shoved the man off her. She arched her back, stretching out the aching muscles. She rolled her head around her shoulders. Her relief at having accomplished her mission was profound. There was nothing to do then but wait until daylight.

But the mercenary had something else in mind.

Before she could brace herself for it, he smothered her in an embrace. His nap seemed to have revived him. His kisses were more fervent than ever. While his tongue playfully flicked over her lips, his hands pulled down the oversized bodice of her dress. He plunged his hand inside and scooped up her breast.

"No!" Garnering her strength, Kerry placed her hands against his shoulders and shoved with all her might. He went toppling over backward and his head hit the dashboard. He rolled to his side and sagged forward. The only thing that prevented him from slumping all the way to the floorboard was his size. His wide shoulders pinned him between the dashboard and the seat.

He didn't move. Didn't make a sound.

Horrified, Kerry covered her mouth and waited several breathless moments. He remained motionless. "Oh, Lord, I've killed him."

She opened the door of the truck. The overhead light came on. When her eyes had adjusted to the sudden brightness, she stared down at the mercenary. Tentatively she poked at him. He groaned.

Her fearful expression turned into one of disgust. He wasn't dead, just dead drunk and passed out.

She tried to pull him up by his shirt collar, but couldn't. Levering herself up on her knees, she tugged on his shoulders until he flopped back, settling into the corner of the cab formed by the passenger door and the back of the seat.

His head was bent over. One cheek was resting against his shoulder. He'd have a crick in his neck by morning. Good. Kerry hoped he did. Anyone who drank himself into a stupor like that deserved to reap the dire consequences.

But his position made him look much less threatening. His eyelashes were long and curled, she noticed, incongruent with the masculinity of his face. With the dome light shining on him, she saw that his hair was dark brown, but streaked with reddish highlights, and that beneath his deep tan, he was freckled across his cheekbones.

He was breathing deeply through his mouth. His lips were slightly parted. With that sulky, full, lower lip, it was no wonder he could kiss— She yanked her mind away from any thought of the way he'd kissed her.

Before she started feeling any softness toward him, she thought about how he might react in the morning. He might not take kindly to being recruited for her cause. He might react violently to finding himself in the middle of nowhere before she had a chance to make her sales pitch. These mercenaries were ruthlessly short-tempered.

She looked at the machete. Acting before she could talk herself out of it, she unsnapped the scabbard and slid the long blade out of it. It seemed to weigh a hundred pounds. She maneuvered it awkwardly, barely saved her thighs from being sliced in two and tossed it onto the ground outside the open door.

Then there was the pistol.

She stared at it for several moments. Her stomach became victim to an odd flurrying. She should disarm him. That would be the smart thing to do, but, considering where the pistol was . . .

Now certainly wasn't the time to get squeamish! When she considered what she'd already gone through tonight, getting timid now was ludicrous.

She reached forward. Chickened out. Withdrew her hands. Closed her hands into fists, then flexed her fingers, like a safecracker about to undertake the challenge of his career.

She reached for the pistol again. This time, before she could lose her nerve, she closed her hand around the butt of it and tugged. Again. Harder. It wouldn't come free of his waistband.

She snatched her hand back and debated her alternatives. She had none. She had to get that pistol away from him, and get it without waking him up.

She stared at his web belt. Closing her eyes for a moment and wetting her dry lips, she gathered her rapidly scattering courage. Forcing down her nervousness, she touched the belt buckle. Using the tip of her index finger, she slid the small brass button forward to release the teeth clamping down into the webbing. Gradually the tension eased. She pressed harder. The teeth popped free. Metal clinked against metal softly.

The mercenary drew a deep breath. Let it out on a sigh. Kerry froze. She inched her hands forward again and, working slowly and carefully, pulled the end of the belt through the brass buckle.

There was no rejoicing. She met with another obstacle.

She touched the heavy metal button of his fatigue trousers. He made a snuffling sound and shifted his legs, drawing one knee up onto the seat. Which rearranged everything.

*Everything*. And wedged the barrel of the gun in even tighter between his stomach and his waistband.

Kerry's hands were sweating.

She dared not think of what he would do if he should wake up and discover her fiddling with the fly of his pants. If he thought she was trying to take his gun away, he'd shoot her with it. And if he thought . . . The other was too horrendous to contemplate.

She reached for the button again, and this time didn't let the purring sound coming from his chest deter her. Her fingers were clumsy. It was no small task to work the button out of the reinforced hole in the stiff cloth, but at last she succeeded. She closed her fingers around the butt of the pistol again, but it still wouldn't come free.

She swore in whispers.

Gnawing on her lower lip, she pinched the tab of his zipper between her thumb and index finger. She had to yank on it three times before it moved. She had intended to lower it only an inch or two, but when it finally cooperated, it unzipped all the way. Suddenly. Shockingly. She dropped the tab as though it had bitten her, then jerked the pistol free.

He snorted, shifted again, but didn't wake up. She clutched the pistol to her chest as though it were the Holy Grail and she'd dedicated a lifetime to searching for it. Her whole body was damp with perspiration.

Finally, when she was certain that he had slept through her fumblings and that she wasn't going to have to use the vicious weapon to protect herself, she dropped it onto the ground. It clattered against the machete. She shut the door of the truck quickly, as though covering up incriminating evidence. A bird protested the noise, then silence fell again.

She sat there in the darkness, thinking.

Maybe her mercenary wasn't such a good choice after all, if he could be disarmed so easily.

Of course he was drunk, and where they were going, he wouldn't have access to alcohol. He had warned off that other soldier with one threatening look. He was physically suited to the job she had in mind for him. She had been close enough to him tonight to know that. Those lean, hard muscles could only belong to a man of strength and stamina. She knew also that once he made up his mind to do something, he was determined. If he hadn't bumped his head against the dashboard, she would probably still be fighting him off.

She wouldn't think any more about him. Suffice it to say that she had done well; she had made a good choice.

With that in mind, Kerry settled into her own corner of the cab, rested her head in the open window and fell asleep to the steady rhythm of his gentle snores.

It seemed that she had barely closed her eyes when she was awakened by a litany of words she had only seen scrawled on the walls of public restrooms. There was movement beside her and scalding blasphemy.

The beast was coming awake.

# *Chapter 2*

All the jungle animals were waking up. Rustling leaves marked the progress of reptiles and rodents. Birds chattered in the branches of the trees overhead. Small monkeys screeched as they swung from vine to vine in search of breakfast.

But even their shrill racket took second place to the vivid cursing inside the cab of the truck.

Kerry cowered against the driver's door as she watched her mercenary come awake with about as much humor as a fairy-tale ogre. In fact he resembled an illustration she remembered from a childhood picture book with his hair sticking out at odd angles, his ferocious scowl, and his heavily shadowed jaw. Grunting and groaning, he leaned forward, unsteadily braced his elbows on his knees and held his head between his shaking hands.

After several moments, he moved his head around—it seemed to cause him agony—and looked at Kerry through bloodshot eyes. They had as many red streaks in them as the eastern sky. Without saying a word, he fumbled for the door handle, unlatched it and virtually rolled out of the truck.

When his feet struck the ground, lushly carpeted and spongy as it was, he let loose a string of blistering curses, products of a fertile imagination. That set off the noisy wildlife again. He clasped his head, and Kerry couldn't tell if he was trying to hold it on or tear it off.

She opened the door on the driver's side. Cautiously checking the ground for snakes first, she placed her sandaled foot in the deep undergrowth and stepped out of the truck. She considered picking up one of his weapons, either the machete or the gun, but decided that he was in no condition to do even the most defenseless animal any serious harm.

Gambling her safety on that decision, she crept around the hood of the truck and peered down the opposite side of it. He was braced against it with only his bottom touching. His feet were planted solidly in front of him, as though he had carefully put them there and didn't dare move them for fear of falling off the planet. He was bent forward at the waist, still cushioning his head between his hands.

When he heard her tread in the soft undergrowth, which must have sounded like a marching army to his supersensitive ears, he swiveled his head around.

Under the baleful gaze of golden brown eyes, Kerry halted.

"Where am I?" The words were garbled, ground out by a throat abused by tobacco and alcohol.

"Montenegro," she replied fearfully.

"What day is this?"

"Tuesday."

"What about my plane?"

He seemed to have a difficult time keeping her in focus. The sunlight was growing brighter by the moment as it topped the trees. He squinted against it until his eyes were almost closed. When an extremely vocal bird squawked noisily overhead, he winced and cursed beneath his breath.

"Plane?"

"Plane. Plane. Airplane."

When she only stared back at him apprehensively, he began searching through the pockets of his shirt with a great deal of agitation and practically no coordination. Finally, from the breast pocket, he produced an airplane ticket and what appeared to be an official exit visa. The whimsical government of Montenegro was stingy with visas. They weren't issued very often and were more valuable than gold. It took a king's ransom in gold to have one forged.

He shook the ticket and visa at her. "I was supposed to be on an airplane last night at ten o'clock."

Kerry swallowed. He was going to be upset. She braced herself for his wrath. But she tilted her head back fearlessly when she told him, "Sorry. You missed it."

He turned around slowly, so that his shoulder was propped against the truck. He stared at her with such undiluted animosity that she quavered on the inside.

When he spoke, his voice was whispery with menace. "Did you make me miss my plane out?"

She took a cautious step backward. "You came with me of your own free will."

He took a threatening step toward her. "You haven't got long to live, lady. But before I murder you, I'd like to know, just out of curiosity, why you shanghaied me."

She pointed an accusing finger at him. "You were drunk!"

"Which I'm living to regret."

"How was I supposed to know that you were trying to get on an airplane?"

"Didn't I mention it?"

"No."

"I must have told you," he said with an insistent shake of his head.

"You didn't."

He squinted his eyes and looked at her accusingly. "You're not only a whore, you're a lying whore."

"I'm neither," Kerry declared, blushing hotly.

Those unusual agate eyes traveled from the top of her tousled head to the tips of her toes. But this time, unlike the appreciative way they had moved over her in the *cantina*, they were scornful. His look made her feel exactly like what he was accusing her of being. In the daylight the cheap, ill-fitting dress showed no saving graces.

He asked sneeringly, "What's your gimmick?"

"I don't have a gimmick."

"Was business so bad in the states, you had to come down here to peddle it?"

If Kerry hadn't been so frightened of the latent violence that was causing his muscles to twitch involuntarily, she would have stepped forward and slapped him. Instead she fashioned fists out of her hands, but kept them at her sides.

Through gritted teeth she said, "I'm not a whore. I only disguised myself as one so I could go into that bar and pick you up."

"Sounds like whoring to me."

"Stop saying that!" she cried, as angered by his offhanded assessment of her as by his actual words. "I need your services."

He glanced down at his fatigue pants, which were still unfastened and riding low on his narrow hips. "I think you already had them."

Kerry went hot all over. It seemed that every drop of blood in her body rushed to her head and was pushing against her scalp. She couldn't meet his sardonic eyes any longer and glanced skittishly around the clearing.

He laughed scoffingly. "I don't remember it. How were you?"

She seethed. "You're despicable."

"That rowdy, huh?" he said, rubbing his jaw. "Wish I remembered it."

"We didn't do anything, you fool."

"No?"

"Certainly not."

"You just wanted to look but not touch?"

"No!"

"Then what are my pants doing unzipped?"

"I had to unfasten them to get your pistol out," she flared. "I didn't want you to kill me."

He digested that. "That is still a distinct possibility. And taking away my pistol and machete won't stop me. I could easily kill you with my bare hands. But I'd still like to know why you kept me from getting on that plane. Do you work for the Montenegran government?"

She gaped at him, incredulous that he could think such a thing. "Are you *crazy*?"

He laughed without humor. "That's probably it. It would be just like El Presidente to recruit an American broad to spy for him, damned coward that he is."

"I agree with you that he's a coward. But I don't work for him."

"The rebels, then. What do you do, steal exit visas for them?"

"No. I don't work for anybody in Montenegro."

"Then who? The CIA is in a world of hurt if you're the best they can do."

"I work for myself. And don't worry. I can meet your price."

"What do you mean, my price?"

"I want to hire you. Just name your fee."

"IBM doesn't have that much money, lady."

"I'll pay anything."

"You're not listening. No more jobs in Montenegro. I want out of this godforsaken place." He moved toward her, sinister and steely. "You've screwed up royally, lady. That was the last plane out of here before the government shut down all international travel. Do you know what I had to do to get that visa?''

Kerry was sure she didn't want to know. His slow, threatening approach made her talk faster. ''I'll make the delay worth your while. I swear it. And if you agree to help me, I can guarantee you a way out.''

''How? When?''

''On Friday. I need only three days of your time. You'll go home with your pockets full of money.''

She had his attention. He was studying her thoughtfully. ''Why me? Beyond the fact that I was drunk and easily duped.''

''I need someone with your experience.''

''There are several others still hanging around. Even several in that stinking bar last night.''

''But you looked more . . . suited to the job.''

''What is this job?''

She sidestepped the direct question. First, she had to sell him on the idea of staying in the country for a few extra days. ''It's a tough job. I need someone who has his own weapons available.'' She appealed to his vanity. ''And, of course, the experience and courage to use them if it becomes necessary.''

''Weapons?'' He shook his head in bewilderment. ''Wait a minute. You think I'm a mercenary?''

She didn't have to answer him. Her expression told him that his guess was correct.

Kerry stared at him in mystification as his face broke into a facsimile of a smile. His laugh was hoarse and deep, but eventually it rumbled up out of his chest and finally erupted as a series of dry, hacking coughs. He cursed expansively, but not so viciously as before. He rubbed his forehead and dragged both hands down his haggard face. Then he leaned against the truck, turned his face heavenward, and sighed heavily.

"What's wrong?" Kerry had to ask, though she didn't think she wanted to know. His laughter had held irony, not humor.

"You got the wrong man, lady. I'm not a mercenary."

Her jaw went slack as she stared at him. "That's not true!" How dare he try to trick her this way. "And you called El Presidente a coward. You're just trying to weasel your way out of accepting a challenging job."

"You're damn right I'm a coward," he shouted. "I cover my ass, understand? I don't claim to be a glory guy. But I'm not lying when I tell you that I'm no professional soldier."

She had recoiled at his flash of temper. "But your pistol, your machete—"

"For protection. What kind of damn fool goes into the jungle without any way to protect himself from animals? Of the four-legged variety as well as the two-legged kind." He took another step toward her. "We're in a war zone, lady, or haven't you noticed? Now I don't know what kind of game you're playing, but I'm taking myself back to town right now and throwing myself on the mercy of El Presidente. Maybe he'll still let me leave."

He glanced down at Kerry again, taking in the long, tangled hair and whorish dress. "He likes a bawdy story. I'll tell him one of the lovely ladies of his country enticed me beyond the point of no return. He'll like that."

He stepped around her and headed toward the hood of the truck.

She clutched at his sleeve desperately. "Believe me, this is no game. You can't go."

"Wanna bet?" He wrested his arm free and made for the driver's side of the truck.

"What about all that weaponry?" she asked, pointing toward the bed of the pickup.

He bent down, picked up the machete, and slid it back into its sheath. "You want to see my weaponry? All right."

He strode toward the rear of the truck and heaved one of the heavy bags over the side after removing the tarpaulin with a flourish. "Stand back," he cautioned her theatrically. "I'd hate for any of these to blow up in your face."

With a sharp tug, he unzipped one of the bags. Ready for explosive devises to spill out, Kerry stared down at the contents of the canvas bag with stupefaction.

"That's a camera."

His expression was dripping with sarcasm. "No kidding." He rezipped the bag and set it back inside the pickup. "To be precise a Nikon F3."

"You mean all those bags have cameras in them?"

"And lenses and film. I'm a photojournalist. I'd offer you my card, but a group of guerrillas and I used them to start a cookfire a week or so back and I'm fresh out."

Kerry ignored his acerbity and stared at the canvas bags. She had mistakenly thought they contained the weapons that would have assured her safe passage out of the country. It was several moments before she realized how long she'd been staring, lamenting her monumental error, contemplating her dilemma, and weighing the options left open to her.

She spun around. The man was headed into the jungle. "Where are you going?"

"To relieve myself."

"Oh. Well, I admit I made a mistake, but I'd still like to offer you a deal."

"Forget it, lady. I plan on making my own deal with El Presidente." He thumped his thighs with his fists. "Dammit! I can't believe I was stupid enough to miss that airplane. What enticed me to leave the *cantina* with you? Did you slip me a mickey?"

She took umbrage and didn't even honor the accusation with a denial. "You were drunk before I found you. Why, when you were so bent on making that plane, were you drinking yourself senseless?"

"I was celebrating." His teeth were angrily clenched, so Kerry knew she had struck a nerve. He was just as angry with himself as he was with her. "I couldn't wait to leave this armpit of a country. I'd been grubbing around for days trying to buy a seat on that airplane. Know what I had to do in exchange for that visa?"

"No."

"I had to take a picture of El Presidente and his mistress."

"Doing what?" she asked snidely.

Insulted, he glared at her. "A portrait that I'll probably sell to *Time. If* I ever get back to the United States. Which looks doubtful, thanks to you!"

"If you would just hear me out, I could explain why I needed a mercenary and went to such desperate lengths to get one."

"But I'm not the one."

"You look like one. Why do you think I chose you?"

"I wouldn't hazard a guess."

"I chose you over every other man in that bar because you looked the most disreputable and dangerous."

"Lucky me. Now if you'll excuse—"

"You use a camera instead of a machine gun, but you're of the same breed as these soldiers of fortune." She could still use him. If she had mistaken him for a professional soldier, it was probable that others would, too. "You sell your services to the highest bidder. I can make this worth your while, Mr. . . ."

She stared at him in perplexity.

"O'Neal," he supplied tersely. "Linc O'Neal."

*Lincoln O'Neal!* She recognized his name instantly, but tried not to show that she was impressed. He was one of the most renowned and prolific photojournalists in the world. He'd made his reputation during the evacuation of Vietnam and had recorded on 35mm film every war and catastrophe since. He had two Pulitzer Prizes to his credit. His work was of the highest caliber, often too realistic for the weak-stomached and too poignant for the tender-hearted.

"My name is Kerry Bishop."

"I don't give a damn what your name is, lady. Now, unless you want to see what's behind my zipper after all, I suggest you don't detain me again."

His crudity didn't put her off as it was obviously intended to. It only fueled her resolve. He turned his back on her and went stalking through the trees. Despite her flimsy shoes, Kerry plunged through the wall of green after him.

She caught his sleeve again and, this time, held on. "There are nine orphans waiting for me to escort them out of the country," she said in one breath. "I'm working with the aid of a benevolent group in the United States. I've got three days to get them to the border. On Friday a private plane will land there and pick us up. If we're not at the rendezvous place on time, the plane will leave without us. I need help in getting them through fifty miles of jungle."

"Good luck."

She uttered a cry of disbelief when he turned away again. She clutched his sleeve tighter. "Didn't you hear what I said?"

"Every single word."

"And you don't care?"

"It's got nothing to do with me."

"You're a human being! Barely, granted, but still a human being."

"Sticks and stones—"

"Oh, damn you and your jokes!" she cried. "These are *children*."

His face hardened. It was no wonder to her that she had mistaken him for a mercenary. He seemed untouchable. His callousness was unbreachable.

"Lady, I've seen hundreds of kids blown to bits. Stomachs swelled up like balloons from starvation. Covered in sores and crawling with lice and flies. Screaming in terror when their parents were beheaded in front of them. Tragic, yes. Sickening, yes. Nations of them, lady. So don't expect me to fall on my knees in anguish over nine."

She released him and recoiled as though his heartlessness was a hideous, contagious disease. "You're a horrible man."

"Right. We finally agree on something. I'm not spiritually equipped to take care of nine kids, even under the best of circumstances."

She straightened her shoulders determinedly. Loathsome as he was, he was her only hope. She didn't have time to go back into the capital city and search for a replacement. "Consider this just another job. I'll pay you whatever I would pay a professional soldier."

He shook his head adamantly. "It wouldn't be as much as I'll make off the film I'm taking home."

"Three more days won't matter. Your film will be just as valuable on Friday as it is today."

"But I won't be risking my ass in the meantime. I value my hide almost as much as I do my film. I've risked it too long in this stinking jungle. I have a sixth sense that tells me when to move on." He locked gazes with her. "Now, I don't know who you are, or what the hell you're doing in a place like this, but it doesn't involve me. Got that? I hope you get the kids out, but you'll do it without me."

He turned abruptly and took no more than a few steps before he was swallowed by the jungle. Kerry's shoulders drooped with dejection.

She slowly retraced her steps to the truck. Spotting the pistol still lying on the ground, she shuddered. He might not be a mercenary, but he was just as cold and unfeeling. He was unhumanly jaded and didn't possess an iota of compassion. To turn his back on children! How could he? How could anyone?

She stared at the pistol, wondering if she could force him at gunpoint to help her. The idea was ridiculous, of course, and she dismissed it as soon as it was formulated. She could just see herself toting little Lisa in one hand and the .357 Magnum in the other.

He would probably murder them all in their sleep anyway before they were halfway to their destination or if a better offer presented itself along the way.

Angrily, she whirled around. Her gaze accidentally fell on the bags lying in the bed of the truck. Cameras, she thought scornfully. How could she have mistaken them for weapons and ammunition? They were the tools of his trade, all right, but they were of no use to her.

How low did a man have to stoop before he could place a roll of film above the life of a parentless child? A wretch of a man. A cold-hearted, selfish man, who would rather print pictures of other people than be touched by them personally. A man to whom a roll of film—

Film. Film. Film.

Kerry's heart skidded to a halt. Her eyes rounded with sudden inspiration as she stared at the canvas bags. Before allowing herself time to consider the grave consequences of what she was about to do, she bounded into the bed of the pickup and unzipped the first bag.

Linc felt like hell.

Every time a macaw exercised his vocal talents, the noise went through his head like a spear. His stomach was in turmoil and with the least bit of encouragement would ignominiously empty itself. His teeth had grown fur overnight. He had a crick in his neck. God, even his hair hurt.

Wondering how that was possible, he explored it tentatively and discovered that it wasn't his hair giving him such misery, but an unaccounted for goose egg on his cranium.

But the worst of all his pains was the big one in the butt... by the name of Bishop. Something Bishop. Carol? Carolyn? Damn he couldn't remember. All he knew was that at the moment he'd like to be carving her name on a tombstone after having strangled her with his bare hands.

The little bitch had made him miss that airplane!

Every time he thought about it, he ground his teeth. And because he couldn't cope with his own stupid culpability at the moment, he directed his anger toward the woman.

Damn conniving female. What the hell was she doing in Montenegro to begin with? She was nothing but a meddlesome do-gooder. Nine orphans. How the hell did she think she could secretly transport nine orphans five miles, much less fifty, then catch a plane that was *supposed* to rendezvous . . .

Hell. It sounded like a bad movie script. Unworkable. Implausible. Impossible.

And she had gambled on him risking his neck, not to mention the fortune he stood to make on the photographs he'd taken, to help her. What a laugh! He hadn't stayed alive by being Mr. Nice Guy.

Ask anyone who knew him, and they'd tell you that Linc O'Neal looked out for number one. He was liked. He was respected. He took his turn when it came to buying drinks. But don't depend on him in a pinch, because in a pinch, it was his ass he was concerned about and not the next guy's. He pledged allegiance to himself and himself alone.

He reminded himself of that as he trekked back to where he'd left the woman. He was relieved to see that she had calmed down measurably. She was leaning against the pickup, braiding her hair. The long, dark mass of hair—she had enough for about six people—was pulled over one shoulder. She was working it deftly through her fingers to form a braid as thick as his wrist.

That hair. It was one reason he'd been attracted enough to go with her last night. Hell, the last thing he had needed was a woman. He had *wanted* one, yes. He'd been in Montenegro for six weeks. But he was too fastidious to quench his basic male desires with the tavern whores who nightly bedded soldiers from both sides of the conflict. He'd never been *that* horny.

Last night, of all nights, he had avoided company of any kind. He'd had only one thought in mind: catch that airplane. All he had really wanted was the numbing effect of a few drinks and to get on that airplane and put as much distance between himself and Montenegro as possible.

But the liquor, potent as it was, hadn't been able to wash away the memories of the atrocities he'd witnessed in the past six weeks. So he'd kept drinking the foul stuff. And though it hadn't dulled his memory, it had severely clouded his judgment.

When the woman with that dark hair, lustrous even in the foggy light of the bar, had approached him, his common sense had surrendered to the swelling pressure in his pants. The kiss had been the deciding factor. One taste of her mouth, which had proved to be just as sweet as it had looked, had tipped the scales of his judgment.

Now, he was somewhat relieved to see that he hadn't taken complete leave of his senses last night. She *was* pretty. She *was* clean. Her figure *was* good, though a trifle slender, much too slender for that ridiculous dress. His instinct for women *was* still intact.

But how he could have mistaken her for a whore, he'd never know. He looked more like a mercenary than she did a prostitute. Her hair was dark, so it had been easy to mistake her for one of the local women. But in the dappled sunlight of the clearing, he saw that her eyes weren't brown as he had originally thought. They were dark blue. And her complexion was too fair to belong to a woman of Latin descent. It was almost too fair to belong to a brunette.

Mainly, she didn't have that hard, embittered, weary look of the women who had taken to prostitution to buy something to eat. The Montenegran women who were forced to sell themselves for the price of a loaf of bread grew very old very fast.

This woman still looked fresh and wholesome, and, in the sunlight, unmistakably American. She should be living in a nice house in a Midwest suburb, organizing the Junior League's spring tea. Yet, here she was in a jungle clearing, the morning after pulling off a dangerous escapade. In spite of himself, Linc was curious about her.

"How'd you get the truck?"

She didn't seem surprised by his abrupt question and answered without hesitation. "I stole it. It was parked in front of the *cantina*. The keys were in the ignition. I disguised you as an officer with the jacket and cap left on the seat."

"Ingenious."

"Thank you."

"And you just drove us through the checkpoint, pretending that I was your client for the evening."

"Right."

He nodded in acknowledgement of her cleverness. "I've got a knot on my head."

"Oh, well, I'm sorry about that. You were...I was trying to—" She suddenly broke off. Linc got the distinct impression that she was keeping something from him, something she was glad he'd obviously forgotten. "Go on."

"You bumped your head on the dash."

"Hmm." He studied her for a moment, but let her lie of omission pass. There was no sense in pursuing the subject since their adventure together was drawing to a close. He was now certain that he hadn't had her last night. Drunk as he had been, he wouldn't have forgotten lying between those thighs, whose provocative shape he could see beneath her dress.

Before he got distracted by any more pleasurable thoughts, he turned his attention to what he was going to do once he reached the city. He hoped he would catch El Presidente in a good, receptive mood. "Well, I'm glad we've got the truck. It'll make getting back to the city easier. Are you riding back with me, or do we say our farewells here?"

"That won't be necessary," she said with a cheerful smile.

"What?"

"Driving back to the city."

He assumed an impatient stance. "Look, I've given you my answer. Let's not play any more games, okay? Just give me the keys to the truck and I'll be on my way."

"I don't think you'll be going anywhere, Mr. O'Neal."

"I'm going back to town. Now." He stuck out his hand, palm up. "The keys."

"The film."

"Huh?"

She inclined her head, and he followed the direction toward which she had gestured until he sighted the curls of brown film, now worthless, exposed to the fatal tropical sun.

His blood-curdling cry began as a strangling sound. But when it left his mouth, it was a full-fledged roar of outrage. He whirled around, lunged, grabbed her, and bent her backward over the hood of the truck. His forearm acted as a bar across her throat.

"I ought to kill you."

"You might just as well," she shouted bravely. "What's one more murder? You were willing to sacrifice the lives of nine children to your own selfish pursuits."

"Selfish pursuits! That film represents what I do for a living. You just cost me thousands, lady."

"I'll pay whatever you ask."

"Forget it."

"Name your price."

"I don't want the friggin' job!"

"Because you might have to consider someone besides yourself for a change?"

"Damn right!"

"Okay, then, I'll tell you how you can turn this to your advantage. Let me up. You're hurting me."

She squirmed against him. But immediately became still. His hips were pressing against hers, and her wiggling had a profound and instantaneous effect on him. Against the softest, most vulnerable part of her body, he grew hard.

At the same time she noticed his condition, it registered with him. Instead of moving away from her, however, he pressed closer, fitting himself into the cleft between her thighs. His eyes mocked her insultingly. His breath struck her face in hot gusts.

"You invited me, remember?" he said silkily. "I might take you up on your invitation."

"You wouldn't dare."

His slow smile was anything but reassuring. "Don't count on it, lady."

"You know why I took you out of that *cantina*."

"All I know for sure is that I kissed you and that I woke up this morning with my pants unzipped."

"Nothing happened," she vowed in a voice tinged with anxiety.

"Not yet." He made the words sound like a promise of things to come, but gradually released her and helped her up. "However, business before pleasure. How could this possibly work to my advantage?"

Rubbing her throat and casting him venomous looks, Kerry said, "The story. You would be involved in the rescue of nine orphans."

"And in transporting illegal aliens into the United States."

She shook her head. "We have Immigration's sanction. All the children have been slated for adoption by American parents." She saw a slight alteration in his skeptical expression and took advantage of it. "You'd be right there, Mr. O'Neal, recording it all on film. The story would have much more impact than what you already have."

*"Had."*

"Had," she conceded guiltily.

They contemplated each other warily.

"Where are these kids?" he asked, breaking a long silence.

"About three miles north of here. I left them in hiding there yesterday afternoon."

"What were you doing with them?"

"Teaching them. I've been here for ten months. Their parents are all dead, or considered so. Their village was burned out a month ago. We've been foraging for food and living in temporary shelters while arrangements were being made to get them out of Montenegro and into the United States."

"What arrangements? With whom?"

"The Hendren Foundation, named in honor of Hal Hendren, a missionary who was killed here almost two years ago. His family founded the relief organization soon after his death."

"And you think they'll be at that rendezvous point as they said they would?"

"Absolutely."

"How'd you get your information?"

"By courier."

He barked a laugh. "Who would sell his sister for a package of Lucky Strikes. Which incidentally I need badly," he muttered, slapping his pockets until he found a pack. He discovered it was empty. "Got any?"

"No."

"Figures." He cursed. A long, disgusted breath filtered through his teeth. "Do you trust this courier?"

"His two sisters are among the orphans. He wants them taken out. His father was shot by the regular army as a spy for the rebels. His mother was . . . she was killed, too."

Linc propped himself against the side of the truck and gnawed on his lower lip. He looked down at his film. It was the proverbial spilled milk if he'd ever seen it. Forgiveness would be a long time in coming, but there was nothing he could do to save the film now.

He had only two choices left to him. He could return to the city and beg that despot who called himself a president for mercy. Even if it was granted, he would go home empty-handed. The other choice was equally distasteful. He still wasn't ready to become an ally of this butterfly cum Mata Hari.

"Why did you have to kidnap me?"

"Would you have come with me if I had said 'Pretty please'?" She got only a dark scowl for an answer. "I didn't think so. I didn't think any mercenary would want to bother with a group of children."

"You were right. He probably would have taken your advance money, followed you to the hideout, cut the kids' throats, raped you before killing you, and considered it a good day's work."

She turned pale and folded her arms across her middle. "I never thought of that."

"There's a lot you haven't thought of. Like food. And fresh water."

"I was counting on you...on whomever...to think about all those details."

"Not details," he said with aggravation. "Fundamental necessities."

She resented his speaking to her as though she were simple-minded. "I'm not faint-hearted, Mr. O'Neal. I'll suffer any hardship I have to in order to get those children out of the country."

"They could all die before we cover that fifty miles. Are you prepared for that?"

"If they stay, they'll perish anyway."

He pondered her for a moment and decided that she might not be all fluff after all. It had taken considerable grit to do what she had done last night. "Where is the rendezvous point?"

Gladness shone in her face, but she didn't smile. Instead she turned and rushed to a hollowed-out fallen tree at the edge of the clearing. After poking a stick into it to clean out any snakes that might be harboring there from the heat, she reached in and pulled out a backpack. Unbuckling it as she crossed the clearing, she produced a map as soon as she reached the truck. She spread it out on the sun-baked hood.

"Here," she said, pointing. "And we're here."

Linc had been traveling with rebel guerrillas in recent weeks. He knew where the majority of fighting was concentrated. He looked down at the woman's expectant face, his golden eyes as hard as stones.

"That's troop-infested, solid jungle."

"I know."

"So why there?"

"Because it *is* so heavily patrolled. They use the least sophisticated radar equipment along that stretch of the border. The plane will have a better chance to get through without being detected."

"It's a suicide mission."

"I know that, too."

Angrily, Linc turned his back on her. Damn! She would gaze up at him with that melting look, just as she had in the tavern last night. Only this time he could see her dark blue eyes clearly. That look had made him throw caution to the wind, say, "To hell with common sense," and follow her out of the bar. She might not be a whore, but she sure as hell knew her stuff. She knew how to make a man as hard as steel, but as malleable as putty.

He'd had a helluva lot to drink last night, but he hadn't been so drunk that he didn't remember kissing her, touching her, and liking both immensely. She was a gutsy lady. He grudgingly admired her spunk. But it wasn't her spunk that he wanted to have warm and wanting beneath him. It was her body. He wanted to be wrapped in those shapely limbs and long, silky hair.

He knew, even as he made up his mind, that he was going to pay dearly for making this ill-advised decision.

"Fifty thousand dollars."

After a moment of initial shock, Kerry said. "That's your price?"

"If you can't hack it, we've got no deal."

She set her chin firmly. "Agreed."

"Not so fast. Here are the ground rules. I'm boss, see? No arguing. No bickering. When I tell you to do something, you do it without asking for an explanation." He punctuated his words by stabbing the air in front of her nose with his index finger.

"I've lived in the jungle for almost a year," she said haughtily, wanting to swat that finger away.

"In a schoolhouse with a bunch of kids. That's a little different from tramping through the jungle with them in tow. If we don't get attacked, it'll be a miracle. The only way I'll even chance it is to do everything *my* way."

"All right."

"All right. Let's get started. Three days isn't much time to cover the territory between here and the border.

"As soon as I change we'll pick up the children and gather supplies." She pulled a pair of khaki trousers, a blouse, socks and boots from the backpack she'd taken from the hollow tree.

"I see you thought of everything."

"Including water." She passed him a canteen. "Help yourself."

"Thanks."

She stood there awkwardly, holding the change of clothes against her chest. "Would you excuse me, please, while I change?"

He lowered the canteen from his mouth. His lips were glistening with moisture. He wiped it away with the back of his hand. His gaze never wavered from her face.

"No."

# Chapter 3

"No?"

"Yes."

"Yes, you mean no?"

Lincoln O'Neal crossed his ankles, folded his arms at his waist, and tilted his head to one side. Arrogance incarnate. "No, I'm not excusing you. In fact, I'm not budging."

Kerry couldn't believe it. "You'd be rude enough to refuse me some privacy?" Sharks had kinder smiles than the one he gave her. "Then forget it," she said sharply. "I just won't change until we get to the place where I hid the children."

"I thought you said you weren't faint-hearted."

Her braid almost slapped him in the face when she whipped her head around. The boor was testing her. She couldn't back down from any challenge issued by those sardonic eyes. Even now he could renege on their deal. She wouldn't be at all surprised. He obviously had no conscience. For the time being she had no choice but to play along with his asinine little games.

"Okay. I'll change."

She turned her back on him and reached behind her for the zipper of the dress.

"Allow me."

He moved up close behind her. His hands were large and manly, but sensitive enough to handle intricate cameras and lenses. Apparently he was adept at undressing women, too. The zipper didn't intimidate him or make him awkward and clumsy. It glided down her back without snagging once.

Accepting a dare was one thing, but actually carrying it out was another. She had thought that taking off her dress in front of him would be no worse than slipping out of a cover-up on the beach. But she hadn't counted on his taking an active part in her disrobing, or having him stand so close that she could feel his breath on her back. The sinking sensation in the pit of her stomach threatened to weaken her until she would have to lean against him, as she had a mad desire to do.

Inch by inch she felt her back being exposed to him. As it came open, the zipper left in its wake a ribbon of heat, caused only partially by the sun, mostly by embarrassment and the instinctive knowledge that his eyes were following the widening path of that zipper. It seemed to take forever, but it finally reached the end of its track.

"Thank you."

Kerry wished her words had carried a more authoritative ring and hadn't sounded so breathless. She moved away from him quickly. Hesitating only a few seconds, she lowered the shoulder straps down her arms. The flimsy bodice dropped to her waist. She pushed the dress over her hips and stepped out of it.

That left her standing in nothing but a pair of panties and the strappy sandals. The sun's fierce heat penetrated her naked skin. The humidity settled on it like damp kisses. All the wildlife in the surrounding trees fell silent, as though they were watching from above, awed by her performance.

Her hands were shaking as she hastily stepped into the trousers. She was barely able to button them. Next, she shoved her arms into the short sleeves of her chambray shirt. She buttoned only two of the buttons, then tied the shirttail at her waist. She pulled her long braid from beneath her collar and bent down to pick up that sleazy dress, which, under any other circumstances, she would have been only too happy to discard.

It was when she was bent at the waist that Linc placed his hands on either side of her waist. "Leave me alone," she warned him in a low voice.

"No way, darl—"

The endearment died on his lips when she sprang erect and spun around. His pistol was gripped between both her hands and it was pointed directly at the center of his broad chest.

"You and I have a business arrangement, Mr. O'Neal. It's strictly business. I wouldn't give you the time of day otherwise. If you come on to me again, I'll kill you."

"I doubt that." His features remained unperturbed.

"I mean it!" Kerry shouted. She thrust the pistol an inch closer. "Last night I had to tolerate your disgusting gropings out of necessity, but don't ever touch me again."

"Okay, okay."

He raised his hands in surrender. At least that's what Kerry thought he was going to do. Instead, with uncanny speed and humiliating ease, he knocked the heavy pistol out of her hands. It clattered loudly onto the hood of the truck, then slid to the ground. He pinned one of her arms to her side and shoved the other one up behind her.

"Don't you *ever* pull a gun on me again, understand? *Understand*?" He pushed her arm up higher, until her hand was almost between her shoulder blades.

"You're hurting me," she gasped.

"Not as much as you'd have hurt me if that .357 had gone off," he shouted.

"I'm not even sure how it works," she shouted back.

"All the more reason why you shouldn't have tried such a damn fool thing."

"I'm sorry. Please." Tears of pain and humiliation were stinging her eyes. He relieved the pressure on her arms, but kept her clasped against him.

"I ought to wring your neck for pulling that little stunt," he said. "Instead . . ." He lowered his head toward hers.

"No!"

"Yes."

This kiss was just as possessive as those last night had been. His lips were hungry, passionate, hard, and yet incredibly soft. His tongue slid into her mouth. She tensed, but he brooked no resistance. He investigated her mouth thoroughly. Even though his tongue moved leisurely, Linc was the unquestioned director of the kiss. Kerry was the respondent. In spite of herself, when his tongue glanced hers, it made a corresponding movement.

He raised his head. Her eyes came open slowly, as though she'd been drugged. "Disgusting gropings, huh?" His eyes were maliciously teasing. "I don't think you found my gropings disgusting at all."

With breathtaking boldness, his hand moved to her breast and covered it. He caressed the fullness through her shirt.

"Don't." She dared not say more for fear that the moan of pleasure she felt building behind his caressing hand would work its way up.

"Why not?"

"Because I don't want you to."

"Yes, you do," he said with audacious conceit. "This could prove to be an interesting expedition after all. For both of us. We might just as well set the mood now."

"Please don't." Her voice quavered and became a full-fledged moan when the center of her breast rose up to meet the lazy caress of his thumb.

"You like it," he whispered against her neck.

"No. No I don't."

"Oh, yes." He caught her earlobe between his teeth and tugged on it gently. "Even though you put on this prickly, do-not-touch act, you're a woman who responds to a man." He smiled when a slight repositioning of his hips brought a groan to her throat. He rubbed against her suggestively. "An aroused man sets you off like a flare, doesn't he? Unless that were true, you couldn't have enticed me to go with you last night."

"You were drunk. You would have followed any female from that *cantina*."

"Not so. I was drunk, but I recognized your steamy nature under that cool exterior. Well, nobody stays cool in the jungle, baby. You'll thaw."

"Stop." She put all her strength into the command, so her protest wouldn't sound as feeble as the resolve behind it.

"For now," he said, lowering his hand from her breast. "Because I'm still mad as hell at you for pointing that gun at me. When the time is right, you'll beg me for it."

His audacity had a healthy effect on her. It made her fighting mad. "Don't hold your breath."

She was successful in pushing him away only because he allowed her to. He merely laughed as he bent down and retrieved his gun. He shoved it into his waistband. Kerry watched, until she realized what she was looking at and hurriedly raised her eyes.

He was smiling at her insolently when he said, "Get in. I'll drive. You can put your boots on in the truck."

He had already assumed control, and for the moment that was fine with Kerry. Their embrace had rattled her.

Because she had been devoted to her work with the children over the last ten months, she hadn't missed the companionship of men. There was no one waiting for her to return to the United States. She hadn't been romantically involved with anyone when she came to Montenegro. Because of that lack of involvement with the opposite sex, her entire being had been assaulted by Linc O'Neal's sudden intrusion into her life.

He had created a hunger inside her that hadn't been there this time yesterday. It was both thrilling and shameful. She was afraid of his virility, but fascinated by it, too. He epitomized masculinity in its rawest form. The salty taste and smell of his skin, the roughness of his beard, the huskiness of his voice, all appealed to her. His size and shape and well-honed muscles were a blood-stirring contrast to her femininity.

Unfortunately, he had a rotten character and an annoying personality. If it weren't for the orphans, Kerry would take her bruised lips and wounded pride and flee into the jungle to hide.

She had already had one user in her life. She didn't want another. Her father had been a manipulator and a fraud. At least Mr. O'Neal was straightforward. He freely admitted that he looked out for number one. When her father's corruption had been uncovered, Kerry had suffered in silence out of shame and love. She wasn't about to remain silent with Lincoln O'Neal. She owed him nothing but fifty thousand dollars. He certainly didn't warrant her devotion or respect. If he did anything that wasn't to her liking, she would tell him so with no compunction.

For all her antipathy toward him, she was grateful that O'Neal was with her. She wouldn't even admit to herself how frightened she had been at the prospect of transporting the children through the jungle alone. Their chances of surviving the trip and successfully escaping the country were slim, but at least they stood a better chance with O'Neal along.

"There's a narrow wooden bridge up ahead," she told him now. Once she had directed him to the road, they had ridden in silence. She took petty satisfaction in knowing that he was still nursing a hangover. "Almost immediately after you cross the bridge, there's a path on your left."

"Into the jungle?" he asked, looking up ahead.

"Yes. The children are hidden several hundred yards from the road."

He followed her directions, until the truck's progress was impeded by the density of the jungle. "I'll have to stop here."

"It'll be okay. We shouldn't be here long."

He pulled the truck to a halt and Kerry alighted. "This way." She struck out through the trees, anxious to check on the children. Her long braid became ensnared in vines. Branches slapped against her face and scratched her arms. "We could use your machete."

"Hacking through the plants leaves a trail," Linc said. "Unless it becomes absolutely necessary, we're better off struggling our way through."

Kerry was instantly contrite over her testiness. "Of course. I should have thought of that."

She felt somewhat redeemed when they stumbled upon the hiding place, and it went unnoticed by Linc. She stopped, turned around to face him and was met with only a quizzical gaze before she called a name softly.

"Joe. Joe, it's all right. You can come out."

Linc started at a sound on his left. The thick foliage moved, then parted. Several pairs of coffee-colored eyes stared at him from behind fronds as wide as parasols. A tall, slender youth materialized from behind the leafy, green screen.

The boy, whose age Linc placed at around fourteen, had a brooding face that appeared years older than his gangly body. He regarded Linc with a mixture of open hostility and suspicion.

"This is Linc O'Neal," Kerry told the boy. "He's the one I picked to help us. Linc, this is Joe, the oldest of the group."

Linc glanced at her quickly, wondering if she realized that she had used his first name. She didn't appear to. He stuck out his hand toward the boy. "Hello, Joe."

Joe ignored Linc's hand and abruptly turned his back. In soft, rapid Spanish, he called the children out of hiding. In pairs and singly, they emerged from their cover. One of the oldest girls was carrying a toddler on her hip. She walked directly to Kerry and handed the child over to her.

The little girl wrapped her arms trustingly and lovingly around Kerry's neck. She kissed the child's grubby cheek and smoothed back her hair.

The other children surrounded her. It seemed that each had something vital to impart. They competed for her attention, though she spread it around as diplomatically as a candidate running for public office.

Linc knew only enough Spanish to keep himself fed and from walking into the wrong restroom. The children were chattering so excitedly that he couldn't follow what they were saying to Kerry. Only one word, repeated frequently, registered with him.

*"Hermana?"* he said.

"Sister," Kerry told him absently as she gave the child's cheek a spit bath with her fingers.

"Why do they call you—"

Linc's question was never completed. When realization struck him, his face went completely blank. If he'd been poleaxed, he couldn't have looked more stunned.

Laughing at one of the children's disjointed stories, Kerry glanced up at him and asked distractedly, "I'm sorry, what did you say?"

"I asked why they were calling you sister."

"Oh, I—"

She looked at him then, saw his sick expression and realized the conclusion he had jumped to. He thought Sister Kerry had a religious significance. A speedy denial was on the tip of her tongue, but in a split second, she reconsidered. Why deny what he was obviously thinking? He had accidentally provided her with a way to spurn his sexual advances without jeopardizing his loyalty to their mission.

She searched her mind for a reason why she should set him right, but could find none. She also scratched the surface of her conscience, but didn't delve too deeply. She was doing this for the welfare of the orphans.

Before her conscience had time to rear up and question her motives, Kerry lowered her eyes demurely. "Why else?"

He called upon a deity, but not in prayer.

Kerry reacted with stern disapproval. "Watch your language, please." When he mumbled an apology, she knew her ruse had worked. It took all her acting ability to keep from laughing out loud. "Would you like to meet the children?"

"Are they all as friendly as Joe?" Linc asked.

"I speak English," the boy snapped with fierce pride.

Linc, unruffled by his faux pas, snapped right back, "Then your manners aren't worth a damn."

Kerry intervened quickly. "Joe, would you please stir up the fire? We'll feed the children before we go." Joe cast Linc a resentful glance before carrying out the chore Kerry had assigned him. "Children," Kerry said in Spanish and motioned for quiet, "this is Señor O'Neal."

"Make it Linc," he told her.

She told the children his first name. Eight pairs of eyes stared up at him with curiosity tempered by caution. One by one she introduced him to them. "And the youngest's name is Lisa."

He acknowledged each introduction solemnly, shaking hands with the boys and bowing stiffly at the waist for the girls, who giggled in response. He playfully tapped Lisa on the nose, being careful not to touch Kerry in the process.

He told them hello in Spanish, which just about exhausted his vocabulary. "Tell them that I'll take care of them on the journey." He spoke slowly so Kerry could simultaneously translate. "But they must obey me . . . at all times." He gave her a look that said, "That includes you," before he continued. "When I tell them to be quiet . . . they must be quiet...silent.... No moving...no wandering away from the group . . . *ever*. . . . If they do as I say . . . we'll get to the airplane . . . and it will take us to the United States."

The children's faces glowed radiantly when they heard the last two words.

"If they've been very good on the trip . . . and have done everything I've asked them to . . . when we arrive in the U.S. . . . I'll take them all to McDonald's."

"That's very thoughtful of you," Kerry said softly, "but they don't know what a McDonald's is. They couldn't even imagine it if I tried to explain."

"Oh." He glanced down at the eight faces turned up to him, and his jaded heart twisted. "Well, think of an appropriate reward," he said with feigned impatience.

After eating an unpalatable paste made of beans and rice, they began collecting their scanty provisions. When all that remained to be loaded was the children, Linc brought one of his cameras back from the truck and began snapping pictures.

"Sister Kerry, if you would—"

"Please. Just Kerry is fine."

He nodded brusquely. He hadn't looked at her directly since learning of her vocation. "Would you please assemble everybody for a group picture?"

"Certainly."

In minutes, they were posed for him. The children were excited and smiling. Lisa had her thumb in her mouth. Joe refused to look into the lens and gazed broodingly into the surrounding trees. Kerry's smile was forced.

"Okay, let's go," Linc said as he popped his lens cap back on. Draping the camera around his neck by its strap, he shouldered a bundle of canned food that Joe had scavenged from the nearest village the night before.

"Don't you usually take action shots? Why did you want a posed group picture?" Kerry asked Linc as they tromped toward the truck.

"In case some of them don't make it."

His curt answer brought Kerry, who was carrying Lisa, to an abrupt halt on the jungle path. She turned to face Linc. "Is that a possibility?"

"Where's your head?" At that moment, he would have been hard pressed to specify just what had made him so angry at her. "In the clouds? There are soldiers on either side who would murder these kids in a minute just for the hell of it. For an evening's entertainment."

She quailed, but refused to let him see her trepidation. "You want to back out."

Linc lowered his face close to her. "You're damn right I do. And if you had any sense, which I'm beginning to seriously doubt, you would too."

"I *can't*."

He cursed expansively and didn't apologize for it this time. "Come on, we're wasting time."

When they reached the truck his grim expression reflected his pessimism. The nine orphans were crowded into the bed of the pickup, along with his camera gear, their meager but space consuming supplies, and Kerry.

"I'm sorry you can't ride in the cab," he said, watching as she took Lisa onto her lap. "But if we're stopped, I can pass Joe off as my aid." He glanced down at her disquieting figure, which even her safari attire didn't detract from. "Without that lurid dress, you don't look much like a, uh . . ."

"I understand. The children will do better if I'm back here anyway. Just warn me in plenty of time if you see a patrol. I'll pull the tarp over us."

"It'll be stifling under there."

"I know."

"If we're stopped, the children must remain absolutely silent and still."

"I've explained that to them repeatedly."

"Good," he said with a terse bob of his head. "You've got water?"

"Yes. Do you have the map?"

"I know where we're going." He met her eyes soberly. "I just hope to hell we get there."

They exchanged a meaningful glance before he climbed into the cab of the truck and started the motor.

Kerry had never been more uncomfortable in her life, though she tried to put up a brave and contented front for the children. They were roughly jostled about in the bed of the truck. Its shocks were ineffectual on the washboard jungle road. At least the bouncing motion kept the gargantuan mosquitoes and other biting insects from lighting on them.

They never had to hide under the tarp, but the sun beat down on them mercilessly. And when the trees provided shade, they swapped the fiery sun for humidity so thick it could be cut with a knife.

The children complained of being thirsty, but Kerry carefully rationed their water. Fresh water might not be easy to come by. Besides, the more they drank, the more often she would have to ask Linc to stop. She wanted to avoid asking him for any favors.

He kept driving even after the sun had sunk below the tree line and had pitched the jungle into premature twilight. Darkness had completely fallen by the time they drove through a deserted village. As a safety precaution, Linc had signaled for Kerry to hide herself and the children under the tarp. He circled the village, and when he was satisfied that it was truly deserted, drove a half mile beyond it and pulled the truck into a clearing.

"We'll stop here for the night."

Kerry gratefully took his hand and let him lift her down. She planted both palms in the small of her back and arched it, stretching her cramped muscles.

Linc averted his eyes from her breasts, which were emphasized by her stretching exercise. They strained the sweat-damp fabric of her shirt. He couldn't help but remember how responsive they'd been to his touch. He cleared his throat uncomfortably. "Will you be all right if I walk back to the village and scout around?"

"Of course. Can we build a fire?"

"Yes, but keep it small. I'll take Joe with me. Here," he yanked the pistol from his belt and twirled it, presenting her with the butt of it.

She took it, but looked at it fearfully. "I told you this morning that I wasn't sure how to use it."

He gave her a quick lesson. "If you have to shoot it, be sure your target is as close to you as I was this morning. Then you can't miss." He grinned crookedly. She answered his smile. Then he and the boy faded into the darkness.

She put one of the older girls in charge of the younger children and sent the boys to gather firewood. By the time Linc and Joe returned, Kerry had a low fire going. Joe was carrying blankets. The bodies of two scrawny chickens were dangling from Linc's hand.

"Perfect fire," he told Kerry.

"Thank you."

"These may not go far." Apologetically he indicated the chickens. "But they were all I could find."

"I'll open a can or two of vegetables and make a stew."

He nodded and moved away from her and the children to pluck and dress the chickens. For which she was supremely grateful.

Though they had dozed while traveling, the children were almost too exhausted to eat. Kerry encouraged them, knowing that this might be their last hot meal for a few days.

Eventually they had all been fed and put on pallets in the back of the pickup.

She was sitting near the dying fire sipping a precious cup of coffee when Linc joined her and refilled his cup. "See or hear anything?" she asked in a hushed voice.

"No. Everything's quiet. Which is almost unnerving. I'd rather know where they are."

"They?"

"Everybody but us." He grinned. The firelight caught his wide, white smile.

Kerry looked away from it. It was disturbingly attractive. "You surprised me."

"How?"

"By being so wonderful to the children. Thank you."

"Thank you for the aspirin. They helped improve my headache and my disposition."

"I'm serious. I appreciate your kind handling of these orphans."

"I've done some terrible things in my lifetime, but I've never abused a child," he said tightly. He sipped his coffee and stretched his long legs out in front of him.

She hadn't meant to intimate that he had, but thought it best to drop the subject.

"Tell me about them," he said after a long moment. "Mary."

"She never knew her father," Kerry said. "Before Mary was born he was executed for circulating propaganda. Her mother was sent to prison and is presumed dead."

"Mike."

Kerry had already anglicized their names so that they would start being familiar with the names they would hear in the United States. She told him about the boy. "Carmen and Cara are the courier's sisters. His name is Juan."

"And Lisa?"

Kerry smiled. "She's precious, isn't she? When her mother was only thirteen she was raped by a rebel soldier.

She took her own life after Lisa was born. At least Lisa doesn't know the heartache of having had and lost."

"What about him?"

Kerry followed the direction of Linc's gaze. Joe was sitting at the edge of the clearing, staring out into the dark jungle.

"Joe," she said wistfully. "So sad."

"How old is he?"

"Fifteen." She gave him a rundown of Joe's history. "He has a remarkable mind, but he's a product of his tragic past. Hostile. Angry. Antisocial."

"In love with you."

"What?" She looked at Linc as though he'd lost his mind. "Don't be ridiculous. He's only a boy."

"Who's had to grow up fast."

"But in love with me? That's impossible."

"Hardly. By the time a boy is fifteen he's already had—" He broke off.

"I suppose so," Kerry murmured to cover the awkward pause. "Had you?" She couldn't imagine what had prompted her to ask him that. She didn't dare look at him, though from the corner of her eye, she saw the sudden movement of his head as he looked at her sharply.

"I thought taking confessions was a priest's job."

"So it is. I'm sorry. We were talking about Joe."

"Do you know what he did with that dress you wore last night?" She shook her head. "He burned it in the campfire before he banked the flames." When she gazed at him in disbelief, he nodded somberly. "I watched him throw it onto the coals and stare at it until it was consumed."

"But he's the one who stole the dress. He knew why I had to wear it."

"He also knew it helped get me here. He hates himself for contributing to your shame."

"You're imagining things."

"Nope. He's extremely protective of you."

"He's never been before. We're not in imminent danger. What is he protecting me against?"

"Me."

The firelight was reflected in his eyes, making them appear more golden than brown. He had taken off his bush shirt earlier in the day and was wearing only an army-green tank top. His skin was as smooth as polished wood. The upper part of his chest was matted with brown hair that had the same reddish cast as that on his head. It curled crisply against his tanned skin and seemed tipped in gold whenever sunlight—or firelight—struck it.

Uneasily, Kerry glanced away.

When he finally broke the strained silence, his voice was hoarse. "Why didn't you tell me?"

"There was nothing to tell," she replied honestly.

"I beg to differ, *Miss* Bishop." His face was taut and angry. "Why didn't you stop me from kissing you?"

"If you'll recall, I tried."

"Not very hard."

She stared at him, aghast over his righteous defense of his actions. "I chose being kissed over being killed."

"You were never under threat of dying and you know it. One word. You only had to say one word and I would have left you alone."

"This morning maybe, but what about last night?"

"That was different."

"Because you were drunk?"

"Yes." He could see that she considered inebriation a flimsy excuse. "Well what was I supposed to think?" he demanded defensively. "How is a man supposed to react to a whore's solicitation?"

"I'm sure I don't know," she said coldly.

"Now you do. He reacts to a whore exactly the way I did to you last night. The dress, the hair, the suggestive smile, the whole damn package was an offer no man could refuse. So don't go condemning me for taking your bait!"

"Sister Kerry, are you all right?"

They both looked up. Joe was standing just beyond the circle of the firelight. His hands were balled into fists and his eyes were trained threateningly on Linc.

"It's all right, Joe," Kerry reassured the boy. "Go to sleep. Tomorrow will be a difficult day."

He looked reluctant to relax his vigilance, but eventually he backed toward the truck and climbed into the cab, where it had been decided that he and Linc would sleep.

Kerry and Linc stared at the dying embers of the fire. The silence was as dangerous as the jungle that surrounded them.

"What made you decide to do it?" he asked.

"I needed someone's help."

"No, I don't mean recruiting me. I meant what made you decide on becoming a . . . you know?"

"Oh." She pulled her knees against her chest and propped her chin on them. "Things. Circumstances."

He was going to be furious if and when he ever discovered the truth. This morning's rage would be mild compared to the hell he would raise when he found out. She already dreaded the day. But until they were out of danger and in the United States, she had to continue with her lie. It served as protection against him.

And, if she were scrupulously honest, protection against herself. For all his rough edges, Kerry found him attractive to a disturbing degree. Lincoln O'Neal could have stepped out of a feminine fantasy catalog. He was ruggedly handsome, lived an extraordinary life-style, courted danger, and flaunted his disregard for established rules of behavior.

He would be an excellent lover. He had treated her roughly; his caresses had been somewhat crude; but his brazenness had held an appeal all its own. He was the kind of challenge no woman could resist. A maverick to tame. A hellion to redeem.

Kerry could deny it until she turned blue in the face, but the truth was that he had aroused her. So, to keep herself from doing something extremely foolish, she would consider herself as unavailable as he thought her to be. In a way, she was even now taking a vow of chastity.

He was impatiently jabbing a stick into the fire. Frustration was evident in his every movement and in the gritty sound of his voice. "Being what you are, how could you do what you did last night?"

"I was desperate. Surely you can see that now."

"But you were so damned convincing."

She felt flattered and ashamed at the same time. "I did what was necessary."

She could feel his gaze on her and couldn't prevent herself from meeting it. Across the fire, they stared at each other. Each was remembering his caresses, the forbidden places where he had touched her, the thorough, intimate kisses they had shared. Their thoughts ran parallel. They were on tongues, and breasts, and innuendoes that would have been better left unsaid.

Linc was the first to look away. His expression was tense. He swore beneath his breath. "Maybe you missed your rightful calling. You played your part so well," he said scornfully. "But then you had to, didn't you? You had to be certain I'd go along with you, so you lured me with a few feels. A few tastes of you—"

"Stop it!"

"Until I was crazy with lust and not thinking too clearly."

"I lied to you, yes!" she cried. She feared the seductiveness of his words and had to stop them. "I tricked and deceived you, yes. Suffered your insufferable embraces. I'd do it again if that's what it took to get these children to safety."

"Remember me in your prayers tonight, Sister Kerry," he growled. "I sure as hell need them."

He quickly tossed the dregs of his coffee into the fire. The live coals hissed like a serpent. A cloud of smoke rose up between them, symbolic of the hell he was going through to keep himself from touching her.

# *Chapter 4*

They came out of nowhere. The brush on either side of the road shifted and moved; suddenly, the truck was surrounded by guerrilla fighters who seemed to have sprouted from the trees.

Linc stamped on the brakes. They squealed as the truck skidded to a halt on the narrow gravel road. The children screamed in fright. Kerry, her screams mingling with the others, pulled little Lisa closer.

When the dust settled, everything was as motionless as a photograph. No one moved. Even the jungle birds sensed impending danger and were silent in their hideouts overhead.

The band of rebel fighters held M-16s and Uzis at their hips. The automatic weapons were, without exception, aimed at the truck and its terrified occupants. The guerrillas' faces were young, but sinister. Some had yet to grow their first whiskers, but they had the implacable eyes of men who weren't afraid either to kill or be killed.

From the looks of their clothing, they had been living in the jungle for a long time. What hadn't been purposely streaked with mud for camouflage was stained with sweat and dirt and blood. Their muscles rippled. The glaring sunlight was reflected off their sweat-oiled skin. Their bodies were lean, hard, as unyielding as their menacing expressions.

Linc, having been in every war zone since Vietnam, recognized the unchanging, uncompromising expression of men who had been killing for too long. These men were inured to death. A human life, even their own, held little value for them.

He knew better than to do anything stupid in the name of heroism. He kept both hands on the steering wheel where they could easily see them. About the only thing he, Kerry and the children had going for them was that they obviously weren't part of El Presidente's army. If they had been, the truck wouldn't have been stopped, it would have been destroyed and they would be jungle fodder by now.

"Kerry," Linc called back to her, "stay where you are. I'll handle this. Keep the children as calm and quiet as possible. Tell the guerrillas that I'm going to open the door and get out."

She delivered Linc's message in Spanish. There was no response from the ring of hostile faces. Linc took that to mean that there was no argument. He slowly lowered his left hand. Several of the soldiers reacted instantly.

"No, no!" Kerry shouted. Rapidly she begged them to hold their fire and explained that Señor O'Neal only wanted to talk to them.

Bravely Linc lowered his hand again and pulled on the door handle. Warily he stepped out. With his hands raised above his head, he moved away from the truck.

Kerry gasped inaudibly when one of the guerrillas lunged forward and snatched the pistol out of his belt. He was told to unholster the machete and, even though he wasn't fluent in Spanish, he understood the threat underlying the barked order and complied without hesitation.

"We're taking the children to a town near the border," he said in a loud, clear voice, "where there's food and shelter for them. They're orphans. We're not your enemy. Let us—"

Linc's explanation was brought to a violent halt when one of the guerrillas stepped forward and backhanded him across the mouth. His head snapped around, following the impetus behind the blow. Linc, who had mastered street fighting before he had cut all his molars, came back with his fist clenched and his teeth bared. Before he could launch a counterattack, however, the soldier punched him in the stomach. Linc went down in the dusty road. The corner of his lip was dripping blood.

Kerry vaulted over the side of the pickup and ran to where Linc was lying, clutching his bruised ribs. She ignored the automatic rifles pointed at her and faced the guerrilla.

"*Por favor, señor*, let us talk to you," she said hurriedly.

"I told you to stay out of this," Linc growled, coming up on one knee. "Get back in the truck."

"And let you get beaten to death?" she hissed down at him. Swinging her long braid over her shoulder she faced the man who had hit Linc. The insignia on his beret designated him the highest ranking rebel in the group. "What Mr. O'Neal told you is true," she told him in Spanish. "We're only taking the children to a safer place."

"You're in a truck belonging to El Presidente." He spat in the road near her feet. Kerry held her ground and prayed that Linc would.

"That's right. I stole it from El Presidente's army."

One of the soldiers roughly hauled Joe out of the cab and conducted a search of it. He came back to his leader, carrying the uniform jacket and cap. The leader thrust them at Kerry accusingly.

She said, "The careless officer left them in the truck when he went inside a tavern to drink and enjoy the women." That produced a stir of resentment among the guerrillas.

"What's going on?" Linc asked. He was standing beside her now. A thin trickle of blood was oozing down his chin, and he was subconsciously rubbing his left ribs. Otherwise he seemed unharmed. Just virulently angry.

"He asked me why we were driving an army truck. I had to explain about the uniform."

Lisa began to cry. A few of the other children were whimpering in fright. The captain of the band was getting nervous. He glanced up and down the stretch of road. He rarely exposed his men to snipers for this long.

He rattled off a series of terse commands. One of his men jumped into the cab of the truck, ordering Joe into the back with the rest of the children.

"What now?" Linc asked Kerry.

"He's taking us to their camp."

Linc muttered a curse. "For how long?"

"I don't know."

"What for?"

"To decide what to do with us."

With rifles at their backs, they were nudged forward. Kerry called out to the crying children, telling them that she would see them shortly. She couldn't bear the sight of their frightened, tear-streaked faces as the truck rolled past. The commander told the soldier who was now driving the truck to take the cutoff. Apparently the camp wasn't far away.

The soldiers slipped through the jungle soundlessly. They moved through the undergrowth without disturbing a single leaf. When Linc tried to make further conversation with Kerry, he was warned to be quiet. The command was issued so threateningly that he obeyed it, though his jaw was bunched with anger.

They reached the guerrilla camp just as the truck was driven into the clearing from the opposite side. Kerry asked permission to go to the children and it was granted. They poured over the side of the pickup, scrambling toward her, seeking reassurance.

Joe was shoved against the side of the truck along with Linc. Linc's camera bags were heaved over the side and opened. Each piece of photographic equipment was examined.

"Tell them to get their goddamned hands off my cameras," he shouted to Kerry.

She shot him a glance that warned him to keep his voice low and his temper under control. She faced the leader. "Mr. O'Neal is a professional photographer. He takes pictures and sells them to news magazines." He seemed impressed, though still suspicious.

On a sudden inspiration, Kerry looked at Linc, where he was being held at gunpoint against the side of the truck. "Do you have a Polaroid?"

"Yeah. Sometimes I use it to set up shots, to check the lighting angles."

"And film?" He nodded.

She turned to the guerrilla, whose dark eyes were moving over her in a most disconcerting way. She ignored his blatantly sexual appraisal. "Would you like Mr. O'Neal to take a picture of you and your men? A group portrait."

She could tell instantly that the idea appealed to the guerrillas. They began joking among themselves, poking each other playfully, using their automatic weapons like toys.

The leader roared for silence, and, as quickly as the joviality commenced, it ended. They all became stock still.

"Wanna fill me in on what the hell is going on?" Linc demanded in a tightly controlled voice.

Kerry told him what she had suggested. "We might bribe our way out of this with a few photographs."

Linc glanced around at the group of hostile men. "They might get their pictures but murder us all anyway."

"Then you think of something!" she whispered tartly. "Even if we do get out alive, this is wasting precious time."

Linc looked at her with grudging respect. Most women would have dissolved into hysterics after the ambush. He knew from experience that her sharp mind could devise alternate plans as the situation called for them.

"All right. Tell the leader to line them up, call off this bozo," he said, glaring at the man who had the barrel of his M16 imbedded an inch in his belly, "and let me get my camera ready."

She told the rebel what Linc had said. When she saw that he still wasn't as keen on the idea as his men were, she spread it on thick. "Señor O'Neal is famous. A prize winner. The photographs of you and your men will appear in magazines everywhere. They will demonstrate to the world your fighting spirit and bravery."

Sullenly the guerrilla pondered what she said, then abruptly broke into a wide grin of approval. His men, who had lapsed into expectant silence, began chattering and laughing again.

"Get your camera," Kerry told Linc. "Start with a Polaroid so they can see immediate results."

Linc thoroughly enjoyed shoving aside the soldier who had been ordered to guard him. He used the heel of his hand rather more roughly than necessary and was rewarded by a scowl. He bent over his camera bag, cursing as he dusted off his expensive equipment, which had been heedlessly dropped onto the ground.

While he was loading his cameras with film, having decided that these pictures would not only be lifesaving, but profitable, too, Kerry assembled the soldiers. They stood proud and tall, showing off their Uzis like fishermen with the day's largest catch.

"They're ready," she told Linc.

"How are the kids?" he asked, as he peered through the viewfinder and motioned for the guerrillas to move closer together.

"Fine. Joe's watching them." She knew now why Linc had all those web-fine lines radiating from the corners of his eyes. He squinted into cameras a lot.

"Tell them to hold still," he said. She did. "Okay, on the count of three."

*"Uno, dos, tres,"* she counted.

The shutter clicked and the camera ejected the exposed automatic film. Kerry took it from Linc and asked, "Can you take another?"

"Yep. Give them the countdown."

After several had been taken, Kerry took the Polaroid pictures to the leader. His men inched closer, looking at the snapshots until they were fully developed. Laughter broke out. Mild insults were exchanged. They were apparently pleased with the results.

While they were passing the pictures around, Linc ripped off several frames with his power driven Nikon. Some of these men, had they been born elsewhere, would be gloating over high school graduation pictures and toting baseball bats instead of machine guns. The contrast between their innocent delight over the snapshots and the grenade-decorated belts at their waists would make photographs that bore the famous Linc O'Neal stamp of excellence. His photographs were wordless editorials.

"Now, while they're in a good mood, let's get the hell out of here," he told Kerry beneath his breath. "You do the negotiating, since you seem to be so good at it."

Kerry didn't know whether to take that as a compliment or an insult, but she didn't dwell on it. They needed to be on their way as quickly as possible. Every hour counted. They had only two more days to make it to the border in time. Traveling with the children was slow. They hadn't covered nearly as much ground as they should have, though Linc had been driving them relentlessly.

Kerry tentatively approached the band of guerrillas. As unobtrusively as possible, she got the leader's attention. "May we leave now?"

As though a switch had turned them off, the soldiers fell silent. They all watched their leader closely, gauging his reaction and anticipating his decision.

The opinion of his men was important to him. He wanted them to hold him in the highest esteem and wouldn't dare lose face in front of them. Knowing this, Kerry pleaded her case.

"You are brave fighters. It doesn't take much courage to terrorize children. El Presidente's men are the cowards who make war on women and children, not soldiers like you." She made a gesture that encompassed the entire group.

"Would you butcher helpless children? I don't believe you would because you fight for liberty, for life. You've all left behind children of your own, or brothers and sisters. These could be your children." She nodded toward the truck where the children were huddled. "Help me. Let me move them to a safer place, away from the fighting."

The leader focused on the children. Kerry thought she discerned a flicker of compassion, or an emotion very near to it, in the man's impenetrable eyes. Then he looked at Linc and his expression became hostile again.

"Are you his woman?" he asked Kerry, hitching his chin toward Linc.

Kerry glanced at Linc over her shoulder. "I—"

"What'd he ask you?" Linc didn't like the look on the rebel's face.

She met his burning gaze across the clearing. "He asked if I was your . . . woman."

"Tell him no."

"No? But if he thinks—"

"He'll use you to get to me. Tell him no, damnit!"

She faced the commander again. "No. I'm not his woman."

He stared at her with cold calculation. Then, in a move that dismayed Kerry, he began to smile. The smile broke slowly across his dark, foreboding face and grew into laughter. Soon he and all his men were laughing at something only they understood and found amusing.

"Yes, you may go," he told her in Spanish.

She looked at her feet in an attitude of humble appreciation. *"Gracias, señor."*

"But first I want your man to take my picture again."

"He's not my man."

"You lie," he said softly.

Kerry shuddered at the triumphant gleam in his eyes. "No. He's not . . . he's not anything to me. I only hired Mr. O'Neal to help me get the children to safety."

"Ah," he said expansively, "then he won't mind if I have my picture taken with you."

She met his gloating sneer with an expression of astonishment and fear. "With me?"

*"Sí."*

Several of his men grunted their approval and congratulated him on his shrewdness with hearty slaps on the back.

"What the hell is going on?" Linc, standing with his hands on his hips, was demanding an answer from her as she slowly turned around.

"He wants his picture made."

"So move out of the way and I'll take one."

"With me. He wants his picture made with me." Her gaze skittered up to Linc's. His face looked as dangerous as any belonging to the men who were crowding behind her. He cast a malevolent look toward the leader.

"Tell the bastard to go to hell."

She smiled a wavering smile of gratitude. She was afraid Linc might have considered it expedient for her to have her picture taken with this animal. Proudly she turned and walked back to the leader. His eyes, directed toward Linc, were filled with malice. He reached for Kerry, encircled her wrist in a grip as hard as iron, and yanked her toward him.

"Let me go!" She wrestled out of his grip. Several machine guns were snapped into readiness, but she kept her chin up. Her expression was one of haughty contempt. "I won't have my picture made with you."

"Then your man will die," the fighter warned sibilantly.

"I don't believe so. You're not a cold-blooded murderer." She rather suspected that he was, but knew that wasn't the image he wanted to project to the free countries of the world.

Joe ordered the children, some of whom were crying, to stay where they were. He moved to Linc's side. The leader ordered two of his men to watch them. The rest of the soldiers scattered around the clearing. All of them kept their guns trained on the photographer and the adolescent boy, whose face was working with fury.

The guerrilla leader laughed nastily and wrapped his large hand around Kerry's neck. She kept her posture stiff, her body unbending. "Take your hands off me." He only drew her closer.

"Damn him," Linc snarled from behind her. "Let her go!" he shouted to the commander.

"Why are you being so stubborn, gringa?" the rebel asked in a lulling voice. "You deprive yourself of much pleasure."

Suddenly, Joe burst into the open. He was tripped by a booted foot and went sprawling in the dirt. The soldiers laughed, none louder than the leader. The guerrilla who had tripped him, put the barrel of his automatic rifle at the base of Joe's skull and ordered him not to move.

"Oh, God," Kerry breathed. Was her stand against the whims of the rebel going to cost Joe his life? She vacillated.

"Tell him you're a nun," Linc said.

"You read the newspapers, Linc."

Right. He did. Churchmen and women were no longer spared bloody deaths. Indeed, they were sometimes the targeted victims of the cruelest executions.

The leader took hold of Kerry's long braid and began winding it around his meaty fist.

"You sonofabitch!"

Linc lunged across the clearing. A rifle butt was slammed into his middle. He went down with a grunt of pain, but came up fighting.

"Linc, no!" Kerry cried as she spun around to see what was happening.

The leader pulled a pistol from the holster at his hip. He took quick aim on Linc.

Kerry grabbed his arm. "*Por favor*, no."

"Is he your man?"

She stared into his obsidian eyes, knowing that what he had wanted most to do was frighten and humiliate them. "Yes," she declared defiantly. "Yes, yes, he is. Please don't kill him." Again and again she repeated the imploring words. Finally the guerrilla lowered the pistol to his side. He issued orders sharply and quickly

Kerry rushed to Linc's side and assisted him to stand upright. "Hurry. He said we could go."

Wincing, holding one arm across his middle, Linc glared at the leader. He wanted to pound that arrogant face to a pulp, and if it weren't for Kerry and the children, he'd risk his life to do it. But she was tugging on his sleeve and pleading with him to get into the truck. Knowing that he was doing the wise thing, if not the thing he wanted to do, Linc turned away from the open challenge in the guerrilla's eyes.

He gathered his cameras and film rapidly as Kerry herded the children into the back of the pickup. Bravely, she pushed aside the soldier who was holding the gun on Joe and helped the boy to his feet. The glower he gave the leader was as malevolent as Linc's.

"Please, Joe, get inside the truck," Kerry said. "I'm fine and we're all alive. Let's go."

She stepped into the back of the pickup and gathered the smaller children against her. Linc came to the end of the truck. "I need my pistol and machete." She asked the leader if he would return them.

"Tell your man to get in the truck and close the door."

Kerry relayed the order to Linc. He grudgingly carried it out. The guerrilla swaggered over to the truck and laid the machete at Kerry's feet. "I am no fool. I will not return the gun."

Kerry passed along the message to Linc. He seemed inclined to argue, but changed his mind. He engaged the gears and drove the truck out of the clearing. Following the winding track through the jungle, they soon reached the road.

Before pulling onto it, he braked and stepped out of the cab. "I know it will he hotter than hell, but pull that tarp over you. We're not going to take any more chances."

He helped spread the canvas covering over the group of huddled children and gave Kerry a piercing look.

"Did he hurt you?"

"I'm fine," she said gruffly, lowering her gaze from that incisive, golden one.

He pulled the tarp over her. Moments later she heard the door closing. The truck wheezed into motion.

"What do you think?" Kerry asked in a low voice.

"It looks deserted."

At the edge of the jungle, they had been watching the sugar plantation house for several minutes. There had been no sign of movement.

"It would be wonderful to spend the night under a roof."

Linc glanced down at Kerry. When he had finally stopped the truck—having accidentally spotted the roof of the vacated plantation house—and peeled back the tarp, she and the children had looked like a wilted bouquet. Some of the children had fallen asleep against Kerry, burdening her even more. But not a single complaint had been forthcoming. Her endurance seemed unflagging. But now he saw the traces of weariness around her eyes and mouth.

"You stay here. I'll take Joe and scout around.

They were back in ten minutes. "It doesn't look like there's been anyone here in a long time. I think it will be all right. Do you want to ride or walk?" he asked her, getting behind the steering wheel of the truck.

"I think we've all had enough of the truck for today. The children and I will walk."

She escorted the children across the sprawling yard of what must have been a lovely estate. It, however, like everything in the Central American country, had suffered the ravages of war. The white stucco walls were scarred and pockmarked with bullet holes. Vines had flourished to a fault. They had choked to death the other plants growing beneath the wide veranda, which now sagged in disrepair. Most of the windows had been broken out. The front door was missing.

But the large rooms had been shaded from the merciless sun and offered a welcome coolness that felt wonderful to Kerry and the children after having spent silent, sweltering hours beneath the tarpaulin in the back of the truck.

There was no electricity or gas in the kitchen, and Linc vetoed the idea of building a fire, so their supper consisted of cold beans straight from the can and sliced Spam. Luckily, even though the pipes were rusty, the water that came out of them was cool. Kerry bathed the children's faces and hands and put them on pallets in one of the well ventilated rooms.

From his lookout post at one of the wide front windows, Linc watched her as she moved among the children. She patiently listened to their lengthy prayers and told them of all the glorious things that awaited them in the United States.

The moon had come up over the tops of the trees and shone onto her hair through the windows. Earlier she had unraveled her braid and combed through it with her fingers. Now her hair shimmered like a skein of black silk over her shoulders and back, catching the silver moonlight on every strand, as she moved from one pallet to another. She lifted Lisa onto her lap, kissed the top of her dark, glossy head, and rocked her gently as she softly hummed a lullaby.

Linc wished to heaven he had a cigarette, anything in fact, to distract him. Even when he wasn't looking at Kerry, he was aware of her every movement. And, curse him, he felt twinges of jealousy that it wasn't his head cushioned on her breasts.

He would surely be damned. He deserved to be. Because even now, knowing that she was chaste, he was hard and hot with the desire to be inside her. He wanted to touch her again. But not in the same way. He didn't want to *subject* her to his caresses. He wanted to treat her to them. He didn't want her humiliated and tearful beneath his hands. He didn't want her still and unmoving with defiance and disgust. He wanted her responsive and receptive, moaning with pleasure.

God, what was the matter with him? His thoughts were no purer than those the guerrilla fighter had no doubt been thinking. He didn't want to consider himself on that low a level, but apparently that's where he belonged. He was going to hell for what he was thinking, but he couldn't for the life of him stop thinking it.

He had been without a woman too long, that's all. But he'd been without women for long stretches of time before and had survived. He hadn't ever been consumed with the thought of having a woman as he was now. And his desires had been focused on the female sex in general, not a single member of that group.

Never before had he been unable to concentrate on anything except his feverish, thick, aching sex, which embarrassingly strained the front of his pants at inconvenient and unexpected times, like when Kerry had turned to him with a cup of water between her hands—giving him a drink before taking one herself, bearing it like a peace offering, proffering it with a silent thank-you in her deep blue eyes.

He was angry with himself for seeing her as a desirable woman and not as what she was. His anger sought an outlet. There was no dog to kick, no missed nailhead to curse. His only scapegoat proved to be the woman who was responsible for making him act and think like a goddamned fool.

"They're all asleep," Kerry said softly as she moved toward the window.

Linc was sitting on the sill, one knee raised to ease the pressure in his groin. Kerry seemed oblivious to his black mood, oblivious to everything but the unspoiled beauty of the night. She drew a deep breath, unaware that it made her breasts lift and swell and push against her shirt until their shape was emphasized for the man who couldn't keep his eyes off them to save his soul.

"Why didn't you tell him right away that you were a nun?"

She looked at him quizzically, surprised by the harsh question. "I didn't think it would do any good."

"It might have."

"It might have also turned his attention to one of the girls."

Unspeakably vile things like that happened in time of war. Men would do things they ordinarily would find abhorrent. Linc couldn't argue the point with her. He knew she was right. But an inner demon was compelling him to hurt her, to make her suffer as he was suffering.

"I just don't get you, lady. You make out like a saint, but you seem to enjoy using that body and face of yours to drive a man crazy. I ought to know."

He slid from the window sill and loomed over her. "Is that how you religious types get your kicks? Is that part of the convent training? Flirting, but never coming across? Promising, but never fulfilling?"

"That's disgusting, even coming from someone as low as you. I became an unwilling pawn between you and that ape in a stupid masculine contest of wills. I stood up to him, which apparently earned his respect. Then I begged him to keep you alive."

What she said had merit, making him all the madder. "Don't do me any more favors, okay? Or were you enjoying the attention so much it didn't even seem like a favor?"

"I put up with his lewd flirtation because I had to. Just as I did with *you*."

"And both times you sacrificed yourself for the children's sake," he sneered.

"Yes!"

"That's a hoot."

"I'm not surprised you don't understand. You've never thought of anybody but yourself. You've never loved anybody but Lincoln O'Neal."

His hands shot out, grabbed her by the shoulders, and jerked her up against him.

Joe instantly materialized out of the darkness. His liquid eyes glittered in the moonlight. They were murderously focused on Linc.

Linc cursed, released Kerry, and turned away. He was angrier at himself than at either of them. He was the one behaving like a madman. "I'm going to take a look around. Stay here." He stalked out, wielding his machete as though he would welcome something to slash into.

Kerry watched his tall shadow blend into the others on the far side of the yard. Joe worriedly whispered her name. She laid a reassuring hand on his arm and smiled halfheartedly. "I'm all right, Joe. Don't worry about Señor O'Neal. He's just edgy."

The boy didn't look convinced. Kerry wasn't convinced herself. It was a mystery to her why Linc was so angry. Why did their conversation always end in a shouting match? They swapped nasty insults like petulant children. The horrible episode with the guerrillas should have drawn them closer together, created a bond, instead it had wedged them further apart. In a very real sense they had saved each other's life today, yet to hear them, one would think they were bitter adversaries. Her feelings toward him were ambivalent. She needed time and space to think them through.

"I'm going to take a walk outside, Joe."

"But he said to stay here."

"I know what he said, but I need some air. I won't go far. Keep an eye on the children for me."

Joe wouldn't deny her request. Kerry knew she was taking unfair advantage of that as she left him standing watch over the sleeping children. She slipped through the dark rooms of the plantation house and, wanting to avoid Linc, exited through a screened porch at the back of it.

The stones of what had once been a terrace were broken and crumbling. Grass was growing up through the cracks. Kerry wondered how many parties had been held there. What had happened to the people who had enjoyed a gracious life-style there? They had obviously been affluent. Had they exploited the land and the laborers, as the propaganda posters proclaimed?

And Kerry Bishop wondered if she had ever met the owners of the house. In that previous lifetime, had she been introduced to them in a gracious salon while wearing a designer dress and nibbling on canapes?

She pushed that disturbing thought aside and strolled down a weeded path. The evening was blissfully cool. She followed the path through the formal garden and beyond.

The sound of running water attracted her attention. She almost stepped into the flowing stream before she saw it. It was an uncovered treasure. In the moonlight, it looked as sparkly and bubbly as champagne.

She hesitated only a moment before sitting down on its rock-strewn bank and unlacing her boots. Seconds later, she was standing in swirling, cooling water up to her knees. It felt delightful. Reluctant to leave it for even a second, she stepped back onto the rocks and unfastened her khaki pants. When she went into the water the second time, she was wearing only her shirt and panties.

She submerged herself in the natural whirlpool. The gurgling water washed her gritty, sun-baked skin, which was salty and itching with dried sweat. The swift current worked like massaging fingers to rid her muscles of their fatigue and tension. She ducked her head and let the water close over her scalp and flow through her dusty hair.

Her bath would have been divine had Linc's words not come echoing back to her. How could he possibly think that she had enjoyed the guerrilla soldier's attention? Strange, that while the guerrilla's touch had repulsed her, Linc's caresses hadn't. Originally she had been just as frightened of him, mistaking him for a man as bloodthirsty as the ones they had encountered that day. But she'd never been revolted by his touch. Disturbed, yes. Aroused, yes. But never had she found his kisses repulsive. And should he ever kiss her again—

She never got to complete the thought.

An arm closed around her midriff just beneath her breasts and hauled her out of the stream. Before she could utter a single sound, a hand was clamped over her open mouth.

# Chapter 5

Kerry fought like a wildcat.

She bit the meaty part of his hand below his wristbone and earned a grunt of pain for her efforts. But when she tried to work her mouth free to scream, his hand only mashed against her lips bruisingly. The sounds she tried desperately to utter were stifled.

She kicked backward against his shins, wiggled and squirmed, scratched and clawed, twisted and turned. But his strength was far superior to hers. His arms felt like a vise about to crush her ribs.

"Shut up and be still for crissake."

Kerry went limp. Her captor was Linc.

While it was infuriating that he would frighten her this way, she was thankful that it was he and not a guerrilla fighter who was dragging her deeper into the jungle and away from the house.

"Um-um-um."

"Shh! Shut up."

His words were nothing but hissing breaths close to her ear. Then new sounds registered with her, sounds she hadn't noticed before, but which were frightfully distinctive and familiar. The gruff laughter of men. The lilting, melodic tones of conversational Spanish spiced with vulgarities. The clanging of aluminum cooking pots and the clinking of armaments.

Soldiers were making camp somewhere nearby.

Gradually Linc eased his hand away from her mouth. Her lips were bloodless and numb from the pressure he had applied, but she forced them to move, forming words that were mouthed almost without sound.

"Who are they?"

"I didn't wait to ask."

"Where?"

"On the front lawn of the estate."

Her eyes widened in alarm. She turned on her heels and was about to charge through the brush. Linc's arm shot out. His hand grasped a handful of her wet shirt and, using that as leverage, hauled her back.

"Let me go!"

"Are you nuts?"

"The children."

"They're safe."

While this terse conversation was taking place, he was dragging her through the dark, dense foliage. "Get in there." He moved aside a vine as heavy and thick as a velvet drape and impatiently motioned her in.

"But the children!"

"I told you, they're safe." When it became obvious that she was going to argue, he spread his hand wide over the top of her head and shoved her down. Her knees buckled beneath her and landed jarringly on the fertile undergrowth. Before she had time to regain her balance, he gave her shoulder a push. She fell over onto her side and rolled into the leafy lair. He scrambled in after her and dropped the natural curtain behind them.

He fit his body against hers like a second skin to maximize the room in their hiding place. "Now lie still and stay quiet," he whispered directly into her ear. "Don't move. Don't make a sound."

Kerry would have protested had his arm not increased its pressure against her midriff. It was a reflexive motion Kerry understood, since she heard the sounds only seconds after Linc had. Someone was thrashing his way through the jungle, muttering to himself in vernacular Spanish as he came nearer.

His booted feet came dangerously close to where they lay, so close that the downward slash of his machete stirred the plants screening them in the darkness. Kerry sucked her breath in and held it. Linc, whose warm breath had been fanning her neck, did the same. They didn't move so much as an eyelash.

The soldier went past them, but they didn't relax. Through the jungle floor, they could still feel the vibration of his footsteps. And as they had expected, he retraced the path he had taken and came near them again, stopping only inches from where they lay behind the vine.

Kerry heard the sound of his slipping his machete into its leather scabbard, then the scratch of a match being struck. The pungent aroma of marijuana smoke filtered down to them. The soldier had decided to take a break from the arduous job of killing and looting.

Linc pressed his face into the nape of Kerry's neck, and they lay motionless and soundless. She thought of a hundred hazards that could reveal them. An untimely cough. A sneeze. A snake.

She shivered, only partially because her shirt was clinging to her wetly. The shudder was one of stark terror. What if they were discovered? And what about the children? Were they really safe, or had Linc just told her that to get her to cooperate in these self-preserving measures?

No, he wouldn't do that. But he might. He had told her once that he looked out for himself above anybody.

Thankfully, the soldier didn't smoke for long. He must have pinched out the cigarette because the sickly, sweet fragrance faded away. They heard the rustling of his clothes as he repocketed the joint, then the soft, rhythmic clank of his water canteen bouncing against his hip as he moved away.

Linc waited a full five minutes from the time they last heard his shuffling tread before the pressure of his arm around Kerry relaxed and he lifted his head. For several moments neither did anything but breathe deeply, gratefully refilling their deprived lungs with air.

"What was he saying?" Linc whispered when he felt it was safe to do so.

"He was complaining that his sergeant sent him out on that scouting mission."

"Anything about us?"

"No."

"Good. I guess they don't know we're here. Are you all right?"

She was scared half to death, but she answered, "Fine. The children?"

"They're safe. I think."

She craned her head around to look at him. "What do you mean you think?"

"Shh. Relax. They were safely hidden when I came looking for you." Over her shoulder she studied his shadowed face. "I swear it," he said, offended by her suspicion.

Kerry was ashamed of her momentary lack of trust. Linc O'Neal was a scoundrel, but he wouldn't sacrifice children to save his own hide. Even he wasn't that unscrupulous. "What happened?"

Speaking in whispers that were barely louder than a deep breath, Linc related what had happened. "I heard their trucks approaching while I was taking that last look around. I figured that if we had thought the deserted house would serve as a good camp, then soldiers would too. I ran back, found you gone, and hustled the children into the root cellar beneath the kitchen."

"I didn't know there was one."

"I hope the soldiers don't either," he said grimly. "I put Joe in charge and threatened him with castration-by-machete if he left the cellar before I came to get them. He argued with me, of course, and wanted to go searching for you."

"I shouldn't have left."

"A little late to be thinking of that, Miss Bishop." His low volume didn't soften the stern reprimand.

She thought of several biting comebacks, but saved them. Her primary concern was for the children. "Were the children afraid?"

"Yeah, but I calmed them down, tried to make a game out of hiding. They have water. I promised them a treat if they didn't make a sound. I told them to go to sleep and said that when they woke up, you'd be there."

"Do you think they understood?"

"I hope to God they did. When he wasn't arguing, Joe was translating for me." Worriedly he added, "I'd hate to have to explain nine hidden children to this bunch of cutthroats."

The memory of the commander and his rough, insulting touch still made Kerry feel slightly sick to her stomach. "Are they the same ones we encountered today?" she asked with dread.

"I don't know. But they probably aren't any better, whatever side of the conflict they're on. I thought it best just to stay out of their way."

"I agree. What about the truck?"

"Luckily, I hid it under brush after we unloaded it."

She lay still for a moment, trying not to think about the way Linc's legs were pressed against hers. As precisely as her wet shirt was plastered to her torso, his legs were molded to every contour of hers.

"I told you to stay in the house," he said abruptly. "You agreed to do everything I told you to."

"I needed some air," she snapped.

Knowing that he was right stung her pride. It had been reckless of her to leave the house, especially at night. Now, if any harm came to the orphans, she would have to take the blame upon herself. It would be entirely her fault.

"Well you could have gotten a lot of air...through the bullet holes in your body." He unleashed his frustration. "You almost got yourself killed, along with the rest of us. I hope you enjoyed your bath."

"I did. Brief as it was." Suddenly she drew herself up more tensely. "Linc, I left my clothes-"

"I stuffed them behind a banana tree. Let's hope they're not discovered."

"Why didn't you just bring them with you?"

"Look, lady," he said snidely, "I've only got two hands. I couldn't collect your clothes *and* haul you out of your bath *and* keep you quiet all at the same time. So I stashed the clothes. Okay? If the soldiers had found you before I did, they would have stripped you naked anyway, and believe me, base as you may think I am, I have more respect for your modesty than they would have."

Kerry wished he hadn't made even that veiled reference to her nakedness. Now that they were out of immediate danger, she could turn her thinking to her scanty attire and her forced proximity to Linc.

How long would they have to stay hidden, lying close together, unable to move or speak above a whisper? They couldn't relax their guard for a single moment. Since they weren't hidden beneath the house as the children were, the density of the jungle at night was the only place they could hide. To go in search of another hiding place would be risky. She was just coming to realize how uncomfortable the next several hours would be.

And not only in terms of being cramped and cold. Linc's nearness was playing havoc with her senses. She gravitated toward the security his virile frame promised. Her chilled body sought the warmth of his.

"Whatever they're cooking smells good," she remarked to take her mind off him.

"Don't think about it." His own stomach rumbled hungrily. She angled her head back a fraction and glanced over her shoulder at him. "It's probably iguana...or worse," he said in an attempt to banish both their hunger pangs.

"Don't say that," she murmured, shifting her legs slightly. "I keep imagining creepy-crawly critters moving over me."

"Be still." He clenched his teeth. The slightest movements she made caused her hips to press against the curve of his lap. She was already fitted securely into that notch, and the merest shifting motion of her legs caused her bottom to rub against him.

"I'm trying," she said, "but my muscles keep cramping."

"Are you cold?"

"A little," she admitted.

The jungle was like a sauna in daylight hours, steamy and airless. But they were lying on the damp ground. Sunlight had never penetrated this dense foliage and, as a result, it was abnormally cool beneath the vine. She was so clammy that her teeth had begun to chatter.

"You'd better take off that wet shirt."

Ponderous seconds ticked by. They lay as tense and motionless as they had while the soldier was nearby. Kerry wanted to negate his idea outright. But before she could even form the words, she shivered uncontrollably. Under the circumstances, any maidenly protests would sound ridiculous.

But to lie in Linc O'Neal's arms wearing nothing but panties . . . ?

"I'm all right," she said stiffly.

He sighed with exasperation. "I'll take my shirt off. You can wrap yourself in that."

She reconsidered, knowing that catching cold would certainly be untimely. "All right," she said reluctantly. "How . . . how do we do it?"

"Let me go first."

Moving as little as possible, he wedged his hand between her back and his chest and unbuttoned the few buttons on his bush shirt. With excruciating care not to move a single leaf, he eased himself into a half-sitting position and shrugged the shirt off his shoulders and down his arms. The effort made him short-winded. He was panting by the time he worked his arms free of the sleeves.

"There," he sighed. "Now you."

Kerry was grateful for the darkness which hid them. At the same time, it lent intimacy to their awkward situation. She rolled her lips inward around her teeth and squeezed her eyes shut for a moment, trying to muster her slipping courage before reaching for the buttons of her own shirt. That was the easy part. The difficulty came when she tried to peel the clinging, damp fabric away from her skin.

"Sit up as far as you can," Linc suggested.

She detected the hoarseness in his voice and passed it off as caution against discovery. She didn't dare entertain the notion that there might be another reason behind it.

Moving carefully, she raised herself until she could prop her weight on one elbow. Then, lifting and lowering her opposite shoulder repeatedly, she tried to work the wet shirt free.

"Here, let me help."

She felt the warm pressure of Linc's hand on her shoulder. It moved down her arm, taking the shirt with it, inch by slow inch. At her elbow, he had to give it an extra tug. His knuckles bumped into the side of her breast.

They froze.

"Sorry," he said at last.

Kerry said nothing. The lump of embarrassment lodged in her throat wouldn't have allowed a word to get past. He slipped the sleeve down until she pulled her hand from it. The position she had to maintain, compounded by tension, had strained all her muscles to the aching point. Tiredly she lay back down and released a grateful breath. The air cooled her back as Linc moved the wet cloth aside.

"Can you manage the rest?" he asked.

"Yes, I think so."

She rolled backward, actually bringing herself closer against him, while she pulled the other sleeve from the arm she'd been lying on. As soon as the shirt was off, she rolled forward again, hoping that in those brief few moments her breasts hadn't been as vulnerable as they had felt. It was so dark that she doubted he could actually see her. But they both knew that she was completely uncovered.

It was a disturbing thought.

So much so that, when he draped his shirt over her, she clutched at it, pulling it against her chilled skin. It was both a relief and a hazard. It provided warmth and covering, but it also smelled like him. Linc's scent filled her head and had an intoxicating effect. Holding his garment against her was like being wrapped in his arms.

"Better?"

She nodded her head. Her hair was heavy and wet. She gathered it in her fist and shifted it above her head. But that left her neck and shoulders bare. Now she could feel each breath he took. She knew without looking that he was wearing only the army-green tank top, and that above the deeply scooped neckline grew an impressive pelt of chest hair.

"You're still shivering." He laid his arm over her and drew her back against him.

Closing her eyes tightly didn't help to dispel her memory of his arms, leanly bunched with muscles, ribboned with healthy veins. She had seen him shirtless that morning while he washed. As he sluiced water over his head and chest, she had noticed his sleek musculature.

Now she wished she hadn't paid such close attention. The muscles she had admired that morning were pressed against her back. She felt them twitch, contract and relax, as though they were as jumpy as her nerves.

That morning, the sun had streaked his hair with russet highlights and made his body hair glow a reddish-gold. She could feel its crinkly patterns now against her bare skin. And she knew that his shoulders were sprinkled with freckles, as his cheekbones were.

"Are your legs cold?" Not trusting her to give him an honest answer, Linc ran his hand down the outside of her thighs and felt the goose bumps. "I'm going to put my legs over yours. Don't be alarmed."

She could almost laugh. *Don't be alarmed.* A ludicrous statement. Like, "Don't turn around, but isn't that Prince Charles and Lady Di coming through the door?" Or like the dentist saying as he lifts his drill, "You might feel a slight tingle but don't let it bother you."

It was impossible not to be alarmed. When he laid his thigh across hers, it brought the full solidity of his maleness directly up against her bottom. The rough cloth of his fatigue pants pleasantly abraded her sensitive skin.

"Aren't you cold, too?" she asked in a high, thin voice.

"No. I've got on pants and you're wearing nothing but—"

Right. Stop right there, O'Neal. Don't say it. It was better left unsaid. Neither of them needed to be reminded that all she was wearing was a pair of panties, and that they were sheer and skimpy and damp. Better that they direct the conversation toward anything—books, movies, politics, the weather—than to even make mention of her attire, or lack thereof.

"I still have my canteen. Do you want some water?"

"No," she replied breathlessly. She didn't want him to move. Every time he moved, she felt him. Vividly. And her mind kept reverting to when she was trying to get the pistol out of his waistband and how his body had looked. What she had only guessed at then, she could feel pressing against her hips now.

How long would this night last? Hours. And what if the soldiers didn't break camp and pull out at daybreak, as she and Linc had tacitly assumed they would? She didn't think her pounding heart could stand the strain. Something had to be done, said, to relieve the tension.

"Tell me about yourself, Linc."

God, she didn't want to know about him. If she were smart, she didn't want to know that he sensed her with every nerve fiber in his body. They were alive and kicking, feeling her, smelling her, tasting her. She didn't want to know how his blood vessels were pumping with desire for her.

He had raced back to the house, the convoy of military trucks only minutes behind him. He had bounded into the large living room, already issuing orders for her to get the children and their pallets up and into the kitchen. He had been dumbfounded when Joe told him that Kerry wasn't there, that she'd left the house.

Cursing her even while he spoke soothing words that the children couldn't even understand, he herded them into the dark, dank cellar. It was spooky, but it provided a perfect hiding place. As he sealed the door and moved a cabinet over the floorboards, he cursed the headstrong woman who was loose in a jungle crawling with guerrilla fighters when she could be safely hidden.

Only fear for her safety had contained his fury as he had dashed through the darkness looking for her. He remembered seeing the creek when he had previously scouted around the deserted estate. The refreshing water had tempted him into taking a quick dip. Acting purely on a hunch, he had followed the vine-choked path toward it.

He had felt both murderous and profoundly relieved when he discovered Kerry splashing in the shallow water. Taking time only to hide her pile of clothing in the brush, he'd lifted her out. Snatches of erotic pictures were emblazoned on his brain.

He knew that her breasts were full, and that her nipples were so pointed and pink that a man would go through hell for a chance to touch them with his tongue. He thought about her breasts now, lying soft and unrestrained beneath his shirt and he ached to touch and reshape them in his hands. And a while ago, when she had rolled onto her back, he had known that all he had to do was lower his head and . . . God, it had been agony not to.

He knew that her derriere was taut and rounded, cute and saucy and sexy as hell. And now that sweet little butt was cuddling his sex. It took every ounce of self-discipline he possessed not to groan out loud with the thought.

He tried not to think of the way her hair had looked with the moonlight shining on it, or the way that silvery light had turned her eyes as deeply mysterious as sapphires. Her lips were strictly off limits. Yet the memory of their taste lingered in his mind. He couldn't allow himself to think about the most vulnerable, most alluring part of her neck being only inches from his lips.

For someone already denied heaven, one more wicked thought didn't matter. But he would die and see the gates of hell before the night was out if he continued torturing himself this way.

They needed diversion. Anything. To get their minds off what must surely be as discomfiting for her as it was for him, though for different reasons.

"What do you want to know?" His voice was little more than a growl.

"Where did you grow up?"

"St. Louis."

"Tough neighborhood?" she asked instinctively.

He scoffed. "Lady, you can't even begin to imagine."

"Your parents?"

"Both dead now. My old man raised me. My mother died when I was just a kid."

"No brothers or sisters?"

"No, thank God."

"Why 'thank God'?"

"Because things were rough enough as it was. My dad worked all the time in the brewery. I was on my own after school until late every night. You see, he resented being stuck with me when my mom died. He was a foul-mouthed, mule-headed, hard-drinking man. His ambition extended only to having enough money to pay the rent and buy whiskey. The last thing he wanted was to take care of a kid. I left home as soon as I got old enough. I only saw him twice after that before he died."

"What happened to him?"

"He was bowling one night with a bunch of his cronies and just dropped dead of a heart attack. They buried him beside my mother. I was in Asia. They sent me the details of it in a letter."

Kerry didn't know what to say. She'd never known anybody who had come from that kind of environment. "When did you get into photography?"

"High school. I was flunking something...I don't remember what now...so they stuck me in the journalism class that put together the school newspaper. They gave me a camera and appointed me photographer as a punishment."

He chuckled softly. "It backfired. By the end of the year, I was hooked."

"Where did you go to college?"

"College?" He barked a scornful laugh. "Cambodia, Vietnam, Africa, the Middle East. I got my formal education on the Golan Heights, and in Beirut and Belfast, and in refugee camps in Biafra and Ethiopia."

"I see."

"I seriously doubt that," he said bitterly.

Kerry didn't know whether his resentment was directed toward her, toward his unloving father, toward his lack of formal education, or a combination of all of them. But she felt it safer not to pursue it.

It was he who finally broke the silence. "What about you? What kind of childhood did you have?"

"Charmed." Kerry smiled with remembrances of golden times. Before they were tarnished by scandal. Before the nightmare. Before the bubble burst. "Like you, both my parents are dead now, but I had them when I was growing up."

"You went to parochial school, of course."

"Yes," she answered truthfully.

"Let me guess. You wore navy blue pinafores over stiff white blouses. And pigtails so tight they made your eyes water. White stockings and black patent shoes. Your face and hands were never dirty."

She laughed softly. "You're remarkably accurate."

"And you were taught social graces along with Latin and Humanities."

She nodded, thinking back on all the formal salons she had sat in with her parents, listening to boring conversations, which to a teenager with a passion for the Rolling Stones, had had no relevance. She had never been at a loss as to which fork to use and had always politely thanked the host and hostess for the evening's entertainment. Linc had had a latch-key, and she had had personalized stationery.

"Yes," she replied, "my father's work involved considerable travel. You and I might have been in some of the same places at the same time."

He uttered another of those humorless laughs. "Honey, you don't even know about some of the places I've been in."

"I'm not *that* innocent."

"Compared to you, Sister Kerry, Rebecca of Sunnybrook Farm led a wild life."

Though she couldn't see his face, she could imagine the sneer on his lips. Knowing now how different his background was from hers, she could understand why he might ridicule her previously sheltered life and lack of worldly experience.

She lapsed into silence. Apparently he was of the same mind. He adjusted himself more comfortably against her. Miraculously they fell asleep.

Kerry came awake suddenly. Every muscle in her body was tense and quivering. "What is it?"

"Shh." Linc laid his fingers against her lips. "It's only rain."

The huge drops fell heavily on the plants surrounding them. They landed in hard splats. It sounded as though their shelter were being pelleted with BBs. "Oh, Lord," Kerry whimpered and ducked her head so low that her chin almost touched her chest. "I hate this."

Even though the broad leaves of the vine covering them provided some protection from the torrent, rainwater still trickled through the foliage and dripped chillingly onto her exposed skin. Her muscles were cramped. She longed to stretch her limbs in all directions in order to ease their aching and to restore circulation.

"I can't stay in here. I've got to get out."

"No," he said sharply.

"Just for a minute. To stretch."

"And get soaked in the process. Then when you crawl back in, you'll be even more uncomfortable. No, Kerry."

"We could sneak back into the house," she said in a hopeful rush.

"Uh-huh."

"No one will be watching. We could go through the kitchen and join the children in the basement. They must be terrified."

"They're probably asleep. Besides, they have Joe."

"No one would see us."

"It's too risky. The soldiers are bound to have posted a watch."

"I don't want to stay here any longer!"

"And I don't want to be shot! I don't think you want to be gang raped either." She sucked in her breath quickly. "Now hush about it. We're not leaving until I say so."

The racket around them was deafening. It was raining buckets. Kerry felt the jaws of claustrophobia closing around her.

"How much longer?" she asked.

"I don't know."

"Dawn?"

"I hope."

"What time is it?"

"Around four I think."

"I can't stand it any longer, Linc." She hated the tremor in her voice, but she couldn't control it. "Truly, I can't."

"You've got to."

"I can't. Please let me stand up."

"No."

"Please."

"I said no, Kerry."

"Just for a minute. I've got—"

"Turn around."

"What?"

"Turn around. Face me. Switching positions will help."

Her muscles were screaming for her to move. She turned onto her back, then did another quarter turn to bring herself face to face with Linc.

He laid his arm across her waist and sandwiched her thighs between his. She placed her hands on his chest and buried her face in the hollow of his shoulder. Tucking her head beneath his chin, he held her close. She basked in the warm security he provided until the noisily splattering rain abated.

Kerry never knew how long they stayed like that. It might have been hours or merely minutes before she gradually became aware that the rainfall had ceased and that the silence was as loud as the downpour had been. She stirred and would have put space between Linc and her, had there been any space available.

"I'm sorry," she whispered.

"It's okay."

"I panicked. Claustrophobia, I guess."

"You woke up frightened. You're cold, hungry, uncomfortable. So am I. But for the time being, this is the best we can do."

His voice sounded funny. She didn't have to ask why. Her own was none too steady. The feel of his breath against her face, the way his fingers were moving comfortingly through her hair, the heat rising from the places where skin contacted skin were the reasons behind her tremulousness.

"Why did you do it, Kerry?"

"What?"

"Commit yourself to a vocation so unsuited to you."

Oh, that. She felt wretched about her lie. With the exception of their bitter quarrels, he had treated her honorably since he had mistaken her for a nun. If he had continued to be aggressive and abusive, she would have taken a blood oath that her life was committed to a religious order. But his nobility demanded the truth. At least a partial truth.

Yet, she stalled. "Why do you say it doesn't suit me?"

Linc's head was whirling with discrepancies. Kerry felt more womanly than any woman he'd ever held in his arms. He couldn't reconcile this young, beautiful, desirable woman with his concept of a nun. The sweet pressure of her breasts against his chest, the way her mouth had yielded to his those few times he had kissed her, just didn't jive with black habits and cloistered abbeys. He was street wise enough to know that some first impressions were sound. And he'd bet his life on this one.

In answer to her question he said, "You don't look like any nun I ever saw."

"Nuns look like everybody else."

"Do they all wear bikini panties?"

She blushed hotly. "I . . . I happen to like frilly underwear. That's not a sin. Feminine things appeal to me because I'm a woman."

*That* he didn't need to be reminded of. She was a woman, all right. He could feel her womanliness with every masculine cell in his body.

"You just don't have a holy aspect." She stiffened with the affront, but he held her tighter. "I don't mean that you're unholy, it's just that . . . hell . . ."

He paused for a moment, searching for words. "I mean, didn't you ever think about having kids? You're great with these orphans. Didn't you ever want to have kids of your own?"

"Yes," she answered honestly.

"And a, uh, you know, a man?"

"I've thought about that, yes," she said softly. She wondered if he could feel her heart pounding against his chest. Her answer was truthful. But she'd never thought about having a man as powerfully as she was thinking about it now.

She was recalling the masterful way his tongue had parted her lips and moved inside her mouth, and the manner in which his hands had been both caressing and commanding. She had felt the grinding thrust of his hips against hers. Total possession by this man must be an ultimate sexual experience for a woman.

"You've thought about making love with a man?"

She nodded, rubbing her nose in his crisp chest hair.

"You've wondered what it feels like?"

She held her lips tightly together to stopper the longing groan that pressed against them from the inside. "Of course."

He sifted his hands through her hair. "If he knows what he's doing, a man can give you pleasure. Pleasure never dreamed of."

She was liquifying, melting against him. She wondered how he could continue to hold her when surely she must be dissolving in his arms.

"Aren't you curious to know how it feels?"

"Yes."

"Well then," he asked, hoarsely, "won't you feel cheated if you don't ever experience that?"

She held her breath for what seemed like an interminable length of time before blurting out, "I haven't taken any final vows yet."

He flinched reflexively. *"What?"*

"I said—"

"I heard what you said. What does that mean?" His breath was hot, as hot as the widespread hand branding the skin on her back.

She was sorely tempted to tell him the truth then and there. Seconds after the words were out of her mouth, he would be making love to her. Of that she had no doubt. Swollen and hard, his manhood pressed against her belly. She was dewy and achy with desire for him. What transporting ecstasy it would be to—

But no. Her attention must be focused solely on the nine orphans. Their lives were in her hands. If they were to survive, they needed all the odds in their favor. Neither she nor Linc could be distracted for a single instant.

If they became lovers, that would not only be a distraction, but a complication. When this was all over, when they were safe in the United States, their relationship would be a heart-rending dilemma to her and an albatross to him.

Kerry couldn't give herself to any man lightly, yet that's the way this man of vast experience would take her. She had no doubt that when Linc had referred to a man who knew how to give a woman pleasure he was speaking of himself. But that's all it would be to him. Pleasure. Mutual but temporary. Involvement with a man like Linc O'Neal would only open up oceans of regret for her.

She chose her answering words carefully. "It means that I'm still considering what to do with the rest of my life." It wasn't a lie. It was a solid truth. She hadn't planned her future beyond getting the nine children into the United States.

She felt his heavy sigh; it seeped out of him gradually. And with it, his tension. His compliance with her silently expressed wishes made her feel even worse about her deception.

She remained lying in his arms, but there was a tangible difference in the way he held her. Soon, grayish light began filtering through the branches of the vine. Straining their ears, they could hear sounds of morning activity coming from the soldiers' camp. The smell of coffee and food made them both delirious with hunger. Several times they heard men moving through the jungle, but none came as close as the soldier had the night before. Finally, they picked up the welcome sound of truck engines being pumped to life.

Linc waited about fifteen minutes before he lifted the vine and crawled out. "You stay here."

Kerry obeyed him. She was actually grateful for the moments of privacy. She pulled on her own shirt, which was still damp, and ran her fingers through her hair. It was a mass of tangles. She was still working her fingers through the knotted strands when the curtain of leaves was lifted.

"It's all right," Linc told her. "They're gone."

# Chapter 6

Kerry sank down onto the bank of the river. She was thoroughly dispirited. Her shoulders sagged with defeat. The toddler, Lisa, seemed to have gained fifty pounds overnight. Kerry couldn't hold her for another minute without dropping her. She set the child on the ground beside her.

"Now what?"

She got no answer. Several moments ticked by. Even the children were still, as though realizing that they faced a serious problem that might not have a solution. Shading her eyes with her hand, Kerry glanced up at the man standing beside her.

Hands on hips, one knee bent, brows lowered, eyes glowering, mouth frowning, it wasn't difficult to assess Linc's mood. Kerry watched his lips form a crude expletive that he didn't dare speak aloud in front of the children, even though they didn't understand English.

She diplomatically let a few more moments go by before she tried again. "Linc?" His head snapped around and he glared down at her. "How the hell should I know? I'm a photographer, not an engineer."

Linc immediately regretted lashing out at her. It wasn't Kerry's fault that the heavy rains the night before had caused local flooding and that the wooden bridge he had planned to use to get across the river had been washed out.

It wasn't even her fault that he was in such a foul mood. She was the reason for it, but she wasn't to blame. Ever since he had helped her crawl out of the cover where they had passed the night, he'd been ready to take somebody's head off at the slightest provocation.

"You'd better put these on." He angrily tossed her her clothes after he'd retrieved them from where he'd hidden them the night before.

She hadn't taken issue with his brusqueness, but had quickly stepped into her khaki trousers. Unable to tear his eyes away from her long, lovely, fantasy-inspiring legs, Linc had watched every supple movement. His loins had ached with the recollection of her thighs being entwined with his.

Had it really happened? Had he only dreamed that her body perfectly complemented his? Had she curled up against him, actually seeking contact, or had he just wished it so hard that it had seemed real?

Maybe so, because all morning they had fenced with each other. They hardly behaved like two people who had slept together like lovers. They hadn't even been friendly. She'd been cautious and wary of him; he'd been truculent and quarrelsome.

When they returned to the house and found the children in the kitchen instead of in the cellar, Linc had yelled at Joe. "I thought I told you to stay down there until I came to get you."

"I heard the soldiers leave," the boy shot back. "I knew it was safe."

"You don't know sh—"

"Linc!"

"When I tell you do to something I expect you—"

"Linc!" Kerry had shouted again. "Stop yelling at Joe. All the children are safe, but you're frightening them."

Linc had cursed beneath his breath as he headed for the front of the house. "Get them ready. I'll be back in five minutes."

Luckily the truck was where he had left it the evening before, concealed by jungle vines. He slashed at them viciously, working out some, but only some, of his frustration.

"The children are hungry," Kerry told him from behind the screened door when he bellowed from the front lawn for them to load up.

Stormily he had followed her back into the kitchen, where the orphans were gratefully eating stale bread and bananas. Kerry had helped them wash their faces and hands, which had become grimy in the cellar. None of them looked at Linc directly, sensing his mood, but he felt eight pairs of eyes frequently glancing in his direction. The ninth pair, belonging to Joe, openly defied him. Animosity simmered between the man and the adolescent boy, who hadn't taken kindly to the blistering lecture.

Little Lisa had squirmed free of Kerry's arms and crossed the kitchen floor bearing a dry crust of bread. Her eyes were sympathetic and imploring as she gazed up at Linc and tugged on the knee of his fatigue pants to get his attention. He looked down at her. She offered him the crust of bread wordlessly. But her eyes, as dark and rich as chocolate syrup, spoke volumes.

Linc crouched down, took the piece of bread from her, and ate it. *"Muchas gracias,"* he said and cuffed her on the chin. Lisa flashed him a dazzling smile before shyly scampering back to Kerry.

It was a while before he had cleared his throat enough to say gruffly, "Let's go."

When all the children had been placed in the truck, he drew Kerry aside. "Call off your watchdog."

"What are you talking about?"

"Joe. Make it clear to him that I didn't compromise you last night. I'm afraid to turn my back on him for fear he'll slide a knife between my ribs."

"Don't be ridiculous."

"Tell him!"

"All right!"

Those had been the last words they had exchanged until now, when, with her eyes shaded from the glaring sun, she had looked up at him and spoken his name.

Apparently her nerves were just as frayed as his. She lashed back. "That's what I'm paying you for, Mr. O'Neal. To come up with ideas. To improvise."

"Well, maybe you should have checked out my credentials more carefully before offering me the goddamn job."

Kerry had no argument for that, so she clamped her mouth shut and returned her stare to the rushing water.

Why did she always make him look like a snarling beast in front of the kids? They were watching him as though he were a cross between Jack the Ripper and Moses, afraid of him, but looking to him for leadership.

He blew out an exasperated breath. "Give me a minute, Okay?" he said, raking his fingers through his sweat-damp hair.

The bridge was clearly indicated on the map, but apparently hadn't been that substantial. The rising current, due to last night's torrential rains, had been sufficient to tear it from its moorings.

The truck had rolled to a stop where the road ended in the swirling, murky water. The children had piled out and now stood on the bank, looking to him for answers he didn't have. Joe seemed to derive a perverse satisfaction from their predicament; his lip was curled with smug derision. And quite clearly, Kerry was leaving the solution up to him. As she had pointed out, that's what she was paying him for. He would have to earn every red cent of that fifty grand.

He gnawed on his lip as he studied the river. Then he went back to the truck, picked through the supplies in the bed of it, and returned to Kerry. "I need to talk to you."

She stood, brushed off the seat of her pants, instructed the children not to get too close to the water, and followed him. When they had moved out of earshot, she asked, "What do we do now?"

"I have a suggestion, and please hear it out before you fly off the handle." He fixed his golden stare on her. "Let's load the kids up, turn around and go back the way we came. Let's throw ourselves on the mercy of the first troops we see."

He paused, expecting an explosion. When it didn't happen, he pressed on. "It won't matter which side we align ourselves with, El Presidente's or the rebels. Whichever it is, we'll appeal to their vanity, tell them what a humanitarian gesture it would be for them to help us. We'll promise to propagandize their cause to the world if they'll only help us."

He laid his hands on her shoulders and appealed to her earnestly. "Kerry, the kids are hungry and we have no more food. Our clean water is running out, and I'm not sure where we'll find more. I don't know how in hell to get across that river without risking all our lives. The truck is almost out of gas and there are no Exxon stations in the jungle.

"Even if we do make it to the rendezvous point, how do you know for certain that this Hendren fellow will be there to pick us up and whisk us away into the wild blue yonder like some Sky King?"

He saw her eyes darken and hastened to add, "Look, this was a noble idea. I admire you; I really do. But it wasn't a very practical plan, not very well thought out. Now you'll have to admit that." He smiled at her engagingly. "What do you say?"

Kerry drew a deep breath, though she never released him from her gaze. When she spoke, her voice was level and calm. "I say that unless you want my knee rammed into your crotch, you'd better take your hands off my shoulders."

His smile collapsed. His face went comically blank. His hands fell quickly to his sides.

She pivoted stiffly and marched away. But she got only a few steps away from him before he lunged, shoved his hand into the waistband of her pants and yanked her to a teeth-jarring halt. "Just a damn minute," he shouted. He spun her around. "Didn't anything I said to you register?"

She tried to wiggle free, but this time his hold on her was inescapable. "I heard every patronizing, condescending, chicken-hearted word."

"You're determined to go on?"

"Yes! Once we cross the river, it's only a few more miles to the border."

"It might just as well be a thousand."

"I promised these children that I would get them to the families waiting for them in the United States, and that's what I'm going to do. With or without you, Mr. O'Neal." She pointed her index finger at the end of his nose. "And if you desert us now, you'll never see a penny of your precious money."

"I care more for my life than I do the money."

"Well you've got a better chance of keeping both by getting us to that airplane instead of turning yourself over to a band of guerrillas. What happened to all your warnings about getting shot and gang raped? Do you really think that I'd ask a *favor* from any of these troops?"

"Most of them, whichever side they fight for, come from Catholic backgrounds. Your profession would protect you."

"It hasn't protected me from you!"

His face turned stony. Before Kerry had time to regret her words, he yanked her high and hard against him. He snarled, "Wanna bet?"

Fleetingly she recalled the many times he could have taken advantage of her and hadn't. Unable to meet that fierce, masculine glare, which was as hard and unyielding as the lower part of his body, she moved her gaze down to his throat where she spotted his pulse beating as rapidly as her own.

"I'm sorry," she said breathlessly. "I shouldn't have said that."

"You sure as hell shouldn't have." He shoved her away, but she got the impression that it was to spare himself embarrassment and not out of any kind feelings toward her. His strong fingers were still curled around her shoulders.

"Don't be deceived," he said in a voice that throbbed with passion. "Just because I haven't touched you, doesn't mean that I haven't thought about it. A lot. You're not concealed by a habit yet. When you go flashing that dynamite body of yours around a man, you had better be willing to accept the consequences. Some might have even fewer scruples than me."

Her head came up slowly, until her eyes again met his. "Then why would you even suggest that I turn myself and these children over to the soldiers?"

He released her. Each of his ten fingers let go separately, as though being individually pried away. "I had to see how tough you really are."

She looked at him aghast. "You mean . . . this was all . . . you didn't really mean—"

"That's right. This was a test of your mettle. I had to know if you've got guts."

She backed away from him. Her hands were balled into fists as though prepared to hit him. Dark blue eyes narrowed to threatening slits. "You son of a bitch."

Linc's lips quirked. Then he threw back his head and laughed. It was a loud and wholesome laugh, so loud that it disturbed the birds and small monkeys in the branches overhead. They squawked and chattered in protest. "Damned right, Sister Kerry. I'm a son of a bitch. And I'm gonna get worse. If we make it through this alive, you're gonna hate me before we're through. Now, round up the kids while I get everything ready."

Before she could tell him just how loathsome she thought his tricky tactics were, he was stalking back toward the truck. She had no choice but to do as she was told. The orphans were hot, hungry, thirsty and exhausted, so she tolerated their querulousness. She answered their whining questions as best she could, but her attention was really on Linc. He was busy securing the end of a rope, which had been in the back of the pickup when she stole it, to the trunk of a tree. Tying the other end around his waist, he waded into the swift current.

"What are you doing?" she called, surging to her feet in alarm.

"Just keep everybody back."

The children fell silent. All stood in tense silence as Linc made unsteady progress across the muddy river. When he reached the middle where it was too deep to stand up, he began swimming. Numerous times the swift current sucked him under. And each time, Kerry clasped her hands together, holding her breath, until she saw his head break the surface again.

At last he made it to the opposite side. The water dragged at his clothes as he pulled himself up the spongy bank. Once he reached firm ground, he dropped to his knees, hung his head, and gulped air into his lungs.

When he had regained his breath, he selected a stout tree trunk and tied the rope around it. He tested it several times before wading into the river again. He pulled himself across on the rope. It wasn't as strenuous as swimming, but even so, it was exhausting work to fight the current. It took him several moments to recover once he had reached them.

"Got the idea?" He was bent at the waist, his palms resting on his knees, when he lifted his head and glanced up at Kerry. His hair was plastered to his head. Several sodden strands striped his forehead. His eyelashes were wetly clumped together. Kerry was tempted to comb the hair off his forehead and touch his bristly jaw. To keep from touching him, she actually had to squeeze her fist so tightly that her nails bit into her palm.

"Yes, I get the idea, but what about the truck?"

"It stays. We go the rest of the way on foot."

"But—" The objection died on her lips. Only minutes ago he had tested her fortitude. He had all but promised her that the going from here on would be a nightmare. She had insisted on bucking the odds. "All right," she said softly. "What do you want me to do?"

"You take Lisa. Carry her piggyback. I'll get Mary. Joe," he said hitching his chin toward the eldest boy, "you get Mike this time. You and I will have to make several trips I'm afraid."

The boy nodded his head in understanding.

"I can make more than one trip," Kerry said.

Linc shook his head no. "You'll need to stay on the other side with the children. This is no joy ride, believe me. Explain the procedure to them, and for god's sake stress to them that they must hold on tight."

As she translated for the children, she tried to make crossing the river sound like a grand adventure, at the same time emphasizing how treacherous it could be and how vital it was for them to hold on to the adult carrying them.

"They're ready," she told Linc as she bent down and let Lisa climb onto her back. The child's arms folded around her neck and her ankles criss-crossed in front of Kerry's waist.

"Good girl, Lisa," Linc said, tousling the child's glossy hair.

When she beamed a smile up at him, he returned her grin and patted her back. Kerry looked up at him, marveling over his soft expression. He caught her surprised look, and they exchanged a brief stare before he turned away and leaned down so Mary could climb onto his back.

"Have you got your passport?" he asked Kerry.

They would have to travel light from now on. She had discarded everything she didn't absolutely need. "It's buttoned into my shirt pocket."

"Okay, let's go." He led the way into the churning water.

Kerry tried not to remember all the tales she had heard about the jungle river creatures. She ignored the slimy things that bumped into her feet and legs as she sought firm footing on the slippery mud of the river's bottom. She crooned comforting words to Lisa, but the reassurances were meant for herself as well as for the crying child.

The rope, not too strong to begin with, was slippery now. It was difficult to hold on to. If it hadn't meant the difference between living and drowning, she would have let go long before she reached the middle of the river. By then her palms were bleeding.

When she stepped onto nothingness and her feet were swept from beneath her, she was terrified of never breaking the surface. Finally she pulled herself up and made certain that Lisa's head had cleared, too. Gallons of water had rushed up Kerry's nose and into her eyes and mouth. She was blinded and gasping for air. But she forced herself to work her way along the rope, going hand over hand.

After what seemed like hours instead of minutes, she felt strong hands molding to her armpits and lifting her out of the water. With Lisa still on her back, she collapsed into the soft, warm, squishy mud of the river bank and sucked in coveted air. Linc lifted Lisa off her back. Kerry's muscles quivered with exertion, but she pulled herself to her hands and knees and eventually rolled to a sitting position.

Linc was holding Lisa in his arms. Her face was buried in his throat. Her tiny hands were clutching his soaked tank top. He was stroking her back, kissing her temple, rocking her gently back and forth, and murmuring words of encouragement and praise, even though she could understand only his inflection. Kerry envied the child. She wanted to be rocked. Held. Kissed. Reassured.

"You did fine," he said.

It was hardly a lavish compliment, but Kerry had only enough energy to give him a wavering smile anyway. He pulled Lisa away and, after kissing her cheek, passed her to Kerry. Mary was sobbing quietly nearby. Kerry gathered the two girls and young Mike in her arms. They made a pitiful, soggy, sorry-looking group, but all were grateful to be alive.

"Keep this," Linc said, dropping the machete, the only weapon they had, down onto the ground near Kerry's feet. "You okay?" he asked Joe.

"Of course," the boy said haughtily.

"Let's go then."

They waded back into the water. Kerry didn't know where they found the strength. She could barely keep her head up. Linc and Joe made three more trips each, until all the children had been safely transported across the river. On the last trip, Joe helped one of the older girls along, while Linc carried two backpacks, crammed with their meager supplies.

Tears formed in Kerry's eyes as she watched Linc sling his camera bags into the muddy waters of the rushing river. He had ripped the plastic lining out of one of the bags and wrapped his film cannisters in it, then strapped the makeshift package to his torso with his webbed belt.

Kerry had felt contrition as she watched him carry out this sobering task. She had manipulated this man unmercifully. He would be home, safe in the United States, pursuing his profession, if it weren't for her.

The only thing that eased her conscience was looking into the hopeful faces surrounding her. And she knew that, if she had it to do over again, she would take whatever measures were necessary to guarantee these orphans a brighter future.

As soon as Linc reached the bank after crossing the river for the last time, Kerry expected him to collapse and rest. Instead his movements were quick and lively.

"Hurry, Kerry, get all the children back into the trees. Have them lie down and tell them not to move."

Even as she carried out his instructions, she asked him. "What's the matter?"

"I think we're about to have company. Quick now! Joe, tell those girls to be quiet. Everybody lie down."

After having made certain that they'd left no traces behind and slashing the rope from the tree trunk, Linc dove for cover in the deep undergrowth beneath the trees. He lay on his stomach beside Kerry, staring out over the river. His breathing was rapid and heavy.

"You're exhausted," she whispered.

"Yeah."

His eyes didn't waver from the truck on the other side of the bank. Much as Kerry had despised that pickup, she missed the security of it now. "Do you think someone is following us?"

"I don't think they were deliberately following us. But someone is behind us. I heard them."

"Who?"

"It won't matter when they see the truck belonging to El Presidente's army and the rope."

"If it's El Presidente's men, they'll wonder what happened to their comrades and come checking on them," she said musingly. "And if it's part of the rebel army..."

"You got it," he said grimly. "Shh. There they are. Pass it along that no one is to move a muscle."

The whispered command was passed from child to child as a Jeep chugged out of the jungle on the far side. Several others could be seen behind it.

"Rebels." Linc whispered a curse. He would have preferred the regular army since they had deserted a government truck.

Several guerrillas alighted, holding their automatic weapons at their hips ready to be fired. They approached the pickup cautiously, fearing that it might be booby-trapped. When they were satisfied that it wasn't, they examined it thoroughly.

"Recognize any of them?"

"No." Kerry listened hard, trying to catch the gist of their conversation over the roar of the water. "They're speculating on why the truck wasn't just turned around when it came to the washed out bridge. They're wondering if the soldiers crossed the river by holding onto the rope."

"Only a fool would try crossing that river on a rope," Linc muttered.

Kerry looked at him quickly. He glanced down at her from the corner of his eye. They exchanged a brief smile.

On the far bank, one of the guerrillas produced a pair of field glasses. "Lie still," Linc hissed. The soldier studied the river bank through the binoculars and said something.

"He saw our footprints in the mud," Kerry interrupted. "He's telling the others that there are several of us. Around a dozen."

"Pretty damn smart."

"Now he's saying—" She gasped sharply when more guerrillas moved into view.

"What is it?"

"The one on the far left—"

"Yeah, what about him?"

"That's Juan. Our courier."

By now the rebel's two sisters, Carmen and Cara, had spotted him. One gave a soft cry and made to rise. "Get down!" Linc's order, for all its lack of volume, carried with it unarguable authority. The young girl froze. "Tell her to stay put. He might be her brother, but the others aren't."

Kerry conveyed the message in whispers, but in a considerably softer tone than Linc's. Carmen whispered something back, her face working with emotion.

"What did she say?"

"That her brother wouldn't betray us," Kerry translated.

Linc wasn't convinced. His eyes remained on the far river bank. The soldiers were conferring while they lounged and smoked and relieved themselves. Occasionally one would gesture across the river. One reeled in the rope and examined it. He gave it one swift tug between his hands. It snapped in two.

Kerry looked at Linc. He shrugged. "I told you only a fool would try it."

Some of the rebels offered opinions. Others seemed supremely unconcerned and dozed as they leaned against their Jeeps. The one identified as the courier who had made arrangements for the orphans' escape kept glancing furtively toward where they lay hidden in the brush. After almost half an hour, the one obviously in charge ordered them all back into the Jeeps.

"What's the consensus?" Linc asked Kerry.

"They're going to try another road and cross the river farther downstream." She was leaving something out. Her guilty expression told him so. He took her jaw in his large hand and forced her head around. His eyes demanded the truth. "Then they're going to come back this way and keep looking for us," she added reluctantly.

He swore. "That's what I was afraid of. Okay, let's start moving." He checked to make certain that all the Jeeps had turned around and disappeared into the jungle before he lined the children up safari-style. He would lead, Joe would take up the rear. Kerry was to keep to the middle to encourage laggers and make sure no one wandered off the path Linc would cut with the machete.

"Tell them we'll be moving quickly. We'll take breaks, but only when absolutely necessary. Tell them not to talk." He relaxed his stern demeanor when, at Kerry's translation, the children looked up at him fearfully. "And tell them how proud I am of them for being such good soldiers."

Kerry turned warm beneath the heat of his eyes. She was included in his compliment. After she passed it along to the orphans, they smiled up at him.

They fell into line and struck out through the dense jungle, which would have been impenetrable were it not for the merciless hacking of Linc's machete. Kerry kept her eyes trained on his back. Before wading into the river, he had tied the sleeves of his bush jacket around his waist and fashioned a sweat-band for his forehead out of a handkerchief. The muscles of his arms, back, and shoulders rippled with each upward swing and downward arc of the huge knife. Kerry let that supple rhythm entrance her. Otherwise, she wouldn't have had the energy to place one foot in front of the other.

Her aching body cried out for rest, her dry mouth for water, her empty stomach for food. When she was certain that she would drop on the next step, Linc halted and called a rest. Bearing Lisa, who had fallen asleep in her arms, Kerry slumped to the ground. The children all did the same, dropping in their tracks.

"Joe, pass around that canteen, but be sure to ration the water." Silently the boy moved to obey Linc's request. "How long have you been carrying Lisa?" he asked Kerry as he dropped to his knees beside her and offered her the canteen that had been hanging from his own belt. She in turn raised it to Lisa's parched lips.

"I don't know. For a while. She was too exhausted to take another step."

"I'll carry her from now on."

"You can't carry her and cut a path at the same time." She lifted her heavy hair off her neck, knowing that she would never take a hairbrush for granted again.

"And I can't afford to have you collapse on me. You're not having your period or anything like that, are you?"

She gazed back at him in speechless astonishment. She didn't even realize that she let go of her hair and let it fall back to her shoulders. She ducked her head. "No."

"Well, that's good. Now take a drink of water." After she had recapped the canteen and handed it to him, she said, "I'm sorry about your cameras."

"Yeah, so am I. We'd been through a lot together."

She could tell by his grin that he was teasing her. "I mean it. I'm sorry you had to destroy them."

"They can be replaced."

"What about your film?"

"I hope the containers are as watertight as they're advertised to be. If they are, I'll have a helluva story to sell when I get home." He stood up. "I'll carry Lisa, and no more arguments about it. We can't go much farther before dark."

He offered his hand to her. Kerry accepted it gratefully and relied on him to pull her to her feet. He swung Lisa onto his back, hoisted her into a comfortable position, and moved to the head of the line again.

Kerry felt dangerously close to tears.

She became immune to the buzzing insects, the slithering progress of jungle reptiles close to her feet, the sweltering, steamy afternoon heat, the raucous chatter of monkeys and the keening of birds. She concentrated solely on following Linc's lead and staying on her feet even when her body threatened to fold in upon itself and never move again.

The sun had long since set and the shadows of the jungle were dark and threatening before Linc stopped. He had stumbled upon a shallow stream beneath a slender waterfall which trickled between two vine-shrouded boulders. He eased Lisa off his back and rolled his shoulders to work the knots out.

The orphans were too tired to complain. Some of them were already asleep as Kerry circulated among them carrying canteens of cool water fresh from the stream. There was no food to distribute, and even if there had been, they were too exhausted to eat it.

Kerry longed to take her boots off and put her feet in the water. Indulging in that luxury was out of the question, however. Her feet might swell so much that she couldn't get her boots back on. Should they be attacked, she wouldn't have time. And from the way Linc was circling the perimeters of their resting place, attack seemed a very real possibility.

He moved toward her and sat down. His deep frown prompted her to ask, "Did they follow us?"

"I don't think they followed our trail, but they're on our heels just the same. I can smell the smoke from their campfires. Apparently they don't think we pose much of a threat." As he talked he was making a thick paste out of a handful of dirt and drops of water from the canteen. "Keep the children quiet. Take cover if anyone you can't identify approaches."

Terror smote her chest. "Where are you going?"

"To their camp."

"Their camp! Are you crazy?"

"Undoubtedly. Or I wouldn't be here in the first place." He gave her a wry grin. Kerry couldn't have fashioned a smile if her life depended on it. Linc motioned Joe over to them. "Will you go with me?"

*"Sí,"* the boy said.

"Smear some of this mud on your face and arms." Linc extended his hand. Joe scooped a large dollop of the mud from Linc's palm and began spreading it over his exposed skin as Linc was doing.

With apprehensive eyes, Kerry watched them methodically preparing to do battle. "Why are you going into their camp?"

"To steal weapons."

"Why? We've come this far without weapons."

She struggled to keep the tears out of her voice, but they were there. And even though it was too dark for Linc to see her stricken features, he could hear the stark fear in her voice.

"Kerry," he said gently, "do you really think that either side in this damn civil war is going to let an airplane from the United States land, then let us waltz on and fly off just like that?" He snapped his fingers.

It was a rhetorical question. He didn't expect an answer and didn't get one. He went on. "*If* the plane is there as you seem to believe it will be, and *if* we get on it at all, it will be amidst gunfire, probably from all directions. I can't fight off two armies with one machete."

The thought of gunfire appalled her. But she realized that what Linc said was true. The fighters in this war weren't likely to wave bye-bye from the ground as they took off in an airplane.

Why hadn't she thought of the actual escape before? Reaching the rendezvous point had been her primary goal. Probably because of the tremendous odds against achieving that, she hadn't thought beyond it. What would happen to them? The children? Joe? Linc? Her stubbornness had put them all in life-threatening danger. She mashed her fingers against her lips to stifle a sob. "What have I done?"

Linc took her in his arms and drew her close. "Don't chicken out on me now." He hugged her tight. Placing his mouth directly over her ear, he whispered, "You've been terrific. And it just might turn out all right after all."

Kerry wanted him to hold her longer—forever—and was disappointed when he released her. He handed her the machete. It weighted her arm down like an anchor. "Use it if you have to. We'll be back as soon as possible."

He moved away from her. She reached for him, but grasped at air. "Linc!"

His shadow solidified in front of her again. "What?"

She wanted to throw herself at him and beg him not to leave her alone. She wanted to cling to him and never let go. She wanted to be embraced, sheltered, protected from the million and one dangers lurking in the jungle at night. She wanted him to kiss her one more time.

She willed her chin to stop trembling and said shakily. "Please be careful."

It was awfully dark. He was virtually invisible with the mud smeared over his features. She might not have even known he was there if it hadn't been for his breath settling in warm gusts over her face. She sensed that he wanted to hold her as much as she wanted to be held. The tension in his body conveyed his reluctance to leave her.

But he didn't touch her again. Instead he only said, "I'll be careful."

Seconds ticked by before she realized that he and Joe had disappeared into the black shadows surrounding her. She and the eight children were alone.

# *Chapter* 7

It was almost daybreak before Linc and Joe returned. Kerry, who had been dozing, was so relieved to see them unharmed that she didn't immediately comprehend their defeated expressions.

Their postures heralded the failure of their mission. Both went directly to the stream and scooped up generous handfuls of water, washing off the camouflaging mud as they drank. When Linc finally turned around, he stared at Kerry through dejected eyes.

"What happened?" she asked.

"We didn't get anything," Linc told her, keeping his voice low. "Couldn't even get close. They were on alert and didn't relax their guard for a single minute. We circled the camp all night, hoping to find a goldbricker asleep at the switch. There was no such soldier in that whole outfit."

He backed against a tree and slid down its trunk, bending his knees as he went, until his bottom touched the ground. Then he rested his head against the tree trunk and closed his eyes. "Anything happen here?"

"No. The children slept. A few of them woke up saying they were hungry, but I managed to lull them back to sleep."

Joe, in a poignant imitation of Linc, sat leaning against another tree and closed his eyes. He was a man now, having done a man's job. He might resent Linc, but he held a grudging admiration for him, too. Kerry touched Joe's knee and, when his eyes opened, gave him a smile that said, "I'm proud of you." The boy smiled back.

She left him to rest and sat down beside Linc. "How much farther to the border?" she asked.

"About a mile."

"We won't have any trouble making it there by the deadline."

The plan was to meet the plane at noon, in hopes that if any troops were nearby they would be sleeping off their midday meal and the afternoon heat.

"I just wish to hell I knew what we were going to do once we get there."

Linc's weary sigh had a frightfully pessimistic sound to it. Kerry clutched at straws. "If we can't board the plane without risking the children's lives, we'll just slip across the border."

"And then what?" Linc asked impatiently. His red-rimmed eyes opened and focused on her. "It's just more of the same over there." He indicated their jungle surroundings with a flip of his hand.

"For miles there's nothing but jungle. God knows how far it is to the nearest outpost of civilization. And the neighboring country doesn't want Montenegran refugees adding more of a strain to their struggling economy. You'll find them inhospitable if not downright hostile. If we *could* convince them to give the kids political asylum, what do we do in the meantime? Where are we going to get food for supper tonight? Water? Shelter?"

His negativity sparked Kerry's temper. "Well then you think—"

*"Shh!"*

Joe sprang to his feet, poised to listen. He cocked his head to one side. After a moment, he shot them a warning glance and silently crept forward. Kerry made a move to detain him, but Linc's fingers encircled her wrist like a manacle and jerked her back down beside him. He shook his head vigorously when she opened her mouth to speak.

Joe disappeared into the deep green shadows of the jungle. The waiting seemed interminable. Linc eased himself up to his haunches and scanned the area with piercing eyes. Kerry felt useless. She only hoped that none of the children woke up making noises.

No more than a minute had elapsed before Joe stepped through the trees, closely followed by a guerrilla fighter. Recognizing him instantly, Kerry stood and rushed toward him, avoiding Linc's precautionary restraint.

"*Hola*, Juan," she whispered.

*"Hermana,"* he responded with a respectful inclination of his head.

Linc joined them. His guard was relaxed now that he recognized the soldier as the one Kerry had pointed out to him the day before. He looked like all the others, except that he was younger than most, sixteen maybe. His features hadn't hardened into a cold mask yet, though he already had the alert bearing of a trained guerrilla fighter. He and Kerry carried on a low, rapid conversation. When he gave Linc a suspicious once-over, she explained who he was.

"He's brought us two guns," she told Linc. "He says they're all he could smuggle out of the camp."

She shied away from the machine guns as Juan handed one to Linc and the other to Joe. Linc checked them both out. "Perfect working condition. Ammo?" The rebel handed him several clips of ammunition.

"Thanks."

*"De nada."*

"Ask him if his group knows who we are and what we're up to?" Linc told Kerry.

"No, he says," she told Linc after translating his question and hearing Juan's answer. "Since we were in the government truck, they think we're inexperienced stragglers or possible deserters looking for a band of rebels to join. They intend to follow us until they find out."

"That's what I was afraid of." Linc gnawed on his lip for a moment. "Ask him what would happen if he explained to his commander who we were. Would he let us go?"

The soldier listened, then shook his head vehemently. Kerry translated his quick response. "He says that they probably wouldn't kill us, but that they would try to take the airplane for their own use. Our only hope, he says, is to get to the plane as quickly as possible. He'll try to divert his squadron away from the designated landing place."

"Does he realize that some of his own men might get shot if they try to stop us?"

Kerry smiled ruefully at Juan's answer. "He says that some deserve to be shot."

Linc stuck out his hand and the young man shook it solemnly. "Anything you can do to help, buddy, I'll appreciate." Linc's tone didn't need any translation.

Kerry suggested that Juan wake up his sisters and tell them goodbye. He crept over to where they were sleeping. His face softened as he gazed down at them, but he motioned for Kerry to let them sleep.

He murmured something to her. His face and voice were earnest, his eyes shimmering with tears. Then, after one last glance down at the sleeping girls, he silently nodded farewell and melted into the jungle.

"What did he say?"

Kerry brushed the tears from her eyes. "He didn't want his sisters' last memory of him to be a goodbye. He knows it's doubtful that they'll ever see each other again. He wants them to start a new life in the United States. He said to tell them that he is willing to die for the freedom of his country. If they never hear from him again, they're to find comfort in the fact that he died happy, knowing that they were safe and free in America."

They fell silent, and for a long moment none of them moved. Any commentary on the young soldier's sacrifice would be superfluous. Words, no matter how poetic, wouldn't do it justice and would only sound banal.

Linc forced himself out of the reflective mood and asked Joe, "Do you know how to use that?" He nodded down toward the Uzi the boy held in his hands.

While Linc was instructing him, Kerry moved among the children, rousing them, but telling them to remain as quiet as possible. She gave them fresh water to drink and promised that there would be food for them on the airplane. Surely Jenny and Cage had thought of that.

When they had gathered what pathetically few possessions they had left, they began the final leg of their journey to the border. Kerry insisted on carrying Lisa so Linc would have more freedom of movement. Not only was he carrying the machete now, but the blunt-nosed machine gun, too.

It was almost eleven o'clock before they reached the edge of the jungle. A wide strip had been bulldozed out of it so that the border between Montenegro and its neighbor could be easily distinguished. Between the two green walls of solid jungle, there was a swathe of open territory about as wide as a football field.

"There, that's where he supposed to land," Kerry said, pointing toward the open space. They remained behind the shelter of the trees, but could easily see the clearing. "See that old watchtower? He'll taxi up to that and turn around."

Linc, squinting against the brightness of the sun, studied the area. "All right, let's move as close to it as possible. Tell the kids to stay together and well behind the tree line."

"Do you see anything?"

"No, but I've got the feeling that we're not the only ones taking cover in the jungle this morning. Let's go."

They moved laterally, always keeping several yards of jungle growth between the clearing and their parallel path. When they came even with the abandoned watchtower, Linc halted them. "We'll wait here." He consulted his wristwatch. "It shouldn't be long now."

Linc told Kerry to make sure all the children understood the need to run in a crouching position should they be fired upon. "Tell them not to stop running for any reason. *Any* reason, Kerry. Make certain they understand that."

They prepared the children as well as they could, then Linc drew Kerry aside, out of earshot, and sat down to wait. "He's got fifteen minutes," he said, glancing at his wristwatch again.

She said confidently, "Cage will be here."

Linc's eyes, as sharp as a gold-plated razor, sliced down to her. "Who is this Cage Hendren anyway?"

"I told you. He's a Texan whose missionary brother was shot by one of El Presidente's firing squads a couple of years ago."

"I know all that. But who—or what—is he to you?"

If she didn't know better, she would think Linc was jealous. "My good friend's husband."

He stared deeply into her eyes as though looking for signs of duplicity. "What was he to you before he married your good friend?"

"Nothing! I didn't even know him. I met Jenny first, through the Hendren Foundation."

He looked away, staring straight ahead. He didn't comment on the information she had imparted, but the tension in his jaw had relaxed noticeably.

"You and I will escort the children out," he said to her, abruptly changing the subject. "Can you carry Lisa?"

"Of course."

"Even at a run?"

"I'll manage."

"Okay, I'll hold back and cover our rear. Joe will stay here until you are all on board."

"Why?" she asked, alarmed.

"To provide cover should anybody start shooting."

"Oh."

"Once you're on the plane, I'll come back for Joe."

What had been left unsaid was that Linc would be exposed to gunfire longer than anybody. His tall frame not only provided the largest target, but he would have to make the hazardous trip across the clearing twice.

"Here," he said.

She gazed down at the packages of film he had laid in her hands. "What's this for?"

"If anything happens to me, at least the film will get out." She paled drastically. "I've been in some pretty tight squeezes, but never quite this tight before. I'm just taking precautions."

"But this film hasn't even been opened," she said, puzzled.

"Yes it has. The boxes contain the film I've used. I replaced it in the cellophane wrappings so it would look like new, unexposed film. That, at least, might protect you if...if anyone caught you with it."

"I don't want to be entrusted with your film, Linc. I might—"

"Look, if target practice for one of those guerrillas pays off, just make sure the film gets processed and the pictures published."

"Don't talk like that!"

He pulled the handkerchief he'd often used as a sweatband from around his head and slipped it over hers, working it down until it hung around her neck. "Didn't knights of old give a lady they admired a token before they went into battle?"

"Don't," she said tearfully. "I can't stand this. I don't want to talk about this. I don't even want to think about it. And you don't admire me."

He chuckled. "Yes, I do. Oh, I'll admit that I could have throttled you when I woke up and found myself shanghaied into a job I didn't want." His face lost all trace of teasing then. "But I do admire you, Kerry. You've been a trooper when you could have been a real pain in the butt. If I don't have an opportunity to tell you later—"

"Stop it! You can tell me anything you want to when we get to Texas."

"Kerry," he said gently, realizing that her distress could jeopardize her courage when she needed it the most, " I don't have any intention of dying in Montenegro. I don't want my third Pulitzer to be awarded posthumously. I've never considered that there was much prestige in winning prizes if you're dead. Besides, I want to collect my fifty grand from you."

He flashed her a brief smile. He had beautiful teeth, she noticed for the first time. They looked startlingly white in contrast to his deeply tanned and bewhiskered face. She didn't know whether to slap him or kiss him.

But she didn't dare let her affection for him show. They couldn't afford to become maudlin now. So she glowered at him. "Any other last requests?" she asked sarcastically.

"If you make it and I don't, smoke a cigarette for me and have a glass or two of straight whiskey."

"Bourbon or Scotch?"

"I'm not particular."

"Anything else?"

"Yeah. Don't take those final vows."

He moved so fast her mind couldn't register it before he had hooked his hand around the back of her head and pulled her face beneath his. Close. "I'd just as well die a sinner as a saint."

He kissed her.

His mouth came down hard on hers. Her lips parted. His tongue made one sweet, piercing stab into her mouth. The suddenness of it, the masculine claim it symbolized, made her weak. Her hands clutched the front of his tank top and her head fell back. His whiskers scraped her face, but she didn't mind. His tongue, as smooth as velvet and as nimble as a candle's flame, mated with hers and provocatively stroked the inside of her mouth.

An emptiness deep inside Kerry yawned wide, wider, yearning to be filled. Her breasts felt full, as with milk. The nipples tingled with a desperate need to be touched, kissed, sucked. Her womanhood ached deliciously. Reflexively, her hungry body arched against him. Her arms folded around his neck.

Her response drove him a little mad; he deepened the kiss. His broad hand opened wide over her back and pressed her as close to him as possible. The fervency mounted until he made a strangled cry and lifted his head. He stared down into her bewildered eyes. He gazed at her mouth, now full and red and moist from their kiss.

"Godamighty, Kerry," he rasped.

Involuntarily, she ran her tongue over her throbbing lips.

He groaned. "Oh, God, you're sweet." He kissed her again, his tongue thrusting deeply. "And I swear to you that if we had the time—" he kissed her again "—I'd see you, all of you. And touch you. Your breasts, God, your breasts." He passed his hand over them fleetingly. It was a sizzling sensation and she moaned. "And I'd kiss you. Get inside you. Even if it meant being denied heaven."

She wanted him. Yes. But . . . she loved him. She loved him! And, God forbid, should anything happen to him, he would die thinking—

"Linc, there's something—"

His head popped up. "Shh!"

"But I have to tell you—"

"Not now. Be quiet." He pushed her away and stood up, craning his head to see above the trees. He motioned her to silence. Seconds later, her ears picked up the drone of an airplane's engine.

"We've got a lot to talk about, sweetheart, but now's not the time. Get the children ready." He was spurred into action, every muscle of his body tense, but executing movements with amazing calm and agility. "Joe, get into place."

"I'm ready," Joe said, taking cover behind a tree.

The airplane didn't circle the area in reconnaissance. It made one approach. The children were restless with anticipation. Their dreams were coming true. While they all kept their eyes trained on the landing airplane, Linc's were busily scanning the area for any sign of troop movement.

The pilot made a faultless landing and the airplane taxied to a stop directly in front of the old watchtower, in perfect accordance with the plan.

"Go." Linc gave Kerry a gentle push.

Tightly clasping Lisa against her chest, she took several hesitant steps into the clearing.

"Go!" This time Linc roared his command.

Kerry broke into a dead run, yelling for the children to do the same. She could hear the heavy thud of Linc's boots close behind them. They had closed almost half the distance between them and the airplane when the first shots were fired. Kerry froze; the children screamed.

"Go on, don't stop," Linc shouted.

He spun around and sprayed the air with machine gun bullets, aiming in the general direction of their as yet unseen attackers. He saw answering gunfire. The trees seemed to spit flames no larger than those of a cigarette lighter, but he could hear bullets peppering the ground all around him. He rattled off another round and turned to chase after Kerry and the children, who had almost reached the plane. Miraculously none of them had been hit, though some of them were screaming in terror.

The door of the plane was already open. Linc turned again. The wall of the jungle now seemed to be alive with troops firing weapons. Apparently Juan hadn't been successful in diverting them. Linc only hoped that the boy hadn't been found out.

From the corner of his eye he saw Joe leave his cover and fire his machine gun. He shredded jungle plants and sent a few soldiers scampering for cover, before he jumped back behind his tree.

"Good boy," Linc muttered. He glanced over his shoulder and saw that the children were being pulled into the plane. Running backward and firing from the hip, he went to assist them on board.

It was when he glanced behind him again, that he saw Jeeps loaded with troops moving out of the line of trees on the other side of the border. Montenegro's neighboring nation was impartial, but they were coming out to investigate. An officer in the first Jeep, holding a bullhorn to his mouth, shouted an order at him. Linc didn't understand it, but he got the general meaning when the soldiers began firing warning shots.

"Shit!"

Now they had armies shooting at them from both sides.

One of the children stumbled and went down. Linc raced over to him, scooped him up, and ran at a crouch toward the door of the plane.

"Was Mike shot?" Kerry shouted over the whine of the plane's engine and the persistent gunfire.

"Just fell I think. Get in the damn airplane!"

Lisa was being lifted out of Kerry's arms and swung up into the fuselage. Linc shoved Mike toward the pair of reaching hands. The terrified little boy, tears making muddy tracks down his dusty face, was hauled inside to safety. All the children were now inside, except Joe, who was doing enough damage to frustrate the guerrillas and keep them under cover. But his ammunition would run out soon.

"Get in the plane!" Linc repeated to Kerry.

"But you and Joe—"

"For god's sake, don't argue with me now!"

Apparently the man in the plane was of the same mind as Linc. Still protesting, Kerry was pulled inside. "If anything happens to me, get them the hell out of here," Linc shouted to the blond-headed man.

"No!" Kerry screamed.

Linc looked directly at her. The briefest but most puissant look passed between them, then Linc turned abruptly and began running back toward the line of trees, firing the machine gun as he ran.

"What's he doing?" Cage Hendren asked. "Why didn't he get in?"

"He's gone back to get one of the boys. He stayed behind to give us cover."

Cage nodded his understanding as he watched the man run in a zigzag pattern across the clearing. He didn't know who he was, but he considered him a hero. Or a fool.

"Cage, we've got to go," the pilot of the airplane shouted from the open door of the cockpit.

Kerry grabbed Cage's sleeve. "No. This plane doesn't take off without them."

Cage saw the determination on her face. "Not yet," he yelled to the pilot.

"One of these lunatics might hit us. And the other bunch is moving Jeeps—"

"Thirty seconds more," Cage bargained, knowing that the veteran pilot was right. "We've got two more passengers."

Kerry screamed when she saw Linc fall to the ground. "He's all right," Cage reassured her. "He's just reducing the size of their target."

From his battle position, Linc shouted for Joe to run toward the plane while he provided cover by firing at the guerrillas. Joe emerged from the jungle with his machine gun blasting. Rotating as he ran, he fired in all directions. He had almost reached the point where Linc lay when his left leg buckled and he went down.

"No!" Kerry cried. She tried to jump from the door of the airplane, but Cage caught her shoulders from behind and gripped them hard to keep her inside.

Just then several bullets struck the exterior of the plane. They did no serious damage, but increased Cage's anxiety. The success of the mission depended on getting the children to safety. Could it be sacrificed for two who were apparently willing to give their lives?

He watched Linc belly crawl to where the boy lay sprawled face down in the dirt. He saw them exchange words. "He's alive," Cage told Kerry.

"Oh, God, please don't let them die." Tears were streaming down her face.

"Cage, they're blocking off this makeshift runway with jeeps," the pilot yelled.

The children were all crying in terror.

"Kerry, we've got to go," Cage said.

"No. We can't leave them."

"We might all die if—"

"No, no." She struggled to get away from his restraining hands. "You can take off but leave me."

"You know I can't do that. The children need you."

She sobbed wretchedly as she saw Linc come up on one knee. He gripped Joe under the arm and slowly heaved him to his feet. Joe couldn't support himself. His left leg dangled uselessly. Linc struggled to get one of Joe's arms around his shoulders, then he began backing toward the plane with the boy in tow.

They were pelleted with gunfire. Kerry saw little puffs of dust rising from the ground where bullets struck. Smelling victory, the guerrillas left the cover of the trees and began running across the clearing, firing steadily.

"Kerry—"

"No, Cage! Don't you move this plane a single inch!"

"But-"

She cupped her hands around her mouth. "Linc! Linc! Hurry!"

Linc fired the machine gun at the pursuing enemy until it ran out of ammunition. Then, with a vicious curse, he threw it down and, in a single motion, swept Joe up into his arms like a baby and ran toward the airplane.

"They're coming!" Kerry shouted.

"Start rolling," Cage shouted over his shoulder to the pilot. He leaned as far out the door of the airplane as he could, hand extended.

Kerry saw Linc's grimace of agony a second before she saw the front of his shirt bloom red. She was too hoarse by now to make a sound, but she opened her mouth and screamed silently.

Wounded, Linc kept running, his teeth bared with exertion. He stumbled toward the door of the plane, making a Herculean effort to hand Joe up to Cage.

Cage gripped Joe's shirt collar and pulled him inside. Under his own strength and despite the pain, the boy crawled out of the way. The plane had gained momentum now and Linc was having to run to stay abreast of the door.

"Give me your hand," Cage shouted.

Linc reached as far as he could, stumbled, but miraculously stayed on his feet. Then, with one last burst of energy, he grasped Cage's hand and held on. His feet went out from under him. He was dragged a considerable distance before Cage, with Kerry's clawing assistance, managed to pull him inside. He fell in, rolled to his back and lay there gasping while Cage secured the door and shouted to the pilot, "Get the hell out of here!"

"Roger!"

They weren't out of danger yet. The airplane was fired upon from all directions before the pilot finally taxied his way clear, and the aircraft became airborne only a few feet above the Jeeps trying to block their takeoff.

The children were huddled together. Most of their tears had dried, but they were wide-eyed and apprehensive over their first airplane ride. They stared at the tall, blond *norteamericano* who was speaking to them in their native language and smiling at them kindly.

Kerry's hands fluttered over Linc's chest. "Oh, Lord. Where are you hit? Are you in pain?"

He pried his eyes open. "I'm fine. Check on Joe."

She crawled over to where the boy lay. His face was ashen, his lips white with pain. Cage shouldered her aside. He swabbed Joe's arm with an alcohol-soaked cotton ball and gave him an injection.

"A pain killer," he said in answer to Kerry's unasked question.

"I didn't know you could do that."

"I didn't know I could either," he said wryly. "One of our local doctors gave me a crash course in nursing last night."

He cut away Joe's pants leg and examined the nasty bullet wound in his thigh. "I don't think it shattered his femur, but it tore up the muscle a bit."

Kerry swallowed the bile that flooded her throat. "Will he be all right?"

"I think so." Cage smiled at her and pressed her hand. "I'll do what I can to clean the wound and keep him comfortable. When we get closer, the pilot will radio Jenny. She'll see to it that an ambulance is waiting for us when we land. And by the way," he said with the smile that had made him a legend with women throughout West Texas, "I'm glad you made it."

"We wouldn't have, if it hadn't been for Linc." Now that Joe seemed to have lapsed into painless oblivion, she moved toward the man still lying prone on the floor of the fuselage.

*"Who?"* Cage asked.

"Linc. Lincoln O'Neal."

"You're kidding!" Cage exclaimed. "The photographer?"

"Somebody call my name?" Linc opened his eyes and struggled to sit up. The two men grinned at each other with the ease of old friends.

"Welcome aboard and pleased to meet you," Cage said, shaking hands with Linc.

"Thanks."

Linc looked at Kerry. She looked back. Cage realized immediately that something was going on there and that whatever it was, he was a fifth wheel. "I, uh, I'll see to the kids. Kerry, maybe you'd better check on Linc's wound. Medical supplies are in here," he said, sliding a first-aid kit toward her. Diplomatically he left them alone.

"What in the hell were you trying to prove back there?" Linc demanded angrily. "I told you to leave without us if anything happened. I ought to bust your butt for disobeying me."

Kerry's encroaching tears were swept away by fury. "Well pardon me," she snapped. "I wasn't waiting for you. I was waiting for Joe. Are you in pain or not?"

"It's a Band-Aid wound," he said, negligently glancing at his bleeding shoulder.

"Cage can give you a shot to stop the pain."

"Forget it. I hate shots."

They glowered at each other. Her lips were the first to quirk with the beginning of a smile. Then his. They surprised all the passengers in the small aircraft by suddenly bursting into laughter.

"We made it!" Linc cried exuberantly. "We actually made it. Hotdamn! You're home free, Kerry."

"Home." She whispered the word like a benediction.

Then her emotions made another swift about-face. She launched herself against Linc's blood-stained chest. And while they hugged each other fiercely, she wept with relief.

# *Chapter 8*

Jenny Hendren had thoughtfully provided food. There were peanut butter sandwiches, oranges and apples, and homemade chocolate chip cookies. Cheese snacks and canned drinks had been kept in a portable cooler. As soon as their hunger had been appeased, most of the children dozed. All the seats had been temporarily removed from the Cessna executive plane, but there still wasn't an abundance of space inside the fuselage.

"How is Joe?" Kerry asked Cage.

He was bending over the injured boy, checking the inadequate bandage he had placed over his thigh wound. "Still out."

"I'm glad you had that injection ready."

"So am I. He'd be in a helluva lot of pain without it. How is the other patient?"

"Ornery, bull-headed, obstinate." Immediately after her tears had dried, she and Linc had moved apart awkwardly. No longer tender and consoling, he'd reverted to being tough and abusive. "He wants to talk to you."

Cage moved over to where Linc was propped against the wall. He looked as disreputable as when Kerry had first met him. He was unshaven. His clothes were filthy and torn and blood-stained. Without the handkerchief sweatband around his forehead, he had to constantly keep pushing his hair away from his face.

"Kerry said you wanted to talk to me." Cage eased down beside the other man.

"You said something earlier about calling ahead to your wife." Cage nodded. "Do you think she could have a camera waiting for me when we land?"

"Linc had to throw his cameras in the river when we crossed it," Kerry explained. "We barely managed to save his film."

Cage, for all his reckless living in years past, looked back at them with surprise and respect. "Sounds as if the two of you had quite an adventure."

Kerry glanced uneasily at Linc. "Yes, we did. You see, the river—"

Cage held up both hands. "I want to hear all about it, but everyone else will, too. Why don't you rest now, then tell it once for everybody?" Kerry smiled at him gratefully. "What kind of camera do you need, Linc?" he asked.

"Got a pencil?"

Cage jotted down the specifications as Linc ticked them off. "I'll see what I can do." He inched toward the cockpit.

"Nice guy," Linc remarked, his eyes still on Cage.

Kerry laughed. "Not always, from what I hear."

"Oh?"

"As I told you, I met Jenny through the Hendren Foundation. She was engaged to Hal Hendren when he was shot."

"Cage's brother?"

"Yes."

"The missionary?"

"Right."

Linc shook his head. "I must have taken a blow on the head I don't remember. Or is this as confusing as it sounds?"

"It is rather complicated. Jenny knew the brothers quite well. You see she grew up with them. The Hendrens adopted her when her parents were killed."

"So they were all one big, happy family?"

"Yes."

Linc's eyebrows shot up and he grinned lecherously. "Sounds kinky to me."

"Hardly. They were reared in a parsonage. Cage's father is a minister."

"Preacher's kid, huh? No wonder I liked him immediately. Bet he's a hell-raiser."

"Until Jenny got hold of him."

Even though Linc was bedraggled, his eyes sparkled. "I think I'm looking forward to meeting this Jenny."

Kerry laughed. "You should be, but not for the reason you think. She's a real lady. She and Cage, who was a lady killer extraordinaire, are devoted to each other. They have one child, a little boy, and she's expecting another. I'm sure that's the only reason she didn't come with Cage to pick us up."

"Well if she had come along, I don't know where we would have put her."

Linc's comment called attention to how cramped they were. They were sitting so close that Kerry's knee was propped on his thigh. As unobtrusively as possible, she moved it away.

Both were remembering the kiss he had given her before the airplane arrived. There were kisses. And then there were *kisses*. And that kiss had been the kind a man gives a woman he wants badly. It had been ravenous and undisciplined and carnal. Each time Kerry thought about it, she trembled with aftershocks. And each time Linc thought about it, his manhood threatened to embarrass him.

"Are you comfortable?" she asked huskily.

His gaze popped up to hers. At first he thought she had read his mind, or, God forbid, noticed the rigidity behind the fly of his pants. Then he realized that she was looking at his shoulder, not his lap.

"No, it's nothing," he said in a strained voice.

She shivered at the blood stains on his tank top. He could have been killed so easily. He had risked his life. It would be impossible to repay him for the sacrifices he had made for her and the children, but she knew that some kind of thank you, insufficient though it would be, was in order.

"Linc?"

Because he couldn't look at her without his desire running rampant, he had leaned his head against the wall of the aircraft and closed his eyes. Now, when she spoke his name with such appeal and laid her cool, dry hand on his arm, his eyes opened slowly and he turned his head to look at her.

"Hmm?"

"What you did back there..." Her voice trailed off and she lowered her eyes. "I want to thank you for everything. I...I..." The right words wouldn't come. She couldn't think of anything to say that wouldn't come close to sounding like a declaration of her love. Unwisely, she blurted out the thing that came to mind. "I'll give you a check for the fifty thousand as soon as possible."

He sat perfectly still for several moments. It was the calm before the storm. He violently jerked his arm from beneath her hand. He wanted to tell her to keep the goddamn money. Money! Is that all she thought this had meant to him?

"Go to hell."

"What?"

"You heard me."

"But I don't understand."

"You've got that right, lady, you don't understand."

"Why are you snapping at me? I was only trying to thank you." By now, Kerry, too, was angry. There was just no understanding this man. He wouldn't let someone be nice to him. He was an unfeeling barbarian.

"So you've thanked me. Now drop it."

"Gladly." She started to scoot away, but noticed the fresh drops of blood oozing down his chest. "You made your shoulder bleed again."

Indifferently, he looked down at it. "It's all right."

She took a square of gauze from the first-aid kit. "Here, let me—"

He caught her wrist before her hand made contact with his injured shoulder. "I said it's all right. Just leave me alone, will you? As you've been so quick to remind me, we have a business arrangement only. That doesn't include tending my wounds." He lowered his voice. "Or kissing. Why'd you let me kiss you back there?" He moved his face closer to hers. "Why'd you kiss me back? Baby, your tongue was just as busy as mine. Don't think I didn't notice. Well, you could have spared yourself the trouble. I would have run just as hard, shot off just as many rounds of ammo, if you hadn't."

Kerry's cheeks were hot with indignation. "That's a horrible thing to say."

"Maybe. But not as horrible as making sexual promises you don't intend to keep." His lip curled with contempt. "We're even now, Sister Kerry. I hired out to do you a service. As soon as you pay me, I'm gone. *Finis.* I'll click off a few shots of the kids getting off the airplane for their first sight of U.S. soil, then I'll split. This whole goddamn mess will be history, and frankly, it can't happen soon enough for me."

Kerry snatched her hand out of his grip, glaring at him with patent dislike. Never in her life had she known anyone so hard and insensitive. "Goddamn mess." That summed up what he thought of the orphans, their ordeal, and her. The disillusionment was cruel, but she had suffered disillusionment before. It was painful, but not fatal. One could survive and live to tell about it.

She put as much distance as possible between herself and Mr. Lincoln O'Neal, found as comfortable a space as the crowded fuselage afforded, and settled down to sleep for the remainder of the flight.

Cage nudged her awake. "We're about fifteen minutes out, Kerry. I thought you might want to rouse the children."

"How's Joe?" The boy was moaning. His eyes were still closed, but he was fitfully rolling his head from side to side.

"Unfortunately he's coming around. But I'm not going to give him anything else. I'll let the doctor take it from here."

"Cage," she said, catching his sleeve when he moved toward the cockpit again. "I don't want to face a crowd of reporters right now. The children will be frightened enough already. We're all so dirty and tired. Can you arrange it?"

He rubbed the back of his neck. "You're big news, Kerry, because of—"

"I know," she interrupted quickly, aware that Linc could overhear everything they were saying. "But I'm sure you understand why I prefer privacy. For me and the children, not to mention the couples who are going to adopt them."

"I understand, but I'm not sure the media will. Reporters have been camped out in La Bota for days, waiting for your arrival." He saw her distress and laid a comforting hand on her shoulder. "But if you don't want to be interviewed or have the children exposed to that kind of mayhem, that's the way it'll be. I'll radio the sheriff now and tell him to cordon off the airport."

"Thank you."

The children, who were all wide awake now, were chattering excitedly as they peered out the windows. Kerry laughed at their bewildered comments about the flat West

Texas landscape, which was so different from the jungle terrain they were accustomed to.

The experienced pilot made another perfect landing. When the plane taxied to a stop, the first priority was to get Joe to the waiting ambulance, which would rush him directly to the hospital. Cage jumped to the ground and conferred briefly with the doctor.

Linc swung down and looked for a pregnant lady with a camera. She wasn't difficult to spot. Kerry was right. Jenny Hendren spelled lady from the top of her glossy brown hair to the toes of her shoes. "Mrs. Hendren?"

"Mr. O'Neal?"

They smiled at each other and she passed him the camera he had ordered. "A Nikon F3 with Tri-X film. I sent Gary to Amarillo to pick it up. We had to call around before finally locating one there."

"Sorry for putting you to so much trouble."

"I just hope it's all right," she said anxiously. "I barely know which end of a camera to point."

Linc didn't know who Gary was, but he was damned glad to have a camera in his hands again. "It's perfect, thanks. I'll settle up with you later."

He tore into a package of film and loaded it mechanically. He raised the camera to his eye just in time to snap off pictures of the paramedics lowering the stretcher bearing Joe out of the airplane. He moved toward it. The boy's eyes were open now. He spotted Linc, the only familiar face among those surrounding him. Linc said, "Hang in there, trooper." For the first time since Linc had met him, Joe smiled. Linc captured that wan smile on film.

The doctor climbed into the ambulance after the stretcher had been loaded. When he turned to close the door, he noticed Linc's wound. "You should have that attended to."

"Later." Giving his minor injury no more thought, Linc swung his camera around toward the door of the airplane.

Inside it, Kerry was speaking with soft reassurance to the children. "Everything will seem different, but don't be frightened. You are very special to the people here. They want you."

"Are you going to leave us?" young Mike asked.

"No. I won't go until I'm sure you are all happy with your new families. Are we ready?" Eight heads nodded solemnly. "Good. Then let's go."

She assisted them to the ground. Cage and Jenny Hendren escorted the pitiful parade toward a waiting van. Kerry did her best to ignore Linc as he took pictures of her. She also tried to ignore the stab of envy she felt when Cage took his wife in his arms, held her close, and kissed her.

Jenny's relief that Cage had returned safe and unharmed was apparent, as was his concern that she was overtaxing herself in her advanced stage of pregnancy. While both dismissed the other's worry, their love shone around them like an exclusive sun.

When all the children had been loaded into the van, Kerry and Jenny embraced. "It's a dream come true," Kerry said to her friend. "Thank you for everything. For making all the arrangements. You've both been wonderful."

"Hush now. You need rest and nourishment. We'll have plenty of time to talk later. Cage," she said, turning to her husband, "why don't you and Mr. O'Neal climb into the back with the children? I'll drive."

"Uh, excuse me, Mrs. Hendren," Linc said. "I'll just get a cab to the nearest hotel and—"

Simultaneously Cage and Jenny burst out laughing. "We only have one cab in town," Cage explained. "You'd be lucky to get him here the day after tomorrow if you called right now. And there's no hotel, although there are several motels."

"Besides," Jenny chimed in, "I wouldn't let you leave without thanking you for all your help. Now get in before we collapse from this heat."

And that, it seemed, was that. Linc got in the back of the van with Cage. Little Lisa, her face a study in uncertainty, held her arms up to him. He settled her in his lap for the ride to the Hendren's house.

"I held the reporters at bay with the promise of a press release, Kerry. You can prepare it whenever you feel like it."

"Thank you, Jenny."

"And, of course, you're staying with us," Jenny added.

"What about the children?"

"We've been loaned several mobile homes. They're at the ranch," Cage said. "We've also got nurses standing by to check them over to the immigration department's satisfaction. It'll take several days for the paperwork to be completed and the adoption papers finalized. That will all be taken care of before their families arrive to pick them up." Cage looked at the circle of young faces surrounding them. "Which ones are the sisters?"

Kerry pointed out Juan's two sisters. Cage smiled at them and told them in Spanish that their new parents were already at the house. "They're waiting for you. You'll meet them as soon as we arrive."

The little girls, who had been inconsolable when Kerry gave them their brother's parting message, clung to each other fearfully and looked to both Kerry and Linc for guidance. He gave them the thumbs up sign and an exaggerated wink. That made them giggle.

Kerry was impressed with the Hendren's house and surrounding acreage and commented on it as they turned off the main highway and drove through a gate.

"Thank you," Jenny said. "Cage had started refurbishing the house before we got married. We've done a lot more work on it since then. I love it."

Cage Hendren had been a wildcatter, and still laid claim to several producing oil wells. But when the price of crude began to drop, Cage could see the handwriting on the wall and began cultivating other businesses, including real estate and beef cattle ranching. He also had a stable full of quarter horses. When the economy shifted, he suffered no tremendous setbacks. They lived modestly by choice, not out of necessity.

There were three mobile homes parked end to end on the near side of the horse barn. Before the van had pulled to a complete stop, Roxie Fleming emerged from one of them at a run, her husband Gary, close behind her.

"That's Roxie," Jenny told them.

"You wrote me about her," Kerry said.

Roxie, buxom and boisterous, would have launched herself at them, had not the easy-going, affable Gary caught her shirttail and held her back.

Cage and Jenny introduced Kerry and Linc to the Flemings. Roxie acknowledged them politely, but distractedly. She was eagerly scanning the faces of the children. "Which ones are Cara and Carmen?" Her voice was about to crack.

Kerry pointed the two girls out. Roxie extended her hands. A tense moment elapsed before the girls separated themselves from the tight little group and baby-stepped their way forward to timidly take Roxie's hands.

As discreetly as possible, Linc took pictures of the heart-wrenching scene. The most poignant photograph he got was one of Kerry Bishop, the person who had made this miracle possible. He knew it would be a good photograph. The reflected sunlight had made diamonds of the tears standing in her eyes.

Kerry descended the staircase with inexplicable nervousness. Perhaps it was because she was wearing a dress for the first time in ages. Well, that wasn't entirely true. She had worn a dress the night she had abducted Linc from the bar, but that wasn't quite the same.

Maybe her heart was pounding because this was the first time he had ever seen her with her hair clean, soft and glowing, her skin smooth and free of grime and her nails buffed to a polished shine.

For whatever reason, her knees threatened to collapse with each step she took.

It seemed that a lifetime had passed since their narrow escape from Montenegro. Yet it had happened only that morning. The day had been spent getting the children settled into their temporary quarters. They had marveled over the "luxuries" they had found in the mobile homes. They had all been given clean bills of health by the nurses. Months ago, when the idea of their being adopted in the United States was first conceived, Kerry had seen to it that each child was vaccinated in accordance with U.S. regulations.

With the aid of the Flemings and Cage's parents, Bob and Sarah Hendren, all the children had been soaped and scrubbed and shampooed and outfitted in spanking new clothes donated by a La Bota merchant. Thanks to members of Bob Hendren's congregation, there was enough food in the kitchen to make the tables and countertops groan. The children had already eaten two full meals.

Roxie couldn't keep her hands off her adopted daughters and had brushed their hair so many times that Gary, almost as guilty of overindulgence as his wife, had warned her that she was going to brush them bald if she wasn't careful. Kerry only hoped that the rapport between all the children and their new families was established as easily.

At her request, Cage had driven Kerry to the hospital. The staff, carefully guarding her privacy, had let her slip in a back entrance to visit Joe. The surgery to remove the bullet from his thigh had been completed. He was groggy from the anesthetic, but he recognized her. The doctor assured her that his leg hadn't suffered any permanent damage.

When Kerry returned, Jenny had insisted that she spoil herself with a long bubble bath. Without a trace of reluctance, Kerry had stripped off the vile clothes she had lived in for almost four days.

Only when she untied the bandana from around her neck did her fingers falter. Since Linc had given it to her, she regretted having to remove it. She laundered the handkerchief in the bathroom sink and hung it up to dry. Unless he asked for it back, she intended to keep it as a memento of her one wild, brief, unconsummated, but no less ardent, love affair.

Now, voices drifted to her from the dining room. Her stomach was queasy with a mixture of anticipation and dread. Bolstering her courage, she stepped through the arched doorway into a mellow pool of candlelight and hesitated on the threshold. Jenny was the first to spot her.

"There you are."

"Wow!" Cage whistled appreciatively. "A little soap and water can do wonders."

Linc said nothing. He was caught in the act of lifting a can of beer to his mouth. It stayed poised there in midair for several counts, before he actually drank from it. Kerry went in and took a chair across the table from him.

"This is so nice of you, Jenny." She gazed in awe at the flower centerpiece, the bright, sterling candlesticks, the china and crystal and silver.

"I thought the two of you deserved a quiet, leisurely dinner. Lunch was rather hectic. Relax and enjoy yourselves. The report from the trailers is that the children are asleep."

"I just hope I don't disgrace myself," Kerry said, running her fingers over the handle of her salad fork. "I've lived in the jungle for so long, I hardly remember how to use silverware properly."

"It will all come back to you," Jenny said with a gentle smile.

"And if it doesn't, we won't mind." Cage passed her a plate filled with food. "We're used to eating with Trent. His table manners are atrocious."

"Cute kid," Linc commented. "He made the others feel right at home."

"Yeah," Cage said. "He taught them by example how to attack a bowl of homemade ice cream."

Laughing, Kerry asked, "Where is he?"

"Blissfully asleep," his mother said wearily. "Eat quietly."

Kerry was surprised at how rich and deep Linc's laughter could be when it wasn't tinged with cynicism. It rolled over her like a wave. Apparently Cage, who was of the same broad-shouldered, slim-hipped build, had lent him a pair of jeans and a shirt. He had showered, and his hair, though it could still stand a trim, had been washed and brushed back. His face had been closely shaved. Without the stubble, his jaw looked even more unrelievedly masculine than before, which was a disquieting thought. She detected the faint outline of a white bandage beneath his shirt.

While they ate, their conversation centered mainly on the orphans. "I distributed copies of your press release to the disgruntled reporters."

"Thank you, Cage."

"We'll tell you about the applicants for adoptions, but tomorrow is soon enough for that."

"Thank you again. I'm so tired, I don't think I could assimilate anything tonight," Kerry admitted. "I'm sure you screened the couples carefully. Are all of them as wonderful as the Flemings?"

"Gary and Roxie are special friends, so we're biased. But we think the others will be super parents, too."

After a pause in the conversation, Jenny smiled at Linc and said, "I never guessed that I'd be so honored as to have a celebrity at my table."

"Where?" he asked, comically turning his head from side to side as though searching for the celebrity.

The Hendrens continued to prod him until he enlightened and entertained them with stories of his adventures as a photojournalist. He downplayed the danger he frequently encountered and embellished some of the more humorous anecdotes.

"But," he said, pushing aside his dessert plate after eating two helpings of apple pie, "this latest escapade in Montenegro was about the scariest situation I've ever been in."

A major portion of the afternoon had been taken up by their recounting their tale. Cage and Jenny, the Flemings and Cage's parents had listened with disbelief as they told them all that had happened to them on their way to the border.

"I'm in no hurry to go back," Kerry said now.

"Neither were we once we got out," Cage said.

Linc looked at him in surprise. "*We?* You were there? When?"

"After my brother was executed."

"I'm sorry."

"No, it's all right. Jenny and I had to go down there and identify Hal's body and escort it back." He reached across the corner of the table and took her hand, squeezing it. "It was an unpleasant experience for both of us." He stared into space reflectively. "Although, if it hadn't been so spoiled by the civil war, Montenegro could be a beautiful place." He gazed at his wife. "The tropical climate was rather sensuous as I recall."

Because Cage and Jenny were looking at each other with such absorption, they missed the fleeting look that passed between their guests. Both Kerry and Linc vividly remembered a night spent beneath the shelter of a vine, a heavy rainfall that surrounded them with a pounding as fierce as that of a heart on fire, and the seductive perfume of jungle flowers, naked skin and earth combined into a potent aphrodisiac.

That night seemed unreal now. It could have happened to two other people in another lifetime. They couldn't have lain together so closely and be this remotely detached from one another now. He couldn't have quieted her fears and dried her tears then and hurt her as he had this morning with his cruel words.

Kerry looked across the table at Linc; he was a stranger. They had shared cups of water and scraps of bread, passionate kisses and equally passionate arguments, and yet she knew so little about him.

"Neither of you has explained how you came to be teamed up," Jenny said. "How did you become involved with Kerry's work, Linc?"

Kerry jumped as though she'd been struck with an electric cattle prod. She met Linc's hard gaze across the table. His expression was smug. He might have cleaned up on the outside, he might look prettier, but he was still rotten to the core on the inside. He was as cunning and calculating as ever, a ruthless street fighter who never cried uncle.

"I think Kerry should be the one to tell you that," he said. *If she dares.* That remained unspoken, but Kerry clearly read the challenge in his eyes.

It was a challenge she didn't dare back down from. Setting her chin at a stubborn angle, she said, "I recruited him." He made a rude, scoffing sound. She flashed him a poisonous look. "All right, I . . . I . . ."

"Shanghaied," Linc supplied drolly.

Kerry sprang to her feet, furious with him for airing their quarrel in front of the Hendrens. "You just won't be nice about this, will you?"

He bolted from his chair. "Nice? *Nice?* You kidnapped me, lady. You deliberately destroyed a month's worth of hard work. You made me miss my plane out of that godforsaken hellhole. You got me captured by a bunch of cutthroats, chased, shot at, nearly drowned and you expect me to be *nice* about it?"

Chest heaving with agitation, he pointed at Kerry accusingly as he addressed Cage and Jenny. "She dressed up like a whore and lured me out of a tavern. That's how she 'recruited' me. I went with her, thinking I was gonna get laid and . . . Oh, sorry, Jenny."

"That's all right," Jenny mumbled.

"He's failed to mention that he was drunk at the time," Kerry sneered. "And I didn't lure him, I dragged him because he couldn't stand up under his own power."

"And that makes it okay?" Linc yelled across the table.

"I thought he was a mercenary," Kerry told their avid listeners. "And he is. He'll get paid for his time and trouble," she said scathingly. "Before you go pinning any medals of valor on him, maybe you should know that he didn't do anything out of largesse. I had to agree to pay him fifty thousand dollars so he wouldn't turn me and the children over to El Presidente."

"That's not why I demanded to be paid, and you damn well know it." Linc moved forward menacingly, as though he was going to climb over the table to get to her. "The money was to repay me for the film you destroyed. That's about how much revenue you cost me. But it doesn't begin to reimburse me for having to put up with you for the last four days." He tossed his napkin down beside his plate. "Cage, would it be too much of an imposition to ask you to drive me into town?"

Jenny Hendren sprang from her chair. "You're not leaving?"

"I'm afraid so, Jenny." Linc liked Cage's wife very much. They had been on a first name basis since earlier that afternoon. She was gracious and kind and straightforward, soft, womanly, and even tempered—everything that Kerry Bishop was not. "Not that I don't appreciate your hospitality."

"But you can't leave," Jenny said imperiously. "Not now." Everyone was surprised by the intensity of her outburst and looked at her inquiringly. Embarrassed, she hastened to ask, "You took all those pictures today to go with the story of your escape, right?"

"Right," Linc answered hesitantly.

"And I'm sure that since Kerry has declined to be interviewed, she's going to grant you exclusive rights to the story. Right, Kerry?"

Kerry hesitated. "Uh, right."

"Well, the story isn't over yet," Jenny said. "Don't you want to photograph the children as they meet their new parents? And you can't leave without knowing how Joe is going to fare."

Linc considered his dilemma. Jenny was right in one respect. The story would be better if he stuck around till the end of it. He'd been on the telephone to several magazines that afternoon and was taking bids from editors who were eager to get their hands on the piece. And, by God, he *was* entitled to exclusive rights to it, whether Kerry had granted them freely or not.

But he didn't think he could stay under the same roof with her for another hour. He'd either make love to her or murder her, and, for entirely different reasons, he was sorely tempted to do both. The balance was precarious. A slight tip in one direction or another and *wham!*, he was going to cook his own goose.

"I don't know," he hedged. "I guess I could get a room in town and—"

"Ouch!"

Jenny's exclamation brought all eyes around to her. She clutched her distended abdomen with both hands, cradling the precious burden it carried.

# *Chapter 9*

Jenny!'' Cage was out of his chair like a shot. Before Linc or Kerry could even blink, he was at Jenny's side and his hands had replaced hers on her swollen stomach. ''Is it . . . what is it?''

She took several gasping breaths, then said, ''Just one of those cramps I think.''

''You're sure? It's not the baby?''

''No, I don't think so. Not yet.''

''Sit down, Jenny,'' Kerry said, scooting Jenny's chair beneath her.

''I'm fine, really,'' she said, easing herself down. ''I had these cramping seizures when I was pregnant with Trent.''

''And they always scared the hell out of me,'' Cage said, running his fingers through his hair. ''Should I call the doctor?''

Jenny raised his hand to her mouth and kissed it. ''No. Don't make a fuss. Sorry I made such a scene.'' She encompassed them all in her apologetic smile.

"You did too much today and were on your feet too long," Kerry admonished gently. "You stay right there and let us clean up the kitchen."

Over Jenny's mild protests, the three of them began carrying the soiled dishes into the kitchen. Cage hovered around his wife. Half an hour later Kerry assisted her upstairs.

No one said any more about Linc's leaving. He didn't even think about the subject himself until he stepped out onto the front porch. When Cage joined him moments later, he said, "I really should go. My being here is putting an extra burden on Jenny."

"We wouldn't hear of it. You're welcome to stay for as long as you like, if you don't mind sleeping in the single bed in Trent's room. And I warn you, he snores."

Linc grinned. "Believe me, anything will be a pleasant change compared to where I've been sleeping." Hearing his own words, his grin faded. He remembered sleeping with only the ground for a mattress and only a vine for a blanket, holding Kerry close. The memory was bittersweet and assailed him with conflicting emotions. "Is that your Vette?" he asked Cage. He had to say something to divert his mind, which seemed to stay on a single track lately.

"Yeah. Want to see it?"

They left the porch and strolled across the yard toward the open garage. Inside it were parked a variety of vehicles, among them the vintage '63 Corvette Stingray that had caught Linc's eye. He whistled long and low.

"It's in showroom condition. How long have you had it?"

"Several years," Cage told him. "It was in bad shape when I bought it. I hired a guy to restore it for me. We'll go for a spin in it tomorrow. It'll still bury you in the seat when you get it up to fourth gear. One of my vices is driving too fast."

Linc withdrew a package of cigarettes from the breast pocket of his borrowed shirt. He'd bummed the pack off Gary Fleming earlier in the day. "Want one?"

"I'd love one," Cage said, but held up both hands when Linc extended the pack to him. "But I've sworn off. When we got together, I promised Jenny that I'd quit."

Linc squinted at his new friend through the cigarette's smoke. "You must have had a lot of vices."

Cage laughed good naturedly. "I did. Too many to count. I've given up most of them." He winked suggestively. "Except screwing. Jenny and I do that a lot."

The men laughed together. "God, that feels good," Linc said after a moment. "I haven't talked with a man who fluently speaks my language in over a month. Heard any good jokes lately?"

"Clean or dirty?"

"Dirty."

While Linc smoked his cigarette, the occasional silences between them were comfortable. They didn't have to work at being companionable because the groundwork for a new friendship had already been laid. It was based on mutual respect, a genuine liking, and perhaps recognition of each other's maverick nature.

That's why Linc didn't take umbrage when Cage said, "About that fifty thousand dollars..."

"I don't want the damn money."

"I didn't think so."

Cage dropped the subject then and there. He didn't probe for answers because Linc didn't seem inclined to discuss the money. Cage could respect that. And Linc liked Cage better for not probing.

"You and Jenny seem very happy together." Talking to a happily married man about his wife was a new experience for Linc, and he felt awkward about broaching the subject.

Cage, however, responded without compunction. "We are."

"You're lucky. I haven't seen too many happy marriages."

"I haven't either. I never take ours for granted though. Jenny gave up a lot to marry me."

"I know you gave up smoking and some hell raising. What did she give up?"

Cage grinned wryly. "Her common sense." They chuckled and Cage shook his head with chagrin. "Marrying her was the only way I could have her, and, well, you know how it is. We do things for a woman that we would never do otherwise."

*You've got that right, buddy,* was Linc's self-critical thought.

"Speaking of Jenny," Cage said, "I'd better go inside and see how she's feeling. Enjoy your cigarette. See you in the morning."

"I'll buy some clothes tomorrow. Thanks for the use of these. Thanks for everything." They shook hands. Cage walked back toward the house and closed the screened front door behind him.

Linc finished smoking his cigarette meditatively. He liked the Hendrens tremendously. He also envied them their closeness to each other. He'd never been that close to another human being. Not to either of his parents. Not to a special friend. Not to anyone.

Cage's and Jenny's gentle teasing was based on affection. The love they shared for their little boy created an almost visible bond between them. By all indications, their bedsheets were kept warm with frequent and ardent activity.

Linc had intercepted numerous loving glances between them. He felt a twinge of jealousy that no one had ever looked at him with such unqualified love. In the farthest corner of his mind, he acknowledged that maybe he'd missed something.

Hell, what was he thinking about? Had a brush with death that morning turned him into a philosopher?

He had it made. He enjoyed a terrific career that involved travel and adventure. It was lucrative. It had won him acclaim. Women were easy to come by. They were drawn to him by his money, his fame, his reputation as a lover. He gave them the expensive gifts, the introductions to influential people, and the pleasure they wanted. And he was interested in only one thing from them. Once his craving for sex was satisfied, he thought no more about them.

The women in his life were bodies only. They were transitory. Women with no substance. Not like Jenny Hendren. Not like—

Uttering an impatient oath, he rubbed Kerry's name from his mind. He also tried to eradicate her image, but was less successful at accomplishing that. He couldn't forget the way she had looked when she came down to dinner. He hadn't expected her to look so…womanly. He had expected a nun's habit.

Instead, she had shown up wearing a dress that was made of some soft material that had clung temptingly to her delicate body. The skirt had whisked against her bare legs. Each time she turned, the shape of her breasts had been clearly profiled for him. Her hair had shone in the candlelight every time she moved her head. Her lips, faintly tinted with gloss, had looked as ripe and juicy as a berry ready to be plucked. And that's all he could taste.

Oh, he had done justice to the meal. His stomach had cried out for the nourishment it had been denied for the past few days. But with every bite of food, he had also swallowed a taste of Kerry.

Linc groaned with resignation as he felt himself grow hard with a desire that would surely condemn him to hell. He couldn't indulge the longing that heated his blood. He could only try his damnedest to cool it.

* * *

"How does that feel?"

"Wonderful," Jenny sighed.

Her husband had found her already in bed when he entered their master bedroom, after having checked on their sleeping son and making certain that the extra bed had been turned down for Linc. Kerry was using the guest bedroom.

Cage had undressed quickly and joined Jenny in their wide bed where he was now massaging soothing lotion onto the stretched, tight, itchy skin of her abdomen. It was a nightly ritual that both of them enjoyed immensely.

"The baby isn't moving very much tonight," he commented.

"She's resting after her performance at dinner." Ever since the doctor had confirmed that she was pregnant, Jenny had insisted that this baby was a girl. She fancied having a blond-haired, tawny-eyed daughter to round out their family.

"That was quite a show, all right."

"What do you mean by that?" Jenny asked testily.

"Only that I wasn't sure if those cramps were real or just your sneaky way of getting Linc to stay."

Jenny moved his hand aside. "I don't like your implication, Cage."

He only laughed at her pique. "That's what I thought. You're guilty as hell. Otherwise you wouldn't be protesting so much." He leaned over and stopped her flimsy denials with a kiss. When he pulled back, he asked, "Should I be jealous?"

"Over what?" She traced the hair on his chest with her fingernail. His kisses still had the power to curl her toes.

"Over your going to such great lengths to keep Linc under our roof?"

"I haven't admitted that yet, but if I did urge him—"

"Urge! I thought you were going to hogtie the poor guy to the dining room chair when he mentioned leaving."

"Well I *do* think he should stay and take photographs of the orphans when they meet their new families. And I *did* have a cramp."

His hands fell still and his handsome face registered concern. "A bad one?"

"No. It was one of those little contractions that don't mean anything."

"Sure?"

"Positive."

He reached for the bottle of lotion and poured some into the palms of his hands. He laid them on her breasts and began rubbing in the scented cream with lulling, circular motions.

She sighed, and her eyes slid closed. Cage gazed down at her with love. "How can you be so very pregnant and still so very beautiful?"

"You think so?" Lifting one hand, she idly brushed a dark blond strand of hair off his forehead.

"Um-huh."

"Do you think Linc thinks Kerry is beautiful?"

"I thought that's what you were up to."

She stared at him guilelessly. "What?"

"Matchmaking."

"Well anyone can tell—"

"Jenny, stay out of it."

"That they're attracted to each other."

"They were practically biting and scratching across our dining room table."

She came up on one elbow. "Well I've known us to bite and scratch some! And over the dining room table, too."

Cage looked stunned, then burst out laughing. "You've got me there. Helluva private party, too, as I remember it." Wrapping his arms around her, he lowered her back to the pillows and followed her down with a lengthy, mouth to mouth, tongue to tongue kiss. When he finally raised his head, her eyes were lambent, but she hadn't dropped their argument.

"I think there's friction between Kerry and Linc because they're fighting a strong attraction."

"What does Kerry say?"

"Nothing, and that's curious, don't you think? She avoids speaking his name aloud if at all possible. After what they've been through, you would think that she'd be dropping his name left and right. She tries too hard not to look at him, but I've caught her at it a thousand times today. Did Linc say anything about it when the two of you went to the garage?"

"Sorry, darling," he said, nuzzling her neck, "I couldn't break a confidence between gentlemen."

"Then he *did* say something about Kerry!"

"No, he didn't. But he's . . . restless. That's the word I'm looking for, I think. His skin is too small for him. He's angry."

"How do you know?"

"Because I recognize the symptoms. I know what it feels like to want a woman you can't have. You're mad at yourself for being hard all the time, and you can't keep yourself from getting hard every time you think about her. It's like if you don't give it to that particular woman, it's gonna fall off." He flicked his tongue over her large, rosy nipple. "And on that note . . ."

"We can't, Cage. The doctor said it's too late."

"I know, but—" He sighed when she placed her hand where he ached to feel it. "Ahh, Jenny." He closed his mouth around her nipple and sucked it gently.

Speaking on short gusts of air, Jenny said, "So, if you didn't talk about Kerry, what did you talk about?"

His hot mouth moved to her other breast. "You. I told Linc you were my only vice."

"Hmm, Cage." She gasped when his tongue played upon her sensitized breast. "He'll think I'm terrible."

"He'll think you're wonderful. What every man wants in a wife. A lady in the parlor—"

"And a harlot in the bedroom."

"Right," he snarled affectionately, sliding his hand between her thighs.

"We can't have—"

"There are other ways."

"But we have guests in the house." Her voice slipped another notch with every feather-light caress of his fingertips.

"That's your problem," he whispered seductively. "You're the moaner."

It was too quiet.

Kerry stood at the window of the guest bedroom, gazing out over the barren landscape, wondering what was keeping her awake when her entire body was crying out for sleep. She had finally come to the conclusion that, after almost a year of living in Montenegro, she was missing the nighttime jungle sounds.

She felt exposed because, save for the mesa forming a silhouette against the sky, there was nothing to break the sameness of the landscape. No encroaching trees, no hanging vines, no dense brush. And no sound.

But then she heard a barely audible sound. A squeak. She glanced down and saw a dark shadow slipping through the gate onto the terrace that surrounded the Hendren's lovely swimming pool.

Linc.

Her heart began its unnatural hammering, as it always seemed to do whenever he was around. This time, however, her rapid heartbeat was partially due to anger. How dare Linc blare out her indiscretion to the Hendrens! She had come to expect nothing but churlish behavior from him, but he had sunk to an all-time low that night at dinner.

His participation in the rescue must have come as a surprise to them. They might have assumed that she would need assistance at some point, but they were no doubt shocked that it had come in the form of a renowned photojournalist.

The orphans had made it impossible for her to de-emphasize the role Linc had played during their ordeal. Because, when in doubt about what to do, they all turned to him for guidance. Even though he didn't speak Spanish, he conveyed messages to them with facial expressions, gestures, and a pidgin Spanish-English that they understood and heeded.

He acted as a surrogate father to all of them, particularly to the younger ones. He might not have wanted the role, but it had been foisted upon him, and he had grudgingly accepted it. In fact, he seemed to enjoy toting Lisa in his arms and entering mock wrestling matches with the boys.

Kerry knew that Cage and Jenny had probably been burning with curiosity. Only politeness had prevented them from coming right out and asking. Linc suffered under no such restriction. Out of pure meanness, he had provided them with all the lurid details of how he had met Kerry while she stood there in mortification.

Throughout the day, she had held her breath, afraid of being exposed as a fraud. She was afraid that someone would mention a name, a name that would undoubtedly trigger a volatile response from Linc. The subject had been stamped around so many times that Kerry had become as nervous as a cat with a long tail.

By one means or another, the truth would come out. He would discover that she wasn't what she had led him to believe she was. When he did, she wanted to be as far away from him as possible. She didn't have to guess what his reaction would be. He would be livid.

That morning, after he had kissed her, she had started to tell him. Fearing that one or both of them might die, she had wanted to confess her lie. But she had been robbed of the opportunity by the arrival of the rescue plane. Then, after they had argued over the blasted money, she didn't want to tell him. It served his mercenary soul right to live under the misconception.

She had felt both relief and despair when, at dinner, he had announced that he was leaving. She wanted him to leave before he found out that she wasn't a nun. On the other hand, the thought of his leaving had crushed her. She would probably never see him again. Such a possibility was devastating. She would always be grateful to Jenny's baby for providing an adequate, but not catastrophic, diversion.

Now, Kerry watched him, unseen, from her darkened second story window as he paced the terrace, smoking. It was consoling to know that he wasn't able to sleep either. She wasn't the only one in an emotional quandary tonight.

Of course what he was feeling wasn't deep emotion. It was lust. She had seen it, blazing in his golden brown eyes, before he carefully screened them. He might be antagonistic toward her, but he wasn't indifferent. Small comfort, that. They were still irreconcilable. He was fighting a contest of wills. She loved him.

She saw him grind out his cigarette in a planter. He looked like a man bedeviled as he raised his hands to his face and rubbed the heels of them against his eyes. She thought she heard a muttered curse, but, because it was so obscene, hoped that she had imagined that.

As she watched, he leaned down and pulled off the boots Cage had loaned him. The boots he had worn out of Montenegro had been so caked with mud that the Hendrens had insisted on throwing them away with the rest of their clothes.

Linc then began pulling at the buttons of his shirt until they were undone. He peeled it off quickly and tossed it onto a patio chaise. A white gauze bandage was taped to his shoulder.

He worked free the buckle of his belt but left the belt in the loops of his jeans. The metal buckle clinked softly as he unbuttoned the top button of his fly.

Kerry covered her mouth to stifle a small, yearning sound when she realized what he was going to do. It was a dark night. The moon was a slender crescent positioned low in the sky and shedding very little light. The evening was warm. The faint wind was as hot and dry as the arid ground it swept over.

It was the perfect night for a nude swim.

Especially if one's body was hot and restless.

Kerry ceased to breathe. In fact, she lifted a hand to the base of her throat as though to verify that she had a pulse, because everything inside her went perfectly still. She was mesmerized by the motions of his fingers as he worked the metal buttons from their stubborn holes. She couldn't actually see his fingers moving, but she could see the movement of his arms and elbows as he struggled with the button fly of the Western jeans.

And then he was hooking his thumbs into the waistband and pushing them down. At about his knees, he let them go. The soft, well-laundered denim pooled around his ankles. He stepped out of the jeans.

And Kerry knew one thing for certain: Jenny bought Cage's underwear. The low-slung, hip-riding briefs were the kind of undergarment a woman liked to see on a man. They were light in color and showed up in stark contrast to Linc's dark, lean body and the surrounding night.

Blood was pumping thickly through her veins.

She saw Linc raise his hands to his waist. His thumbs slid beneath the elastic band. Then . . .

He was splendidly, primally, majestically naked. Rawly, proudly male. And beautiful. So beautiful it hurt to look at him. The sight of his nakedness affected her like a piercing spear through her chest.

She slumped to her knees and rested her chin on the window sill. She exercised no maidenly shyness. Her eyes boldly moved over him. His body hair grew in intriguing patterns and showed up as fuzzy shadows on his tanned flesh. It clustered darkly and thickly around his sex.

He turned. Kerry got a glimpse of a marvelously symmetrical back. Muscled shoulders tapered to a narrow waist, and the sides sloped into a straight, shallow spine. His buttocks were taut. He walked with a swagger that excited and aroused her. His thighs were lean. His calves looked as hard as apples.

Long before she had seen her fill, he dove cleanly into the water. He hardly made a splash. He swam the length of the pool underwater before he surfaced, and then remained in the shadows beneath the diving board for a long while before he began swimming laps. He cut through the water as sleekly as an eel, his arms arcing out of the water and catching the meager moonlight.

Kerry's body ached. Her skin seemed on fire. Her breasts tingled. She covered them with her hands in an attempt to contain that delicious, blooming sensation, but found that touching them brought no relief. It only made them more agitated. The merest movement of Jenny's sheer batiste nightgown against her nipples provoked shameful stirrings deep inside her.

Finally Linc swam to the edge of the pool. He opened his hands flat on the tiles and stiffened his arms, levering himself out of the water until he could get one foot up on the side. He shook the water from his head and peeled his hair back, holding it off his face with both hands behind his head for several seconds before dropping his arms. He ran his hands over his arms and legs, skimming off the water.

Kerry moaned and her body flushed hotly when he ran one hand down his chest and stomach. Before it reached that thatch of dark hair, she squeezed her eyes shut.

When she opened them again, he was stepping into the discarded briefs. He tucked everything comfortably inside before letting the elastic band snap against his waist. Kerry's mouth was dry, but she swallowed hard.

Linc bent at the waist and scooped up the rest of his clothes, then walked toward the back door of the house until he disappeared from Kerry's sight. She didn't move, but maintained her place on the floor beside the window until she heard him come upstairs and go into Trent's bedroom and gently close the door behind him.

Because her thighs had gone the consistency of warm butter, and she felt weak and feverish all over, she virtually crawled to the bed. She kicked off all the covers. She couldn't stand anything abrading her skin. Or rather, being touched anywhere, everywhere, was such a delicious sensation that she thought it best to deny it to herself.

What was this malady? A tropical fever just now manifesting itself? Or was it simply desire for the man she loved?

Linc accidently stumbled onto the intimate scene. He muttered his sincere apologies and immediately withdrew, but Cage and Jenny called him back.

They were sitting at the kitchen table. Cage's hand was splayed wide over his wife's abdomen. Both wore radiant smiles. "Come in, it's okay."

"I didn't mean to interrupt." He felt uncharacteristically gauche and callow.

"You're not interrupting," Cage said.

"Cage loves to feel the baby move."

"What would you say this is, a ballerina or a place kicker?"

Linc grinned self-consciously. "You could stuff what I know about babies into a thimble and there'd still be room."

Cage removed his hand from Jenny's tummy and poured their guest a cup of coffee. "I'm the breakfast chef. What'll you have?"

"Whatever."

"Ham and eggs?"

"Sounds great."

"Orange or grapefruit juice, Linc?" Jenny asked him.

"Orange, please."

She picked the appropriate pitcher off the table and poured him a glass. "You've never been around children?" she asked him nonchalantly.

"Not until this week."

"None of your own?"

Cage cleared his throat loudly, but Jenny didn't acknowledge the subtle reprimand. Linc appeared to be unaware of it. In fact, he was acting rather distracted, as though he were listening for something. "Uh, no, I've never been married."

"Hmm." Wearing a complacent smile that had nothing to do with the innate serenity of pregnancy, Jenny sat back in her chair and sipped her tea.

She ignored Cage's reproachful glance when he returned to the table and slid a plate of food in front of Linc. "Dig in."

"This is great. Where's yours?"

"We ate earlier," Jenny told him.

"I'm sorry I slept so late. Is everyone else already up?"

"I sneaked in early and got Trent out of bed. I didn't want him to wake you," Cage said. "The Flemings and my folks have taken all the kids to the hospital to see Joe."

"Including Trent?"

"He pulled a temper tantrum. Roxie, as usual, gave in. Sarah wouldn't hear of him being left behind either," Jenny told Linc. "Between his grandmother and my best friend, I'm afraid Trent is being spoiled rotten."

Kerry hadn't been mentioned. Linc hesitated to bring up her name, but now, while she wasn't around, was a good time to ask the questions that had been eating at him.

"How did Kerry get involved with your relief organization?"

Both Jenny and Cage tried to mask their surprise. "She never told you?" Cage asked. Linc shook his head and shoveled in another bite of eggs.

"She came to us," Jenny said. "After going through the ordeal of her father's trial, she—"

Linc's fork clattered to his plate. "Whoa, whoa, what trial? What father?"

Cage and Jenny exchanged a glance. "Wooten Bishop," Cage said, as though that explained everything. And it very nearly did.

Slowly Linc pushed his plate aside and folded his arms on the table in front of him. "Wooten Bishop? *The* Wooten Bishop is Kerry's father?"

His hosts nodded simultaneously. Linc expelled his breath on a long gust. "Sonofagun." He shook his head in disbelief. "I never would have put their names together. I remember now that he had a daughter. I guess I never paid much attention to how old she was or what she looked like. I was in Africa when that story broke."

"He tried to shield her from the scandal as much as possible. Of course she was greatly affected by it anyway."

"Obviously," Linc muttered, staring into his coffee cup.

The Wooten Bishop family had been subjected to public scrutiny and ridicule only a couple of years earlier. After a long and illustrious career in the diplomatic corp, Bishop had been called home from Montenegro when it was alleged that he had personally profited from that country's political strife. He had used information made available to him as a diplomat in money-making scams.

When he was found out, all his shady dealings were aired over network television. There had followed a nasty, albeit enlightening, Senate hearing and a subsequent criminal trial. Only one month after his sentencing, he had died of heart failure in a federal prison.

"I asked Kerry about her childhood," Linc said hoarsely. "She said that it had been charmed."

"It was," Jenny said sadly, "before the tragedy. Kerry once told me that something inside Ambassador Bishop snapped after the death of her mother. He was never quite the same."

"Did she know about his corruption?"

Cage shook his head. "No. She suspected, but couldn't believe it. She was shattered to learn that her father had ruthlessly exploited a people who had had so little to begin with. She told Jenny and me that she went through a period of hating him. Then all she could feel for him was pity. It's little wonder that she made such a personal sacrifice to go to Montenegro and try to make up for her father's wrongdoings."

"She had no business going there. She could have gotten herself killed!" Linc exclaimed, banging the table with his fist.

"You've right, Linc." Jenny laid a gentle hand over his. "She came to us, volunteering to go there and teach. We told her that there was plenty she could do here to support the cause without putting herself in danger. But she wouldn't have it any other way.

"I don't think any of us can really appreciate the sacrifices she made," Jenny went on. "Until the scandal broke, she and her family had traveled all over the world. They were highly respected, often guests of royalty and heads of state."

"She's well educated I guess," Linc remarked glumly.

"The Sorbonne."

A muscle in his cheek twitched.

Cage swirled coffee around in his cup. "It was rumored several years ago that there was a romance budding between her and a young man in Britain's royal family. But when I teased her about it, she said that's all it was. A frivolous rumor."

Jenny was reflective. "She hardly looked frivolous yesterday when she got off that airplane. I don't think she's ever been taken seriously. Maybe that's what she had to prove. She went to Montenegro to announce to the world that there was more to her than what was evident on the surface."

"I still don't get it," Linc said, frowning. "It doesn't make any sense."

"What, Linc?"

"Why would a beautiful, charming, intelligent young woman like Kerry, who has everything going for her, give it all up to become a nun? I mean, isn't that going a bit overboard just to make a point? Sure her ol' man got caught with his hand in the till. There was a big scandal. But no... What's the matter?"

"A *nun*?"

# *Chapter 10*

They chorused their incredulity.

Of the three of them, Cage was the first to overcome his astonishment. "Where did you get that idea?"

"She isn't a nun?" Linc croaked.

Baffled, Jenny shook her head. "No."

"Has she ever thought about becoming a nun?" Linc asked. "Taken the first steps?"

"Not to my knowledge."

Linc lunged from his chair with such force that he knocked it over backward. Still shell-shocked by his outlandish presumption, the Hendrens sat mutely and watched him storm from the kitchen and race for the stairs. He took them two at a time. If the door of the guest bedroom hadn't been made of top grade lumber, it would have shattered beneath his hand as he shoved it open. It crashed against the inside wall. He marched in.

The bed was neatly made. The room was empty. The only movement came from the open window overlooking the patio and pool below. Airy curtains fluttered there in the soft, Southern, morning breeze.

Linc spun around and hastily retraced his footsteps to the kitchen. Civilities were the furthest thing from his mind. "You didn't tell me she was already up," he accused his hosts.

Jenny was staring at him apprehensively and fiddling with a button on her maternity blouse. Cage was nonchalantly sipping coffee. It was he who looked up and said innocently, "You didn't ask."

"Where is she?"

"She went horseback riding," Cage told him evenly. "Got up early, even before Jenny."

Linc was holding back his explosive Irish temper with remarkable self-control. The only dead giveaways were the muscles flexing his jaw and his hands, which were held rigidly at his sides while his fingers alternately opened and closed into fists.

"We drank a cup of coffee together, then she asked if she could borrow one of the horses for a while. I helped her saddle it, and she rode off in that direction." Cage hitched his chin toward the endless horizon.

Linc looked in the direction Cage had indicated and studied the prairie through the kitchen window. "How long ago?"

Cage, secretly enjoying Linc's stewing, contemplated his answer to the simple question for an inordinate length of time. "Oh, about an hour and a half, I'd say."

"Can I borrow your pickup?" Linc had noticed a pickup in the garage the evening before. Unlike Cage's other cars, which were polished to a high sheen, the pickup had been scarred by every single mile recorded on its odometer.

"Sure," Cage replied congenially and stood up to fish the keys out his tight jeans pocket. He tossed them to Linc.

"Thanks." He turned abruptly and left through the back door, covering the distance between the house and the garage with the long, angry stride of a man bent on getting swift and savage revenge.

Jenny got up and moved to the window. She watched Linc slam shut the door of the pickup and grind the reluctant motor to a start. He cranked the steering wheel around and drove off in a cloud of dust.

"Cage, I don't think you should have given him the keys. He looks positively furious."

"If Kerry led him to believe that she's a nun, I'm sure he is. And I can't say that I blame him."

"But—"

"Jenny," he said soothingly, moving behind her and encircling her with his arms. He linked his hands together beneath her heavy breasts. "Remember the night I chased down that Greyhound bus you were on?"

"How could I forget that? I've never been so embarrassed in my life."

Smiling at the memory, he placed his mouth close to her ear. "Well I was just as upset then as Linc is now. Hell or high water couldn't have kept me from coming after you. We couldn't have stopped Linc either. If I hadn't lent him my truck, I think he would have struck out on foot to get to Kerry." He kissed her neck. "I just hope that his wild goose chase meets with as much success as mine did."

Linc, pushing the old truck to perform in excess of its capabilities, had murder on his mind, not romance. He scorched the roof of the pickup with curses and disparagements aimed at Kerry's character. When he had exhausted those, he started verbally lambasting his own culpability.

What a damn fool he'd been! She must have been laughing up her sleeve at him all this time. She had duped him not once, but twice. First impersonating a whore, then a nun. Two such diverse personifications, and he'd been gullible enough to believe both of them.

What the hell was wrong with him? Had he been plagued with a jungle disease that ate at his brain? Had Kerry Bishop been slipping a mind-altering drug into his water canteen? How could he, Linc O'Neal, have been so goddamn naive?

He'd been around. He wasn't a lust-blind kid, unacquainted with the wiles of females. Why hadn't he seen past Kerry Bishop's beautiful face and into her devious mind? She wasn't a self-sacrificing churchwoman, but a cunning tease, who evidently had no scruples against manipulating a man to get what she wanted out of him.

Even when she had succeeded in achieving her goal, she had kept up the pretense. "For her own protection," he said through gritted teeth. "To save her sweet neck," he told the dashboard of the truck.

A luscious figure and a gorgeous face had cost him his common sense and quick-wittedness. He hadn't been his cold, calculating, cautious self since he'd left that damn *cantina* with Wooten Bishop's deceitful daughter.

The pickup truck bounced over the uneven road, which was actually no more than a pasture trail. Linc had no idea where he was going, but he was in a hurry to get there. He reasoned that Kerry wasn't well acquainted with Cage's spread either. She probably would have stayed close to the road so she'd be certain to find her way back to the house.

His instincts paid off. After twenty minutes of hard driving over rugged terrain, he spotted a stock tank as large as a small lake. Its steep banks were shaded by the feathery branches of mesquite trees. The spring grass, not yet burned brown by the summer sun, was lush and green. One of Cage's well-groomed quarter horses was tied to the lower branches of a mesquite on the rim of the bank overlooking the placid tank.

At the sound of the approaching pickup, Kerry, who was lying beneath the tree on a blanket she had taken from the tack room and tied behind her saddle, propped herself up on one elbow. She lifted the other hand to shade her eyes. She thought at first that it was Cage driving the truck, but sprang upright when she recognized the long-legged silhouette approaching her as belonging to Linc.

The incline didn't slow him down at all. Within seconds he was looming over her, his booted feet planted firmly on the ground at the edge of her blanket. Her eyes moved up his legs, up his torso, and straight into a disconcerting golden glower. She didn't have to guess at his mood. He was enraged. On the inside, she quailed, though she kept her chin up and met that intimidating stare without flinching.

"You lying bitch."

Kerry didn't even pretend to misunderstand. With a sinking heart and rapidly diminishing courage, she knew that she'd been found out. The only recourse she had was to brazen it out.

"Now, Linc," she said, quickly wetting her lips and holding her hands out in front of her as though to stave him off, "before you jump to any conclusions—"

He effectively cut her off by dropping to his knees and roughly grabbing her by the shoulders. "Before I jump on your bones, you mean."

Her face drained of color. He hadn't made her a seductive promise but a menacing threat. "You wouldn't."

"The hell I wouldn't. But before I do, I want to know why you told me that ridiculous lie."

"I didn't!" She tried to work herself free, but to no avail. The more she struggled, the more inescapable his hold became. "I *never* told you that I was a nun."

"I didn't dream it up, baby."

"You heard the children call me sister and drew your own conclusions. You—"

Her teeth clicked together when he hauled her up closer to his face, which was taut with fury. "But you sure as hell let me believe it, didn't you? *Why?*" he roared.

"To protect myself from you."

"Don't flatter yourself."

She went hot all over at his sneering insult. "I knew what you had in mind. Don't deny it. You were thinking that our escape through the jungle was going to be a lark, during which you planned to use me for a bedmate."

"Me Tarzan, you Jane."

"It was no joking matter. You forced me to kiss you, to change clothes in front of you!"

"I didn't see anything that you hadn't advertised by wearing that cheap dress!" he shouted back. "And whether you admit it or not, lady, you loved those kisses."

"I did not!"

"Like hell."

She had to take deep, restorative breaths before she could continue. "I was trying to think of a way to avoid your unwelcome sexual advances when the children inadvertently provided me with a way."

"Why did they call you Sister Kerry?"

"Because when I first got there, they started calling me Mother. I didn't want them to think of me that way. I was already planning to bring them to the United States for adoption. I thought that being like an older sister would be a healthier relationship. Don't blame me for your own gross mistake."

"What I blame you for is making a fool of me."

"I didn't do it maliciously," she cried.

"Didn't you?"

"No."

"Come now, Miss Kerry Bishop, daughter to one of the chief swindlers of our times, didn't you take delight in playing me like a puppet? Don't you come by those manipulative skills naturally?"

Kerry shuddered at the reference to her father and his corruption. Apparently Linc knew all about her background now. His scorn was well-founded, but it still hurt her to the core that he thought she was capable of such machinations.

"I let you think that I was a nun so that we would be concentrating only on the safety of the orphans."

"My ass. You lied to keep yourself safe from my pawing hands."

"All right, yes!"

"And my leering glances."

"Yes!"

"Not to mention all those kisses you *claim* to have hated."

"Yes!"

"See? By your own admission, you just went on lying."

"I tried to tell you," she cried in self-defense.

"Funny, I don't remember that occasion."

"When you kissed me that last day. Just before we heard the airplane. I wanted to . . .*tried* to tell you then."

"Not very hard you didn't."

"I didn't have a chance. Everything started happening so fast."

"It was a long airplane trip from there to here."

"We argued over the money and I was too angry to tell you."

"What about since we got back? Cage and Jenny would protect you from me, wild animal that I am. Why haven't you told me? You've had dozens of opportunities."

"Because I knew you'd react just as you are. That you'd be angry and abusive."

He lowered his voice to a sinister whisper. "Baby, anger doesn't even come close to describing the way I feel. And you don't know me very well if you think I'd be abusive."

To her humiliation, her lower lip began to quiver. "I never intended for it to go so far. Honestly. I'm sorry, Linc, truly I am."

"It's too late for apologies, Kerry."

"I know I misrepresented myself, but I had no choice. I was desperate. I needed you, but I couldn't cater to your desire. My first obligation was to the orphans."

"Do you think I'd fall for your claims to noble sentiments now?" he asked with a humorless laugh. "No way, sweetheart. I want you humbled. I want you to sink as low on the ego scale as I've been lately. Only that will satisfy me."

"What... what are you going to do?"

"What I told you that first morning I was going to do," he said silkily. "I'm gonna make you beg me for it."

"No!"

The husky exclamation died on Kerry's lips when he pushed her back onto the blanket and followed her down, covering her with his body. He trapped her hands between them. They were useless to her when he secured her jaw with one hand and lowered his mouth to hers.

She struggled, but only succeeded in exhausting her supply of strength sooner. Even her best efforts didn't budge him. Kicking didn't help because he sandwiched her thighs between his. His knees kept hers pinned together. She couldn't turn her head in any direction.

She tried to keep her lips pressed firmly together, but failed. He used his tongue like an instrument of tantalizing torture. It flicked softly over her lips, delved into the corners of them, outlined their shape until her unsteady, frightened breaths became gasps of pleasure. Finally, her lips relaxed and parted, without any force from him.

"That's it, baby. Enjoy."

His kiss was long, sensual, seeking. He firmly slanted his lips over hers, first at one angle, then another, while his tongue moved inside her mouth with sinful skill. She wanted to hate this blatant violation, but she loved it. The texture of his tongue intrigued her. She wanted to feel it not only against hers, but everywhere. She wondered if the myriad textures of his body were this fascinating and thrilling, and yearned to have her curiosity appeased.

But she steeled herself against feeling anything but contempt for him and his hateful kiss. She tried to ignore the heat spilling down her chest and into the lower part of her body, tried to disregard the desire that ribboned through her like a river of wine as golden as his eyes, tried to dismiss the swirls of sensation that licked at her thighs, her middle, her breasts. She wasn't entirely successful, but she forced herself to lie still when she wanted to writhe against him like a cat being petted.

"You might just as well participate," he rasped when he felt her body tense. His lips coasted over her cheek, pecking light kisses on her creamy complexion, now tinted pink by exposure to sun and wind during her morning horseback ride. Linc didn't allow himself to admire it too long. Feeling any tenderness for her was to be avoided at all costs if he were to regain his pride. "Because I'm not letting up until you're crazy with lust. The longer you resist, Kerry, the longer it will take."

"Go to hell."

He made a *tsk*ing sound. "Is that any way for a nun to talk?"

"Don't." When his tongue playfully batted against the lobe of her ear, she tried to sound irritable, but the protest came out as a low groan of arousal.

Linc recognized the sound for what it was. He'd never had difficulty sexually communicating with women, whether they spoke his language or not. It wasn't so much what they said as how they said it. And clearer than the single word of denial, was Kerry's breathless way of saying it.

"You like that?" he murmured, catching her ear lightly between his teeth.

"No."

He chuckled. "We both know you're a liar. I think you like it a lot."

He kissed the soft skin beneath her ear, nuzzled behind it with his nose, flirted with the rim of it with his tongue. It was hard to tell now whether her fitful movements beneath him were meant to put more space between them or to get closer.

His breath was warm as it drifted over her face. It smelled appetizingly of coffee. And that was just one of the reasons why her lips were far more obliging this time when his, with very little pressure applied, settled over hers. His open mouth moved upon hers, separating her lips for his thrusting tongue. As it speared into her mouth, she felt a correlating stab of desire in the depths of her body.

When he raised his head and peered deeply into her eyes, she thought that she might have made an involuntary sound. He asked, "Feel that?"

At first she thought that he was referring to that sweet ache deep inside herself. Then her eyes went wide with alarm when she realized that he was talking about the rigid flesh between his own thighs. She clamped her upper teeth over her lower lip and squeezed her eyes shut. His low laugh was nasty.

"I see that you do. Well, that's how it's been, baby. While you've been playing your devious little games with me, I've been hard with wanting you. All that time we were stalking through the jungle together, I was miserable not only with heat and fatigue and hunger, but with a desire that I couldn't quench. I was ashamed of it because I thought it was a violation of your holiness." He kept his voice as smooth as expensive brandy, but it had a bite as strong as cheap whiskey. "There's nothing holy about you, is there?"

He worked his hand between their bodies. When Kerry realized what he was going to do, she went rigid. "No!" It was a soundless cry.

"Why, Kerry, you surprise me. Don't you want to know the full extent of your powers?"

When he had unbuttoned his jeans, he reached for one of her hands and dragged it down. "No!" This time her protest was stifled by his kiss, a hard, possessive kiss that glued his lips to hers and sent his tongue deep into her mouth.

As he opened her hand over himself, Kerry's brain recorded a thousand fleeting impressions. One prevailed. She wanted to touch him. She wanted to discover. She wanted to catalogue the smoothness, the hardness, the warmth. She wanted to sink her fingers into the hair that was coarse and springy, but soft.

She fought the temptation as long as she could, but self-discipline didn't serve her long enough. Her hand stopped resisting the relentless pressure of his. Of its own free will it molded to his shape and became inquisitive.

Making an animal sound, Linc tore his mouth from hers and roughly shoved her hand away. His breathing was unsteady and rapid. "Not that way, Kerry," he said in a voice hardly above a growl. "You won't get by with that. You never quit playing dirty, do you? I guess it runs in the family. You've always got one more trick up your sleeve. Well, your tricks won't work this time."

Perplexity filled her dark blue eyes, but he didn't seem to notice. He was studying the buttons on her casual shirt. He negligently opened the first one. "I vaguely remember how it feels to touch you. You're small, but nice." The sexist comment brought a wave of resentment rushing through her. He saw the mutiny in her eyes and smiled arrogantly. "And as I recall, your nipples respond nicely."

Her cheeks flared with color, especially when he succeeded in opening all the buttons on her blouse and spreading it open. She and Jenny were of comparable size when Jenny wasn't pregnant. Kerry's breasts filled the cups of the lacy brassiere she had borrowed. With the sunlight pouring over them, there was little left to Linc's imagination.

His eyes turned dark and Kerry thought she saw a muscle in his cheek twitch with something akin to remorse, before his lips formed that hard, unyielding line again. "Open it."

"I won't."

"Then you can explain to Jenny how the fastener got broken," he said, reaching for the clasp.

"You're vile."

"Open it."

Setting her jaw stubbornly, she opened the clasp, but left the cups alone. After muttering a snide thank you, he moved them aside and left her bare to his gaze. It was as scorching as the sun overhead.

Kerry's bravado deserted her. Her eyes closed in shame, so she missed seeing him swallow convulsively. She also missed the spasm of regret that twisted his stern lips as he ran his hands over her. The words he spoke fell like harmful blows on her ears.

"That's what I thought. Not much there, but what there is, is nice."

She slapped at his hands, but he secured her wrists in one manacling hold. She shrank away from his touch when he cupped the underside of her breast and pushed it up. His thumb whisked across the sensitive tip. When it responded, he laughed gloatingly. Again and again he dragged his thumb across the beaded crest, sometimes with agonizing leisure, sometimes with a quick fanning motion, sometimes raking it gently with his thumbnail, until it was quite stiff.

"Very nice," he said hoarsely. "At least to look at, play with. How do you taste?"

Her back arched off the blanket at the first deft brush of his tongue. "No, no," she groaned, rolling her head from side to side.

"I'm not convinced you mean that, Kerry." He spoke directly above her, so that even as he formed the words with his lips, they moved against the aching, throbbing flesh of her nipple.

She made a murmur of protest and had to bite her lower lip to keep from crying out, not in outrage or fear or disgust, but from pleasure. It was exquisite, the touch of his warm, wet tongue against her breast. He licked her until she was wet and glistening, then let the wind dry her while he treated the other breast to the same torturous pleasure.

"Please, no more," she begged.

"A lot more."

She gave an agonized cry when he took her nipple between his lips and held it within the satin heat of his mouth. He tugged on her gently; she made soft moaning sounds with each squeezing, milking motion of his mouth.

"Please, stop," she gasped.

He raised his head. "What do you want?" His tongue moved capriciously over the raised center of her breast.

"For you to stop."

"Why?"

"Because I hate it. Hate you."

"You might hate me. In fact, I'm sure you do. But you don't hate this." Again he touched her with the tip of his tongue. "Do you?" He repeated the question, each time nudging her with his tongue or sipping at her with his lips.

"Yes," she said, shivering with need.

"Do you?"

"Yes."

"Do you?"

"Ye...no, no, no." A sobbing sound tore through her throat.

"I didn't think so."

He lowered his head and kissed her stomach, while he struggled to open the fly of her slacks. Breathlessly, Kerry gasped for air. She was barely conscious of what his hands were doing. All her concentration was centered on his lips as they moved over her flesh, seeming to touch everywhere at once.

She actually raised her hips and aided him when he worked her slacks down. He kissed her protrudent hip bone, swung his head around and kissed the other. His lips brushed her navel, his tongue danced around it and probed it provocatively. He kissed her mound through her panties.

Kerry gave a startled cry and struggled to free her hands. When she succeeded, she didn't fight him. Instead she mindlessly entangled her fingers in his hair. He went on kissing her, leaving her flesh fevered and damp where his mouth had been.

"I thought about this that night you slept in my arms." Linc could barely speak, and even then it was a hoarse whisper. "Your breasts beneath my mouth. Your thighs opening to me."

She didn't remember his getting her panties off, but she suddenly realized that his eyes were hungrily moving over her nakedness. She should have been terrified of his ravenous gaze, but, oddly, she wasn't. Her single thought was that she hoped he was pleased with her.

His fingers sifted through the dark cloud of hair between her thighs. Reflexively her knees came up. He parted them. Then he lowered his head and placed his mouth where she most wanted to feel him.

When his lips touched her, she cried his name. When his tongue touched her, she died a little. Holding her hips between his strong hands, Linc gave her pleasure with the same dedication with which he did everything else.

He stopped short of bringing her to climax, though he brought her to the threshold time and again. Her face was dewy with perspiration when he bent over it. "Tell me you want me."

It was a miracle that he could even form the words in his mind, much less speak them aloud. His body was pulsing with a need so great it surpassed mere desire. God, he needed to be sheathed inside her body, giving her the passion that threatened to kill him if it wasn't shared. He was filled to bursting with his need for her.

And suddenly this revenge seemed a thankless, empty victory. He didn't want to triumph over her. He didn't want to see her cowed in defeat, but glowing with a desire to match his own. He wanted to see joy in her face, not subjugation.

But habits formed in childhood were hard to break. Nobody got the best of Lincoln O'Neal without knowing his vengeance. He'd had to scrap for every ounce of affection and respect he had ever received. He knew no other way to ask than to make it a demand.

"Tell me you want me," he ground out again, clenching his teeth in an effort to keep his body from doing what it was primed to do without playing out this senseless game. He slipped the tip of his organ between the moist petals of her sex.

"I want you," Kerry gasped.

"Inside you," he panted.

"Inside me."

Those two words snapped his control. He slipped into her body and gave a mighty push that sent him straight to her womb. He gave a cry of such anguish and regret that it seemed to echo off the endless sky. He wanted to withdraw, but his control was gone.

Knowing that he would be damned a sinner anyway, and powerless over the demands of his body, he made but three shallow thrusts before his climax claimed him. In sublime surrender, he buried his face in her neck and let the exquisite seizures wash over him. He abdicated control to the natural forces of his own body and filled the woman he had wanted for what seemed like a lifetime with the hot, potent issue of his loins.

For long moments afterward, he lay atop her, exhausted, spent, in blissful devastation. When he finally found the strength to pull himself away, he avoided looking at her. With endearing awkwardness, he draped a corner of the blanket over the lower part of her body. Lying there beside her on his back, he gazed up through the sparse branches of the mesquite tree and tried to think of a name despicable enough to call himself.

Because up until a few seconds ago, Kerry Bishop had been as chaste as the nun she had pretended to be. She had been a virgin.

"Why didn't you tell me?"

"Would you have believed me?"

"No," he sighed, knowing that that was true. He wouldn't have believed anything she had said.

He rolled to a sitting position and hung his head between his wide-spread knees. For several minutes, he mumbled curses and epithets aimed at himself. Then he lapsed into silence. Finally he risked looking down at Kerry. Tears had left salty tracks on her cheeks, but her eyes were clear and staring straight at him.

"Do you, uh, hurt?" She shook her head. He didn't believe her. "Do you have any water?"

"The canteen on the saddle."

He stood and hiked his jeans up his hips until he could rebutton them. He went to the saddled horse, which had been docilely grazing through it all. The canteen was hanging from the pommel by a leather strap. He uncapped it, wet the handkerchief he'd put in his pocket that morning, and carried both the canteen and the soaked handkerchief back to Kerry. He extended it down to her and tactfully turned his back while she used it.

"Thank you."

He turned back around to find her dressed and standing quietly, as though awaiting instructions. He'd not only crushed her physically...God, when he remembered how hard he'd been when he sank into her...but he had wounded her spirit as well. Her eyes were no longer sparkling with lights as pure and fine as costly sapphires. They stared at him dully.

"You'll ride back with me," he said. "I'll tie the horse to the back of the truck."

When that was done, he came to her, took her elbow, and led her over the rough ground with a solicitousness that would have been comical under different circumstances. It was he who winced when she stepped up into the truck.

It took considerably longer to cover the distance back to the house than it had taken Linc to get to the tank. He drove much slower, in deference to the horse that trotted along behind them and out of regard for the discomfort Kerry must be suffering. He knew the rough ride couldn't be comfortable for her and cursed himself as a brute with each bumpy, bone-jarring, teeth-rattling turn of the wheels.

When they reached the house, he pulled the pickup into the garage and cut the engine. They sat in the deep shadows for a moment of ponderous silence, then he turned his head and asked, "Are you all right?"

"Yes."

"Is there anything I can do?"

Kerry glanced down at her hands, which were knotted together in her lap. *You could say that you love me.* "No," she said, choking back tears.

Linc got out. Before he could come around and assist her, she climbed out of the cab and untied the horse. Wordlessly they led him into the stable and turned him over to one of the hands. Still maintaining that strained silence, they headed toward the house.

Everyone was congregated on the terrace. Jenny was bouncing a truculent Trent on her thighs. Cage was sitting in a lawn chair, staring broodily over the waters of the swimming pool, where all the children were splashing in the shallows. Roxie and Gary Fleming were sitting at one of the patio tables moodily sipping cold drinks. Sarah Hendren was clipping roses from an overloaded bush and laying them in the basket that her husband held for her.

The mood, except for that of the gleeful children, was glum.

Cage looked up and spotted Linc and Kerry coming through the gate. It was to her that he addressed his comment. "We've got troubles."

# *Chapter 11*

Kerry struggled up from the swamp of despair into which she had sunk and asked, "What kind of troubles?" She lowered herself into the chair Linc pulled out for her. "Not Joe?"

"No, not Joe," Roxie Fleming reassured her. "Physically he's doing all right, but the doctor told us that he's awfully depressed. Doc suggested that he be moved here this afternoon. He'll recover faster if he's not alienated from the other children."

"Here? Jenny, won't that inconvenience you?"

"Not at all," Jenny told Kerry. "We'll just move an extra bed into Trent's room."

"I'll leave," Linc said bluntly. "Then you'll have plenty of room."

Jenny glanced at him with asperity. "I thought we settled that last night. We're not going to let you leave, Linc. Besides, Joe will feel more at ease with you around."

That argument made sense, so neither he nor Kerry countered it. "Well, if you're sure," Kerry said uncertainly. "It'll only be for another day or so. Just until his adoptive family arrives to take him home."

Gary cleared his throat too loudly. Roxie shifted in her chair. Cage and Jenny glanced uncomfortably at each other.

"Did I hit a nerve?" Kerry asked intuitively. "I must have accidently stumbled onto the trouble spot you mentioned. What gives? Have Joe's adoptive parents had second thoughts since he was wounded in the escape? The doctor assured me that his leg suffered no permanent damage, if that's what's bothering them."

"Actually, Kerry," Cage said with noticeable reluctance, "Joe never was spoken for."

Stunned, Kerry could only stare at him for a moment before crying, "*What?* That was a condition of my bringing the orphans out, that they would have a home ready and waiting for them."

"We know." Jenny's normally serene face was filled with anxiety. "That's why we didn't tell you. Cage and I discussed it and decided that no matter what, we couldn't let you leave any of the children behind."

"Most prospective parents feel that Joe is too old for adoption," Cage said gently.

"I see."

Kerry's shoulders slumped with dejection. According to the clock, it was still well before noon. But it seemed that she had lived a thousand years since she had gotten up that morning. Her heart had already been heavy, knowing that she had fallen in love with the wrong man. That's why she had sought the solitary peacefulness of a horseback ride. Then, what should have been an exultant experience had been a nightmare.

And now this. Just when she was about to accomplish the only worthwhile endeavor in her life, she was met with failure. Poor Joe. He, more than the other children, realized what coming to the United States meant to his future.

"He can't be sent back," she said fiercely.

"You can count on that," Cage said.

Jenny laid a hand on her husband's shoulder as though to hold him back. "You didn't know Cage before he settled down, Kerry," she said, "but he's a dirty fighter. He would take on the Supreme Court before he would let the boy be sent back."

Kerry smiled at Cage. "Thank you. I'll appreciate anything you can do."

"I volunteer my services," Linc said. "And I'd be willing to bet that I fight a helluva lot dirtier than Cage."

"Oh yeah?" The other man sized him up. Then he smiled broadly. "Thanks. I'm sure I can use your help."

"Let's hope it won't go that far." Kerry stood up. "As soon as I change, we'll get to work on it. I have people in—"

"I'm afraid that's not all," Cage told her, indicating that she should sit back down.

She couldn't imagine what news could possibly be worse than what she'd already heard. She eased herself back into the chair, mentally preparing herself for a blow.

"The couple who had spoken for Lisa called this morning," Cage began.

The floor dropped out from beneath Kerry. "And?"

"And, it seems that the lady is pregnant. It was confirmed only two days ago."

Jenny filled the ensuing silence. "They've wanted a baby for years. That's why they jumped at the chance to adopt one of the Montenegran orphans."

Huge, salty tears formed in Kerry's eyes. Not Lisa. She had tried not to form a special attachment to any of the children, knowing that the final separation from them would be heartbreaking enough. But the youngest of them, Lisa, had touched Kerry's heart in a special way, probably because the child had been more dependent on her than the others had been.

"But surely, if the couple considered adoption at all, they've got enough love to give to two children," she said.

"It's not that," Jenny said. "She's had several miscarriages. They don't want to jeopardize this pregnancy. The doctor recommends that she spend the next several months in bed. It would be impossible for her to care for the child."

Beneath his breath Linc said one of the words Jenny had tried to purge from Cage's vocabulary. "Amen to that," Cage muttered.

"I see the problem," Kerry said despondently. "And I understand."

"It was a difficult decision for them. They had looked so forward to getting Lisa."

"Hell, we'd take her in an instant," Roxie said in her lovable, rough way. "But we've already got Cara and Carmen to think of. It won't be so tough now, but college and all..."

Kerry smiled at her and Gary. "You're generous to a fault. You couldn't possibly assume responsibility for another child. It wouldn't be fair to any of you. But I want you to know how much I appreciate the thought."

Kerry sought out Lisa where the little girl was splashing happily in the shallows of the pool. She squealed in delight each time the sparkling water showered her. "She's so adorable. We shouldn't have any trouble placing her in a loving home."

"That's what we thought," Cage told her.

"But tomorrow is the day they meet their families. It will be psychologically shattering if she's left behind."

"We've already put the word out through the branches of the Hendren Foundation. Of course in the meantime—"

"Cage," Jenny interjected warningly.

"In the meantime, what?" Linc asked.

Cage shrugged at his wife helplessly. "In the meantime, she'll be turned over to the immigration authorities."

"Like hell she will," Linc exclaimed.

Kerry's heart felt as hard and cold as a stone in her chest. Lisa would be frightened. She would think that all Kerry's promises had lead to nothing but fear and isolation from everything familiar. "We can't let that happen."

"I'm sure it won't," Jenny said. "Two very special people will be blessed with her." She set Trent down and stood up. "Kerry, Cage has agreed to watch Trent while we go to town and do some shopping. I don't mind if you wear my clothes, but I'm sure you'd like to pick out some of your own."

"What about the children?"

"We're staying with them," Roxie said. "Gary's taken a week of vacation so we could be at your disposal."

"And we'll be here," Bob Hendren said, speaking for his wife, too.

"What about Joe?" Kerry asked. "I should be here when he arrives."

"We'll be back well before that," Jenny said, laughing.

Roxie gave Kerry an affectionate shove. "Go, enjoy, you've earned it."

However, before they left, Kerry circled around to the terrace again after showering and changing. Cage and Linc had donned swimsuits and joined the children in the water. Cage was tossing Trent high over his head, barely catching him before he landed in the water. Linc was playing with Lisa.

Kerry's eyes smarted with a fresh batch of tears as she watched him with the child. His face was split by a wide grin, and his eyes were crinkled with laughter.

Sensing her stare, he looked up at her where she stood on the deck of the pool. His gaze moved over her searchingly. Going warm with embarrassment, Kerry realized that her body was now familiar territory to him. She had no secrets from him. And she wondered, even as his eyes lowered to the spot that had known the touch of his hands and lips and sex, if he knew that she still ached there deliciously.

Lisa raised her arms toward Kerry in silent appeal. Kerry knelt down, and Linc carried the child against his naked chest to the edge of the pool. Kerry bent down to kiss the child on her slippery, wet cheek. "Goodbye, darling."

"Goodbye."

It was Linc who replied. Both surprised, their eyes clashed and held while time seemed to stand still. Then, hastily, Kerry rose and rushed toward Jenny, who was waiting at the car. But her feet didn't move as fast as her beating heart.

The two women made several stops. Kerry, using a line of credit Cage had arranged for her through his bank, bought several changes of clothes, underwear and shoes.

"I never knew a drugstore could be such a wonderland," she exclaimed. She rummaged through the contents of the sack she held in her lap on their return trip to the ranch. "I feel like I've discovered the mother lode. Skin lotion, hair conditioner, nail polish. I'm not accustomed to such luxuries."

"Maybe you should treat yourself to a week at some posh spa. Let yourself be pampered."

Kerry shook her head. "No. Not yet anyway. I've still got too much to do."

Jenny looked at her in alarm. "You're not thinking of going back to Montenegro?"

"No. It's gotten too dangerous. I don't have a death wish." She carefully replaced her toiletries in the sack. "But there's still plenty to do here. Raise money for food. Medicine." Her voice trailed off and her eyes stared sightlessly at the passing landscape.

When Jenny spoke, her voice was quiet. "You can't go on making amends for your father's corruption, Kerry. Sooner or later you've got to get on with your own life."

She sighed heavily. "I know."

"Cage and I let the cat out of the bag this morning, didn't we?"

Kerry started, but she kept her face perfectly composed. "Don't worry about it. Linc had to find out sooner or later."

"I'm sorry. We assumed that he knew who you were. Then when we realized that he thought you were—"

"Please!" Kerry held up a hand to forestall her friend from saying the word aloud. "I'm ashamed enough as it is. Don't remind me of the dirty trick I played on him."

"I know I'm being rude, but I have to ask. Why did you lead him to believe that you were a nun?"

"Jenny, you couldn't be rude if you tried. Naturally you're curious." She chose her words carefully, wanting her friend to understand her motivation. "You know how I coerced him into leaving the *cantina* with me."

"By pretending to be a prostitute."

"Yes. Well, I did things that I thought were, uh, you know, prostitutelike." She glanced away. "Linc is a virile man and he, uh..."

"I think I get the picture. He wasn't ready to call it quits when you explained your situation."

She nodded. "In my position, what would you have done?"

"Probably nothing so ingenious," Jenny said with a commiserating smile. "He was somewhat...upset...this morning when he found out the truth."

"To put it mildly."

"Had he calmed down by the time he found you?"

"No."

Jenny was too tactful to pursue it further. Whatever had happened out there had had an impact on them both. Linc had looked as bleak as Kerry when they returned. And, as Jenny had noticed before, they avoided touching or looking at each other, carrying the avoidance to ridiculous extremes.

"Linc accused me of being a user, just like my father," Kerry said expressionlessly. "And I suppose he's right. I manipulated him." Tears filled her eyes and slipped from her lower lids. When Jenny saw them, she reached for Kerry's hand. "You and Cage are so lucky to love each other the way you do."

"I know. But what we have didn't come easily, Kerry."

Jenny had never confided to anyone, not even to Roxie, about Cage and her. Now was the time. If her story would help Kerry, it needed to be shared.

"The night Hal left for Montenegro, he came to my room," Jenny began. Kerry turned her head in an attitude of listening. "He made love to me. It was my first time." She drew a shaky little breath. "Only it wasn't Hal. It was Cage." Ignoring Kerry's gasp of surprise, she went on before she lost her nerve. "Then when I discovered I was pregnant—"

"You thought the baby was Hal's."

She nodded. "Everybody did. And only Cage knew differently. Hal had been killed. It took Cage months to find the courage to tell me."

"What happened when he did?"

"I was mortified."

"I can imagine."

"I said terrible things to him." She shuddered now with the memory. "I cruelly rejected him. It took a tragedy to bring us back together."

She squeezed Kerry's hand. "Linc reminds me of Cage. They're both volatile men. Short-tempered. There's an air of violence and danger about them. I used to tremble whenever Cage was in the parsonage. I would get as far away from him as I possibly could. Then one day I realized that the very characteristics that frightened me, also attracted me. I wasn't nearly as afraid of his virility as I was of my response to it."

She glanced at Kerry out the corner of her eye. "Cage made me so jittery that I shied away from him. I couldn't deal with the way he made me feel, like I was stepping outside myself whenever he was around.'' She took her eyes off the road long enough to glance across the seat. ''Are you in love with Linc?''

Kerry lowered her head and eloquent tears rolled down her cheeks. She held back sobs only by clamping her trembling lowerlip between her teeth. ''Yes,'' she said on a low moan. ''Yes. But it's hopeless.''

''I thought so, too, at one time. But I learned that the harder it is to come by, the more valuable the love.''

The Hendrens thought that it was important for the children to be exposed to American customs as soon as possible. Kerry agreed. So that evening they cooked hotdogs on the outdoor grill. Later, Cage set up a television monitor and ran Disney movies through the VCR. It was worth all the hardships Kerry had had to suffer to see their joyous faces.

At intermission, they emptied another three freezers of homemade ice cream. Cage's parents passed out cupcakes. Even though well-meaning folks and media were still banned from the ranch, baked goods, clothing, and toys were smuggled in.

Joe, who had been enthusiastically welcomed back into the fold earlier that afternoon, hobbled over to Kerry on his crutches. ''Sister Kerry, didn't you want any ice cream?''

''I'm waiting for the crowd to thin out.'' The children were thronged around Roxie, who was dispensing the ice cream with a long-handled spoon. ''How does your leg feel?''

''A little ache. Nothing more.''

''I haven't had a chance to tell you how brave you were during the rescue.'' The boy made a self-conscious gesture. ''I was very proud of you. Without you helping him, Linc couldn't have saved us all.''

Joe's soulful eyes were downcast. ''He came back for me.''

Kerry, reminded of the animosity the boy had harbored toward Linc, suggested quietly, "Perhaps you should thank him for that."

"He already has."

The voice came out of the darkness behind her. Her knees went weak with the gruff sound of it. When she turned her head, she caught her breath sharply. He had borrowed one of Cage's cars and gone into town on a shopping expedition of his own. He was wearing new stonewashed jeans. They clung to his hips and thighs with a soft, tight fit. He had on a Swiss army shirt made of white cotton. The sleeves had been rolled up to his hard biceps. She smelled cologne on him for the first time and liked his selection. It reminded her of rain and wind. He'd had his hair trimmed, too, but it was still long enough to brush the collar of his shirt.

Linc moved out of the darkness and laid a hand on Joe's shoulder. "He thanked me this afternoon, but I told him it wasn't necessary. He covered my ass. In his own right, he is a freedom fighter for his country."

Joe beamed up at the older man and said proudly, "But now my country is the United States."

No one had had the heart to tell the boy that he, as yet, had no adoptive parents and that there was a very real possibility that he would be returned to Montenegro. Quickly Linc changed the subject. "Did Cage tell you what an uncanny rapport Joe has with horses?"

"He's mentioned it a few hundred times," Kerry said, giving Joe a teasing smile. "You never told me you knew so much about horses."

"I never knew!" the boy exclaimed, his dark eyes shining.

That afternoon, when Joe insisted that he didn't want to lie in bed any longer, he had been taken on a tour of the ranch. Cage had returned to the house with him, marveling over the boy's natural rapport with the animals.

"He seems to speak their language," Cage said, smiling down at the adolescent.

Joe basked in Linc's compliments. In Montenegro, he had seemed old beyond his years. He had shed that untimely maturity along with his hostility toward Linc.

"When you first joined us," he said to Linc solemnly, "I thought you meant to harm Sister Kerry. I know now that you wouldn't hurt her." He didn't notice the slight flinching of Linc's muscles. "I'm sorry I had bad feelings toward you. You brought us to freedom."

Before Linc could make an appropriate reply, Trent Hendren came bounding up to Joe. He halted just short of tackling him, which he would have done if he hadn't been warned earlier about hurting Joe's thigh wound. "Joe, Joe." The child had been Joe's shadow ever since he returned from the hospital. Joe didn't seem to mind. In fact, he assumed a paternal air toward Trent. The child pointed excitedly toward the television screen where another movie was just starting. Smiling shyly, Joe hobbled toward the others with Trent tagging along beside him.

"So much a child, but so much a man," Kerry murmured as she watched him cross the patio.

"And intuitive," Linc said.

"About the horses?"

"About me." She turned her head and stared up at him. "He was right about my hurting you. Only his timing was off."

Her eyes fell away from his piercing stare. "Let's not talk about it. Please."

"I've got to talk about it." He spoke softly, even though it was unlikely anyone would hear them over the antics of Peter Pan and Captain Hook. "Are you in pain?"

"I told you earlier, no."

"Why didn't you warn me?"

"We've already established that, too. You wouldn't have believed me."

"Maybe not this morning, but—"

"When? When, Linc? Think back. At what point during our *friendship* would you have believed me? When would have been a good time to casually drop that into the conversation?" She expelled a long breath. "Besides, what difference does it make? It had to happen sooner or later."

"But not so—"

When he broke off without finishing, she looked at him inquiringly. "Not so what?"

"Roughly."

For a moment they stared at each other. She was the first to look away. "Oh, that, well..."

"Did I hurt you, Kerry?"

"No."

Physically her discomfort had been minimal. Emotionally, it had been fatal. He had taken her out of anger. It hadn't been an act of love, or even of sexual pleasure, but one of vengeance. Her body hadn't been bruised, but her heart had been trampled. He had dealt her emotions a crippling blow, but she would be damned before she let him know that.

She tilted her head to its haughtiest angle. "That's what you want to hear, isn't it? Hurting me would have taken some of the gild off your trophy."

"What do you mean by that?" he asked, lowering his brows dangerously.

"Your sole purpose was to make me admit my attraction to you. You set out to make me beg, remember? Well I did. You got what you wanted, didn't you?"

"No, goddammit."

He moved nearer. His face was dark with anger. She could feel his body heat and, madly, felt cheated for not having felt his naked flesh next to her own. She had shared with him the most intimate act between a man and woman, but she still didn't know the pleasure of her smooth skin rubbing against his hair-smattered body or the delightful friction that caused.

*And, damn him, I still want to know,* her mind cried.

"I wanted to bring you down a notch, but I would never have hurt you. I had no idea when I . . . I wanted to stop as soon as I . . . felt . . ." His eyes coasted down to her mouth. "But once I got inside you, I couldn't stop."

Another of those long stares followed while each remembered the feel of his body snugly embedded in hers. Linc wanted to pull her into his arms again, but knew he couldn't. So he released his frustration by lashing out at her.

"You gotta admit that you're a little old to be having your first lover."

"It was never convenient. My mother died when I was sixteen. After that, I acted as my father's hostess. Boyfriends rarely fit into the embassy's social schedule. And in the last few years . . ."

"You were busy keeping your old man out of jail."

"No," she flared. "I was trying to keep him from killing himself. I didn't have much spare time to cultivate relationships with men."

Linc, sincerely sorry for what he'd said, came back with, "Well, I had no way of knowing all that."

"What you don't know about me would fill an encyclopedia, Mr. O'Neal. From the very beginning, you've jumped to wrong conclusions about me, forming your own erroneous opinions—"

"And whose fault is that?" Anger was the only way to effectively douse the flames in his loins. "Why did you keep me ignorant of the facts, pretending to be what you aren't?" He took another step forward. "You've got your nerve, lady, accusing me of jumping to conclusions. And just for the record, you made a much more convincing whore than you did a nun."

She bristled in outrage. "How dare—"

"Your hands were all over me in that bar."

"I touched your thigh," she shouted defensively. "Low on your thigh."

"The hair. The juicy mouth. The come-and-get-it eyes. That crotch-teasing dress."

"I wish you would forget about that damn dress."

"Not likely, sweetheart. Were all those trappings really necessary? Why didn't you explain to me from the beginning who your old man was?"

"Because, if you'll recall, I thought you were a mercenary, a mean, low, unscrupulous—"

"Cut the insults and answer my question. Why didn't you just sober me up and introduce yourself?"

"Because I didn't know my father's friends from his enemies in Montenegro. He had more of the latter than the former. So to protect both myself and the children, I thought it best not to tell you. The rebels would have murdered me on the spot if they had ever found out. My name was kept a secret."

"What the hell were you doing down there in the first place? For a Sorbonne graduate, you sure aren't very bright."

She let the slight go and addressed the question. "Someone had to go and help these orphans."

"Agreed. *Someone*. You didn't have to go yourself. If you've got fifty grand to pay me, you had fifty grand to pay a mercenary. You could have gotten yourself killed."

"But I didn't!"

"And I don't think you'll be satisfied until you do!"

"What do you mean?" she asked sharply.

"When will you feel like you've made restitution for your daddy's crimes? When they're shoveling dirt over your face?"

Kerry pulled herself up to a rigid posture. "What would you know about moral obligation? You, who spend your life slumming. You, who has never thought of anyone but yourself."

"At least I came by everything I have honestly."

"Oh, you're—"

"I hate to butt in."

Simultaneously, they turned toward Cage. He was wearing an amused grin. "Y'all sure are shouting a lot, and I apologize for the interruption, but something major has come up." He winked at Linc. "No pun intended."

Vivid color flooded Kerry's face. She was grateful for the darkness which hopefully concealed it. "What is it, Cage?"

"Come over here with the rest of the group. Dad has something he wants to say."

When they moved into the circle of light, Reverend Hendren stepped forward. "This will come as a surprise to all of you. Sarah and I have been talking throughout the day and have reached a decision, which we're sure will make our home a much happier one." He turned his head slightly. "Joe, how would you like to come live with us?"

It had been so unselfish and beautiful, what Bob and Sarah Hendren had done. Staring out her bedroom window an hour later, Kerry still got a lump in her throat when she thought about it.

Of course pandemonium had broken out when Bob Hendren first asked that astonishing question. At first Joe hadn't comprehended all that the question entailed. When he did, his face broke into a radiant smile. He nodded his head vigorously and reverted to his native tongue. *"Sí, sí."* When Kerry translated to the other orphans what was happening, they grouped around Joe to exuberantly celebrate his good fortune.

When they had all been put to bed in their respective temporary shelters, Kerry caught up with the older couple.

"I can't tell you how glad I am about what you've done. I only hope that I didn't pressure you into making the decision by what I said earlier today," she said with concern.

Each of them embraced her. Bob said, "We both think this will honor Hal's memory in a special way. We'll only have Joe for a few years before he goes to college. In the meantime, we can make certain that he catches up with his peers academically and socially."

"You see, Kerry," Cage's mother said, "our house emptied of all our children so quickly. Cage was gone, then Hal left. Soon after that Jenny married Cage. Bob and I can't fill those empty rooms. It will be so good having a young person there again. Trent already idolizes Joe, so he'll fit well into the family. And he'll have access to the ranch and the horses he seems to like so well. It all worked out beautifully."

That was one problem that had been resolved, Kerry thought, as she let the curtain fall back into place over the window. Maybe tomorrow would provide a solution to the problem of Lisa's future. Kerry had hugged her tightly when she tucked her into bed. She looked like a little doll in her new dotted swiss nightgown. Lisa had spontaneously returned her hug and kissed her cheek wetly and noisily.

Concern about Lisa wasn't the only burden she was taking to bed with her.

Guilt was a bedfellow. It pressed on her heavily when she recalled the scathing words she had flung at Linc. She had unfairly accused him of never thinking of anyone but himself, when actually he had risked his life countless times to save hers and the orphans'.

Why had she said that? Why did he, more than anyone she'd ever known, provoke her to do and say things that were so out of character?

Her hand paused in the act of pulling back the bedspread when she heard a heavy tread on the stairs. Jenny and Cage had retired to their bedroom as soon as his parents had left for home. The approaching footsteps could only belong to one person. Before she could change her mind, Kerry quickly moved toward the door. She opened it just as Linc was walking past. He looked at her in surprise.

"Is something wrong?"

She shook her head no, already regretting her spontaneity. His shirttail was hanging out and his shirt was unbuttoned. The dark hair in his chest was a tempting sight. She followed its tapering pattern downward. The snap on his jeans was undone. He was barefoot. His hair had been tousled, seemingly by impatient hands. He looked heart-stoppingly wonderful.

When she just stood there rooted to the spot, saying nothing, he said, "I'm sorry if I disturbed you. I went back down to smoke a cigarette and—"

"No, you didn't disturb me," she said on a rush of air. "I...I owe you an apology for what I said earlier." His eyebrow arched inquisitively. "About you thinking only of yourself," she blurted out, by way of explanation. "It was a stupid thing to say after all you did for us. You saved our lives and...and I ask your forgiveness for saying something so patently untrue about you."

When she dared to raise her eyes, she saw that his were slowly ranging down her body, which was clothed only in the nightgown she had purchased that day in town. She was backlit by the lamp on the nightstand. Her body was cast into detailed silhouette inside the sheer fabric.

"I'm glad you stopped me," Linc said huskily. "Because I owe you something, too."

She became entranced by his eyes. "You don't owe me another apology for this morning. You've already apologized."

"I owe you something besides an apology."

"What?"

He backed her into the room. "A whole lot of pleasure."

# *Chapter 12*

The door closed behind him with a soft click of the latch.

"Pleasure?"

"P-L-E-A-S-U-R-E. As in what was missing in your initiation into lovemaking. I took a lot, gave very little. I want to make that up to you."

"You mean you want to . . . uh . . ."

Nodding his head, Linc moved forward with a prowling gait. "Yeah, that's what I mean." Reaching her, he took her shoulders between his hands and drew her against him.

"But we can't." Her protest was as faint as the resistance she exerted when he adjusted his body to fit hers.

"How come?"

"Because we don't even like each other."

He shrugged. "You're all right."

"And every time we're together we fight."

"Makes life interesting and keeps me on my toes."

"You'll always hold it against me that I tricked you."

"But I admire your craftiness."

"In my mind you'll always be a mercenary even though you wield a camera instead of a gun. And—"

"And in spite of all that, we're physically attracted. Granted?"

She stared into his tanned, lean face. Her stubborn will capitulated to the urging of her body. It was awakening, as a morning glory does with the sun. Unfolding itself. Seeking the warmth. Flowering open.

Kerry tried to remember all the reasons why this was untenable and unworkable, and a downright bad idea. But her body had a memory of its own. Her senses recalled each touch, sound, and taste of his lovemaking and wanted to experience them again. Thread by thread her resistance became unwoven.

She laid her hands on his chest. "Granted."

"Then for tonight, can't we set aside all our differences and concentrate strictly on that?"

"Isn't that a rather irresponsible approach to going to bed together?"

"Don't you think we deserve to be a little irresponsible?" His gaze was moving over her face and hair. "After all we've been through?"

"I suppose so." Because his shirt was open, she could feel part of his bare chest against her palms. His skin was hot. The hair that matted it was crinkly and soft. She wanted to feel it against her face, her mouth.

"Don't think about all the reasons we shouldn't, Kerry," he said in a stirring voice. "Think about this."

Cupping her chin in one hand, he tilted her head back and pressed his lips against hers, nudging them apart, and breaching them with his tongue. Kerry's world careened. She did as he suggested and focused all her attention on the kiss, the heat and passion and hunger behind it. His lips were firm, but not forceful. His tongue was bold, but not abusive. Linc used it to make love to her mouth.

When he raised his head, she slumped against him and laid her cheek on his chest. Beneath her ear she could hear his heart pounding. Their kiss had affected him as much as it had her.

"You're good," he whispered to the crown of her head.

"You just haven't had anyone else lately."

"No. You're good."

"I am?"

"Yes, ma'am. Very good. Damn good."

Before she could prepare herself, he tilted her head back again, just in time to meet his descending mouth. He pulled her against him tightly, wedged her thighs apart and tucked the lower part of his body between them. It was a thrilling contact and one that would have made her gasp, had his mouth not held such mastery over hers. His lips ground against hers with a need close to desperation. She recognized the same kind of clamoring need within herself.

Working her hands from between their bodies, she linked them around his neck. When her breasts flattened against his chest, each of them uttered a gratified sound. She laced her fingers through his hair and stretched up on tiptoe. His moan originated in the bottom of his soul. He slid his hands down to her derriere, pressing her higher and harder against the front of his body.

They couldn't continue for long without incinerating. Gradually Linc ended the kiss. His lips, moist and soft, rubbed against hers and his hands moved to the more neutral territory of her waist. It was incredibly narrow and his hands kept gently squeezing it as though marveling over that. Kerry eased down to stand flatfooted again between his wide-spread feet. Her hands glided down to his shoulders, touching his ears, his jaw, along the way. She toyed with the buttons on the epaulets of his shirt.

When she lifted her shy gaze up to his, he did something she'd rarely seen him do. He smiled. She remarked on it, telling him that he had a nice smile.

He laughed softly at the innocent compliment. "I do?"

"Yes. I haven't seen you smile very often. You were usually frowning at me."

"Because I wanted to be on top of you so damn bad."

His emotion-packed words had a profound effect on Kerry's insides. They absorbed them like a blow from a velvet wrapped fist. To put things back on an even keel, she said inanely, "Your teeth are straight. Did you wear braces?"

"Hell no."

"I did."

"I'll bet you were adorable." He pecked a light kiss on the tip of her nose. "But every day you spent in braces was worth it." He ran the tip of his tongue along her upper teeth, barely inside her lips. She shivered with the pleasure he had promised to give her. "Cold?"

"No." Then the absurdity of the question struck her and she laughed. "No," she stressed, shaking her head.

His eyes became as glowing and hypnotizing as lantern light in the middle of a nighttime forest. They were all Kerry could see. Twin stars at the center of this private universe.

"Hot?"

She nodded.

"Where?"

"Everywhere."

He pressed his open palm against her stomach. Never removing his eyes from her face, he slid his hand down, following the tapering line of her body, until his hand conformed perfectly to the delta shape. "Here?"

Kerry made a yearning sound and swayed toward him. "Yes."

"Tender?"

"A little."

"I'm sorry."

"I'm not."

"You're not?"

"No, Linc I'm not."

They kissed, and because it was such a torrid kiss, he removed his hand, caught her, and held her close, rocking her slightly. "We're getting ahead of ourselves," he whispered raggedly. He nuzzled her neck. Kissed it. Touched it with his tongue. "You know the song that goes, 'I want to kiss you all over'?" She made an affirmative motion with her head, though she didn't move it away from the hollow of his shoulder. "Well, that's what I want to do to you. Kiss you all over. And over again."

He encircled her upper arms and eased her away. When her eyes drifted open, he said, "Desire was the only thing that kept me going while we were tramping through that damned jungle. Basically I'm a coward."

"Impossible," she said fervently.

He grinned crookedly. "You caught me on a brave week. Anyway," he said, giving a dismissive shake of his head, "the motivation that drove me was that one day, by some miraculous twist of fate, I was going to have you in bed."

"You don't fool me, Lincoln. Other people might buy that callous air you assume, but I don't. Your motivation was to get those orphans to safety."

He had the grace to look chagrined. "Well it made the situation a helluva lot more bearable to fantasize about you along the way."

"Did you?" She assumed the posture and expression of a practiced coquette, though the gestures came to her subconsciously.

"All the time. Constantly. Continually."

His hands moved over her throat and chest. The pads of his fingers glanced over her skin, barely touching it. Even though they were sensitive to the intricate dials of a sophisticated camera, they were appealingly rough and masculine.

Lightly, he placed his hands on the sides of her breasts. He applied a slight pressure, then relaxed. Several times he did that, making her breasts move beneath the nightgown, which was made of a cotton so thin and airy that her nipples showed up as enticing shadows beneath it, even in the darkness of the room.

"Your breasts fascinated me. The way they moved every time you did. It seemed like your clothes were always getting wet. The night you bathed in the stream. The river crossing. Even perspiration made your shirt cling to you. And I'd see . . ."

He brushed his thumbs over her nipples. Not that they needed any encouragement. His words had already brought them to aching hardness.

"They bewitched me. All I could think of was touching, kissing."

He bent his head and kissed her breast through her nightgown. The wet, stroking caress of his tongue seeped through the sheer cloth and caused it to mold provocatively to the rosy tips. "Nice."

"You said I was small."

"You are. But I never said I didn't like small." He lowered his head to her again and kept up that particular pleasure-giving caress until her knees threatened to buckle beneath her.

"I want to see you." She surprised herself by saying that. But she didn't lower her gaze in maidenly bashfulness. She met his steadily. "Take off your shirt. Please."

Her polite afterthought amused him, but he made no comment on it as he peeled off his shirt. Holding it out to his side, he dropped it to the floor. He stood perfectly still, indulging her curiosity.

She smiled compassionately over the angry red scrape the bullet had left. She wouldn't dwell on how close he had come to being seriously wounded or killed. It made her slightly ill to think about it. She pushed the thought from her mind and, as they had agreed to do, centered her thoughts on loving.

Her touch was delicate and inquisitive when she first laid her hands on the upper, curving portion of his chest. The hair was intriguing, and she combed her fingers through it. It spread in a wide fan shape over his breasts, then funnelled to a silky stripe down the center of his stomach. She bracketed his ribcage with her hands and moved them down as far as his waist, then back up, letting her fingers climb over each rib. They finally came to rest beneath the solid, curved muscles. Her thumbs came dangerously close to touching his nipples before they shied away.

She looked up at him inquiringly. "Touch me like I do you," he said tightly. His face was taut and his breath was rushing between his teeth.

Against her fingertips, the feel of his erect nipples was erotic and exciting. His trembling response to her caress gave her courage. She shed the remains of her shyness and did what she had long wanted to do, she nuzzled him with her mouth. When her lips touched his nipple, both of them sighed with pleasure. She rubbed her tongue against it with no more hurry than a languid kitten at his morning bath. It came as a mild surprise to her that she derived as much pleasure from sucking it tenderly as it obviously gave Linc. Reflexively he thrust his manhood forward, rubbing it rhythmically against her.

When he could stand no more, he pushed her away and angled her head back. "I thought tonight would get you out of my system," he ground out. "Now I'm not so sure. You're a powerful narcotic, Kerry."

He kissed her, sending his tongue into the satiny warmth of her mouth. With an impatience bordering on violence, he ended the kiss. Taking her hand, he led her across the room to a chair near the window. He sat down in it. She remained standing in front of him.

"Take off your nightgown."

Kerry swallowed a knot of trepidation. He had removed her clothing today, but they'd been in an embrace. Disrobing in front of him, strictly for his entertainment, caused her heart to flutter with anxiety.

But with something else, too. The only name she could put to this odd sensation was titillation. She had a deep seated desire to tantalize and dazzle the worldly Lincoln O'Neal.

Her eyes took on a mysterious quality, a seductiveness, a lambency, a knowledge as old as Eve. Kerry turned her back on him. She sensed that he was about to make a protest but withheld it when he saw her cross her arms over her chest and move her hands to the shoulder straps of her nightgown. They were thin. It took the merest flick of her wrists to lower them. They slipped to her elbows. With painstaking slowness she relaxed her arms until they dropped to her sides. When that happened, the nightgown slithered from her body and fell to the floor.

She could almost feel Linc's eyes burning into her back. She knew he was taking in her figure, the way her waist melded into the flair of her hips. Was he pleased? Had he noticed the dimples at the base of her spine? Did he find them cute? Sexy? Fascinating? Was he entranced by the shape of her bottom? Did her thighs look heavy and lumpy?

She stepped out of the pool of fabric at her feet and turned around slowly until she was facing him. She kept her eyes lowered. When she gathered enough courage to look at him, what she saw in his eyes caused her heartbeat to soar.

"Let your hair loose."

That wasn't what she had expected him to say, but the gritty inflection of his voice told her what she wanted and needed to know. He liked what he saw.

She dragged the single braid over her shoulder. The curling end of it lay against her bare breast. Her attentive audience wet his lips. She pulled the rubber band off the end of the braid. Then, unlooping the strands slowly, she made a ballet of unraveling it.

Linc watched every graceful movement of her fingers, as though she were executing an intricate task that required incredible talent and perfect timing. When the entire braid was undone, she tossed the heavy skein of hair over her shoulder.

"Shake your head." Kerry moved her head from side to side. Her hair undulated over her skin in a slow sweep. "Comb your fingers through it." She lifted handfuls of her hair up and away from her face, pulling it through her wide-spread fingers until every strand had been filtered through. It fell over her shoulders and chest, almost reaching the tips of her breasts.

Linc's chest was soughing in and out. She knew that he was about to explode, but when he made his move, she still wasn't braced for it.

His hands shot out and clasped her waist. With one motion, he moved to the edge of the chair and pulled her forward. His open mouth landed with a soft, damp impact on her naked belly and she gave a sharp cry of surprise.

He kissed her fervently, several times, stopping only long enough to move his lips from one spot to another. His arms went around her. His hands cupped her bottom, and his caresses stole her breath with the unrestricted license they took. She laid her hands on the sides of his head, curling her fingers around his ears, and watched as his dear head moved from side to side, branding her with his hot, ardent kisses. His breath stirred the triangle of downy hair before she felt his lips moving in it.

Her knees gave way and she made another whimpering sound that snapped him to his senses. He stood up and enfolded her in his embrace. He murmured endearments spiced with expletives. The words stumbled over one another and became erotic lyrics that thrilled and aroused Kerry even more.

When he slipped his hand between her thighs, they parted without hesitation. It seemed right that he favored that part of her with gentle probings that took his fingers deep inside. She softly cried his name.

"Does that hurt?" Her answer was a wordless, mindless tossing of her head. "I'll never hurt you again, Kerry. I swear it."

As he kissed her, he unzipped his pants and shoved them down his legs. It took some doing, but he stepped out of them without having to release her mouth from his tempestuous kiss.

She felt him, warm and hard and urgent against her. In a leisurely manner that in no way matched their clamorous passions, he smoothed his hand down the back of her thigh and gently lifted it up over his.

When the most intimate parts of their bodies touched, she reacted with total abandonment, throwing her head back until her hair almost reached her waist and arching against him to bring his sex to the very portal of hers.

"Not yet," he whispered.

Then his hand was there again. And his fingers were working magic, discovering secrets, finding the key to what made her woman. When he unlocked it with his exquisite touch, joy and pleasure and love rushed through her. Her nails made dents in his shoulders. Her teeth made imprints on his chest. He welcomed them. He savored each single spasm of pleasure that gripped her.

Kerry wasn't allowed to luxuriate in the sweet aftermath. Weakly she leaned against him, panting softly. He cradled her in his arms and carried her to the bed, where he tenderly deposited her on the pillows. Her eyes were almost too languorous to remain open, but the sight of Linc, naked and proud, bending over her, brought them wide open.

"You're beautiful." She could barely speak the words, but he read them on her lips.

"Who me?" He looked at her with skepticism. It twisted his smile, wrinkled his brow, and narrowed his eyes, making his expression roguish and sexy.

She smiled. "Yes you. And what you did to me. That was beautiful."

"Ah, that I agree with." He was on his knees. He straddled her thighs and ran his hands up and down them.

"I didn't make a fool of myself?"

He touched the moist cleft between her thighs. "It was beautiful to watch. To feel against my fingers."

She bit her lower lip to hold inside the yearning sounds that pushed at her throat. "It . . . I don't think . . ."

"Hmm?"

"I'm not finished," she said breathlessly.

He smiled. "Good, good."

"But I want . . . ahh . . . Linc . . ."

"What? Tell me what you want." He wasn't taunting; he was begging. There was no cruelty on his features. His eyes were imploring. His jaw tensed with need. His face contorted with desire kept bridled too long. His entreaty endearingly vulnerable. "Show me, Kerry. What do you want?"

She placed her hands on the tops of his thighs. When she caressed his pronounced hipbones, he hissed a vivid curse. Her fingers tangled in the dark hair, and he dropped his head forward. And when she cradled his straining manhood between her hands, he released a tremendous groan.

His penetration was swift and deep. Kerry felt again the smoldering heat in the depths of her body. Like glowing embers being fanned, it burned hot, then hotter. When he began to move, she responded, lifting her hips to welcome his thrusts.

"Not so fast. Easy. We're in no hurry this time."

Exercising amazing discipline, he relished her with the appreciation of a viticulturist for a perfect glass of rare wine. As though all of his body were covered with taste buds, he touched her everywhere, sampling her deliciousness.

His restraint couldn't last forever. And soon it was he who was rushing, increasing the tempo. Kerry spun out of control again and this time she took him with her. They whirled in a fiery dance until they either had to burn themselves out or die.

Jenny struggled to a sitting position. "Cage, did you hear something?"

"Yes," he mumbled into his pillow.

"I'd better go—"

He caught the hem of her nightgown. "Stay where you are."

"But—"

"The sound you heard was Linc going in to Kerry's room."

Jenny's mouth formed a small O. She lay back down, lying perfectly still. "Did she invite him in?"

"How the hell do I know? It's their business. Now go back to sleep?"

"Do you think he's still angry with her?"

"Jen-ny," he said warningly.

"Well maybe—"

"Jenny!" His stage whisper shut her up. "This is what you wanted, isn't it? They're together. You've had romantic stars in your eyes for them ever since they came through the door of this house. Now be quiet so Baby and I can go back to sleep."

"Baby wasn't sleeping," Jenny grumbled. "She was kicking."

"Here, scooch back this way." Cage nudged her into the curve of his body where she snuggled, her back to his chest. He laid his hand on her swollen tummy and massaged it gently.

"You know," he commented, as his hand idly moved over her, "I sorta envy ol' Linc."

"That's a terrible thing to say to a fat, pregnant wife!"

"'Fraid I'll go tomcatting around?" She poked him in the ribs with her elbow and he yelped beneath his breath. "You didn't let me finish. I *sorta* envy him. I envy him the fun of the chase. But I wouldn't trade where we are now with where they are in their relationship."

"Me neither."

"Getting you in my house and in my bed was no small feat. Of course anything worth having is worth working for."

"I told Kerry practically the same thing today."

They were comfortable in their love for each other. But it still held elements of excitement, as demonstrated moments later when Cage asked, "Baby asleep?"

"Uh-huh, but mama's wide awake." Jenny turned to face him. "Kiss me."

"We shouldn't Jenny. It's too dangerous now."

"Nothing else. Just a kiss. Kiss me, Cage. And make it count."

"Are you asleep?"

Kerry sighed deeply. "I think I'm dead."

Mischievously Linc blew gently on one of her breasts and, to his supreme delight and amusement, the nipple pearled. "You're not dead."

She pried her eyes open and looked at him slumbrously. She was lying on her back. He was lying on his stomach beside her, propped up on his elbows and staring down at her.

"Do I look frightful?"

"Is this the woman who tramped through the jungle without so much as a lipstick or a hairbrush, worrying now about her appearance?"

"*Do* I?"

"Sexily mussed." He kissed her lightly. "Which is the best way a woman can look."

"Chauvinist."

"Besides, why should you care about your appearance now when you didn't in the jungle?"

"I wasn't sleeping with you then."

"Not for lack of me trying. And actually I did sleep with you. Remember the night under the vine?"

"You weren't my lover then."

"Remember the night under the vine?" he repeated, forcing her to look at him. She nodded. "Did you know that if a man could die of arousal that would have been my deathbed?" She laughed and he frowned. "It's not funny."

"I know. Because I was suffering, too."

"Yeah?"

"Yeah."

He looked at her across the pillow. "You're very pretty."

"You've never told me that before."

"I'm not usually complimentary."

She touched his hair, removing wayward strands from his forehead. "You don't get close to too many people, do you, Linc?"

"No." He saw the wounded expression in her eyes and hated himself for putting it there with his harsh, abrupt answer. He tried to soften it now by laying his hand against her cheek and rubbing his thumb over her lips. "I'm close to you tonight. I'm as close to you as I ever get to anybody. We're close to each other. Let's not spoil it by getting too analytical."

There was so much she wanted to say. Her heart was filled to capacity with love for this man. It demanded to be vocalized. But she knew that saying anything more would drive him farther away, not draw him nearer. So she held her silence.

To lighten the mood, she levered herself up and kissed his forehead. Her hair dusted his shoulder.

"That feels good."

"What?"

"Your hair against my skin."

Inspired then to demonstrate her unspoken love, Kerry began kissing his shoulders, taking careful lovebites that faintly nipped his skin. He made a grunting sound that showed his approval. She folded her legs beneath her hips and leaned across his back, dropping kisses randomly.

She sipped her way down his spine to the shallow dip just below his waist. Her hair followed the motions of her head. It draped his back, shifting and sliding over his smooth flesh as whimsically as the ever-changing surf upon the shore.

She ran her hand over his buttock, and with a gentle squeeze appreciated its firmness. He cast her a sly look over his shoulder and she giggled. "I couldn't help but notice." He grinned smugly, but the expression relaxed and softened into one of sublimity when her hair brushed across his bottom and upper thighs.

"Kerry?"

"Hmm?" She leaned back. He turned over. Her heart stopped.

He repeated her name. There was an unspoken please behind it. And a breathless anticipation he couldn't disguise.

"You don't have to if you don't want to."

Kerry smiled at him lovingly, then lowered her head.

She kissed both his knees and worked her way up his thighs, trailing her hair behind her. She took his breath where next she kissed him. He closed his eyes and sighed her name as the loveplay of her lips and tongue went on and on. Without inhibition. With love. Then, as a refrain, she daintily dipped her tongue into his navel. Her hair swirled around his stiff manhood. The sight was beautiful and erotic and a stunning catalyst.

He lifted her atop him. Kerry gazed down at him with wide-eyed astonishment, but, acting on instinct, impaled herself on him. He sank his fingers into the fleshy part of her hips.

"Do I—"

"Oh, God, yes," he moaned. "Just like that."

She began to roll her hips in a grinding motion. He covered her breasts with his hands, brought the nipples to ripe peaks with plucking fingers, then levered himself up to love them with his mouth.

Closing her eyes, Kerry let her own sensations instruct her on what to do. With each tug of his mouth on her breast, she felt a corresponding contraction in her womb. Inside her he was strong and unyielding, and her only thought was to draw him deeper, make him an intrinsic part of herself. Again that marvelous pressure began to build to insurmountable heights, and she was helpless to stop the avalanche of emotions that overwhelmed her.

Moments later, they lay in a tangled heap of twisted bedsheets and naked limbs. Linc was the first to regain his senses. He could have moved away. He could have left her. But he wrapped his arms around Kerry and held her tightly.

"Kerry, Kerry." There were varying elements in his voice. Yearning. Pleasure. Affection. Mostly sadness.

But Kerry, listening only to the synchronized beating of their hearts, didn't hear that.

# *Chapter 13*

He needed a cigarette.

He could have lit one, but he was afraid the smell of smoke would wake her up. He could have returned to his room or moved to another part of the house to smoke, but he couldn't bring himself to leave her yet. He could have stayed away from her in the first place.

That's what he should have done.

It would have been much more prudent not to have stopped when she opened her door to him last night. He should have accepted her apology, which was unnecessary to begin with, perhaps shaken hands with her, maybe given her a friendly little good-night kiss on the cheek, and then beat it into his bedroom, locking himself in if necessary.

Had he done that, he wouldn't have to hurt her. He could have exited her life as breezily as he had entered it.

Well not quite.

Yesterday morning was still listed in the column of his sins.

He muttered a terse obscenity. No matter how you looked at it, it was a muddle. He was involved with Kerry Bishop. He had been since she had enticed him to leave that *cantina* with her. And he would be until he waved goodbye to her, saying something clever like, "Here's lookin' at you, kid," and riding off into the sunset.

It worked in the movies. Poignant, bittersweet goodbyes made terrific scripts. In real life they stunk.

He placed his forehead against the cool windowsill and pressed hard, as though trying to drive his head through the wood. Saying goodbye was only half the problem. Even after he did, it would be a long time before Kerry was out of his system. He might just as well admit it. She had her claws in him, but good. He was steeped in Kerry, and she was all he could think about.

Her smile. Her voice. Her eyes. Her hair. Her body.

Again he swore and pressed down the swelling flesh beneath his jeans. His body was responding to his recollections of last night. He didn't know how he could possibly get hard again, but he was. He would have thought he'd been pumped dry last night. They had been insatiable. Their lovemaking had been earnest and playful and lusty and tender, but had always, *always*, left them wanting more.

Had he ever met a more responsive woman? In any country? On any continent? At any age? Their loving had gone beyond sexual gratification. Kerry had opened up something hidden deep inside him. It was that element to their lovemaking that he found so disturbing.

Having resisted the temptation as long as he could, Linc turned his head around and looked at Kerry where she lay sleeping. He couldn't hold back the smile that softened his stern mouth and relieved his face of its usual cynicism.

One shapely leg was lying outside the light sheet, which had been their only cover all night. He'd embarrassed her by raising a light bruise on the inside of her thigh with a fervent kiss.

"Who else will see it?"

Laughing, she had thrown her arms around his neck. "Jealous?"

It had surprised him to realize that he was. He had initiated her, by God. He had introduced her to the pleasure her body was capable of experiencing. He, Lincoln O'Neal, had taught her how to give pleasure. The thought of another man enjoying this wonderful, affectionate, sensual woman, whom *he* had discovered, had filled him with a crimson rage.

Now, he could see that slight discoloration on the tender flesh of her thigh and remembered how delightful it had been for both of them when his mouth had put it there. His gaze moved over her. There wasn't an inch of her body that didn't bring an erotic memory rushing to his mind. From the arch of her slender foot to the crescent rim of her ear, he'd caressed, kissed, licked, tasted.

Yet, for all the sensuality she had expressed last night, she looked as innocent as a child now, with her dark hair lying tangled on the pristine pillowcase, and her lips, still rouged by his kisses, slightly parted. Her lashes were dark and feathery, her cheeks creamy.

One breast was peeping from beneath the sheet. With each breath, it rose and fell beguilingly. The tip of it was rosily pink. He intimately knew its texture and taste. How many times during the night had his mouth returned to her breasts, taking and giving pleasure?

With an inaudible groan he turned his head to stare out the window again. The landscape was just being bathed with the glow of the rising sun. Where only minutes ago everything had been gray, now colors became distinguishable. The sky had been a pale noncolor; now it was vividly streaked with the reds and golds of sunrise.

The dawn was a beautiful sight, but it did nothing to lighten Linc's black mood. He had to leave today. Hanging around any longer would be just plain stupid. Any further delay would only make things messier. *Because, face it, you can't stay under the same roof with her without wanting her in bed with you.*

This thing between them, whatever the hell it was, couldn't go on. Sooner or later they both had to get on with their lives. His common sense told him that sooner was better.

Mission accomplished. End of story. Over and out. They'd done what they had set out to do. It was time to move on to other endeavors. She'd gotten all the orphans safely out of Montenegro. They'd all been placed with families, except for Lisa, and that was no cause for alarm. Finding parents for her wouldn't be difficult.

Linc had decided to accept the offer an international magazine had made for his photographs documenting their escape. The price he had demanded would financially sustain him until the next military coup, or airplane crash, or volcanic eruption, or whatever it was that caused mayhem and havoc which people wanted to see pictures of.

Odd, that he wasn't feeling his usual restlessness. He had a wanderlust that had never been quenched. At the drop of a hat he had been ready to pack his cameras and catch the next plane out. Why was he dragging his feet this time?

*That's an easy one, you bastard. Take a look behind you.*

All right, so it was Kerry. He wasn't too anxious to leave her. But what other choice did he have? What could he offer her? A cluttered, dusty apartment in Manhattan where he picked up his mail every month or so. The bathroom doubled as a darkroom. He stored his chemicals in the living room. He didn't own a car. An answering service took his telephone calls. He ate out every meal except breakfast, which he usually skipped. The only appliances in his kitchen were an unstocked refrigerator, which he used only to make ice, and a coffeepot.

But even if he had a fully equipped, lavishly furnished penthouse on Park Avenue, he couldn't ask a woman like

Kerry Bishop to share her life with him. He was from the streets. A thirty-five-year-old hoodlum. He'd had no formal education. He wasn't just rough around the edges, an unpolished gem, he was seedy to the marrow.

She had lived in comparative luxury. She could probably speak more languages than he could name. She was refined, educated, and a member of the socially elite. And whether she believed it or not, no one was going to hold her old man's corruption against her. On the contrary, she was probably admired by many as a tragic heroine.

She was also the best damn thing ever to happen to Linc O'Neal, and he simply couldn't handle it.

Breathing a slow, silent sigh, he crossed the room and gazed down at her. If things were different... But they weren't, and there was no sense lamenting what couldn't possibly be. Life would sure be dismal without her. She was like a spark, constantly ready to ignite, shedding warmth and light on his cold and dreary world.

Linc braced his hand on the wall behind the bed and leaned over the headboard. He was tempted to kiss her one last time, but was afraid that would wake her up. Instead, he touched her lips lightly with his thumb. Lord, she was beautiful. She was exciting. His gut twisted painfully at the thought of never seeing her again after today.

He'd never said the words to another soul. Possibly he'd said them to his mother, but he had been so young when she died that he didn't remember. He knew he'd never said them to the dour, unfeeling man who had sired him. He whispered them to Kerry Bishop now.

"I love you."

Seconds later, her violet eyelids fluttered. He was afraid his confession had awakened her, but she came awake too slowly for that to be the case. She stretched sinuously, raising her arms above her head and pointing her toes as far as they would reach. The movement pulled the sheet away from her breasts and left them vulnerable to his gaze.

His jaw was steely with tension as he restrained himself from leaning down and taking one of those perky, pink nipples into his mouth and worrying it slowly with his tongue until she came fully awake. It cost him tremendous effort, but he kept his features remote.

When Kerry's eyes opened, she had an unrestricted view of his armpit. Impishly, she reached up and tickled it. He lowered his arm and turned away.

"It's early," he said over his shoulder. "You don't have to get up."

"I want to get up if you are. Or could I tempt you back into bed?"

He glanced at her as he pulled on his shirt. Her dark blue eyes were sultry with invitation. The sheet was draped over her lap, but she sat with back straight, breasts bare. Her hair was spilling over her shoulders. Her nipples were high and pointed. She looked like a priestess of some South Seas pagan cult.

He didn't need to be tempted. He wanted her so badly already that he could barely pull the fly of his jeans together.

"No. I need a cigarette."

"You can smoke here."

He shook his head. He heard the apprehension creeping into her voice and avoided looking at her. "I need coffee, too. Do you think Cage and Jenny would mind if I started a pot?"

"I'm sure they wouldn't."

Linc could see in the mirror over the dresser that her eyes were following every single movement he made. Anxiety crept into her expression. She had no doubt expected affection and tenderness this morning. He hadn't even given her a token "morning after" kiss. He couldn't trust himself to. If he ever held her again, he knew he wouldn't be able to let her go.

"I'll see you downstairs." Cursing himself, he headed for the door.

"Linc?" She had used the sheet to cover herself. That more than anything stabbed at his conscience. No longer a beautiful woman, unashamed before her lover, she was now self-conscious in her nakedness. Her smile lacked conviction, but she made a valiant attempt at one. "What's your hurry?"

"I've got a lot to do today. As soon as I shoot the orphans meeting their families, I'm out of here." He couldn't bear her shattered expression, so he turned away and grabbed the doorknob. "See you downstairs."

Once the door was closed behind him, he paused in the hallway. He would have been surprised by the agonized expression on his face. He clenched his teeth to hold back a cry of anguish. Then, expansively cursing life and the tricks fate played on people, he went downstairs.

Kerry let the water of the shower beat against her with punishing force.

It hadn't been a dream. Her body bore the marks to prove it. Even without physical evidence, every precious memory was branded on her mind. Linc had been her lover last night. More than that, he had loved her.

He had been exquisitely tender. Attentive to her every desire and need. Affectionate. Extremely sensual. It was as though he had read her most secret sexual fantasies and fulfilled them.

This morning, he had been a cold, remote stranger, as hostile as when he had first learned that she had shanghaied him. Only this time had been worse. Then he'd been angry. This morning he'd been indifferent. She preferred a negative emotion to none at all.

As she descended the stairs after dressing, her indomitable optimism encouraged her to believe that Linc's distant mood this morning stemmed from his need for nicotine and caffeine, and that after he had had his morning ration of both, he'd be reaching for her again and kissing her with the boundless passion he had demonstrated last night. Maybe he just wasn't a morning person.

She refused to consider the nasty alternative: that she was an "easy lay" and that once he had satisfied his curiosity and gotten his fill of her, he was ready to move on.

But the moment she entered the kitchen, she saw that the latter was true. He glanced up at her indifferently. Not a glimmer of personal feeling was to be found in those implacable golden brown eyes. He gave her a cool nod, then resumed sipping his coffee.

"Good morning, Kerry," Jenny said cheerfully as she spooned Cheerios into Trent's greedy mouth. "Cage, would you please pour Kerry some juice?"

"Just coffee please."

"What would you like to eat?" Jenny moved Trent's glass safely away from the edge of his high chair's tray and deftly wiped milk from his mouth at the same time.

"Nothing, thank you," Kerry mumbled into the cup of coffee Cage handed her. She kept her head down. What had she expected? Professions of love over the breakfast table? He had promised only to give her pleasure. He had kept that promise.

"You look smashing this morning," Jenny said.

"I was just about to comment on that myself," Cage said. "New dress?"

"Yes and thank you." She was wearing a casual, two-piece linen dress in lemon yellow. Her accessories were azalea pink and robin's egg blue. "After bush jackets, anything would look good." Kerry tried to inject some lightheartedness into her voice, but without much success. "Has anyone heard from the children this morning? Are they ready?"

"I checked in on them just a few minutes ago," Cage said. "They're in a state of controlled chaos, but they're getting packed."

"Any leads on Lisa?"

"None so far, I'm afraid," Jenny told her.

Linc scraped back his chair. He hadn't said a word since Kerry came into the kitchen. He hadn't eaten. "I promised Joe I'd carry him downstairs. I'd better go see if I can help him dress." He skulked out.

"Go wash your hands, Trent." Jenny lifted her son from his high chair, a move that earned her a stern admonishment from Cage. "Kerry, there's plenty of coffee. Cage, will you please help me in the laundry room a minute?"

As soon as they entered the utility room beyond the kitchen, Jenny turned to him and asked, "Are you sure you heard Linc go into Kerry's room?"

"Yes."

"When did he come out?"

"What are you, the dorm mother?"

"Did he spend the night?" she whispered.

"I think so, but it's none of our business."

"What's the matter with them?"

"Everybody has an off night now and then."

She shot him a look of consternation. "You never have."

Grinning complacently, he leaned down and kissed her neck. "That's true." Then her mouth got its first honest kiss of the day. "Come to think of it, neither have you."

She squirmed away from him. "You make it impossible for me to remain decent. Ladies as pregnant as I am aren't supposed to feel sexy."

"Their tough luck." Cage reached for her again.

"Cage, stop it. I know what you're doing. You're only trying to distract me from the subject of Linc and Kerry."

"Right. I am."

"We've got to do something."

"No we don't."

"But *what*?" she added, ignoring his response.

"Jenny." He pressed her shoulders between his hands, forcing her to pay attention. "I know I sound like a damn broken record, but I'll say it one more time. It's none of our business."

"They love each other. I know it! I can feel it!"

She was cutest when she was annoyed. He smiled down at her and bobbed his eyebrows suggestively. "You want to feel something? I'll give you something to feel."

"Oh, you're impossible!"

"That's why you love me. Now, unless you want to pay the consequences for locking yourself in the laundry room with a very bad boy, I suggest that we get down to the business at hand. This is going to be a helluva day."

It was almost dusk before the Hendrens and Kerry and Linc sat down on the outdoor furniture on the porch and drew exhausted breaths. The day had been even more hectic than Cage had predicted it would be.

A barbecue picnic had been catered by a local restaurateur to relieve the initial awkwardness of the orphans meeting their adoptive parents.

The couples who had adopted the children were all Kerry had hoped for. She tearfully waved goodbye to the children, confident that each would grow up in a home filled with love.

She had demurred from accepting any praise and shied away from the media. Reporters, who had at last been granted access to the ranch, pressed her for interviews, but she kept them at a minimum. When she did speak with them, she focused their attention on the children who had enriched her life so much over the past year and took little credit for herself.

Roxie and Gary Fleming left for home with their daughters. Reverend and Sarah Hendren had left with Joe only a few minutes earlier. His parting with Linc had been almost too painful to watch. The boy had struggled not to cry. There was a tension around Linc's mouth, too, as he and

Joe solemnly shook hands, exchanging pledges to stay in touch with each other.

Now Trent and Lisa were playing together on the lawn. Lisa gave no indication that she felt rejected. In fact, she hadn't even questioned being left behind.

"There's leftover brisket in the kitchen." Jenny wearily waved her hand toward the house. "Supper is every man for himself."

"No thanks," Cage said, speaking for all of them. "I could drink a beer though. Linc?"

"I really should be getting to the airport."

He was ready to leave. The clothes he had bought in La Bota were packed in a new duffel bag and his new camera and additional lenses were stored in their protective, customized bags. They stood on the porch steps ready to be placed in the car for the drive to the airport. There was a commuter plane to Dallas leaving later that night; there he would make a connecting flight to New York.

Kerry had learned of his travel plans through Jenny. Her heart was breaking, but she refused to show it. She had assumed the same detached air that he had started the day with. Though her image was imprinted on the film in his cameras, she could have been a stranger to him. In a few weeks he probably wouldn't even remember her. She would be just another notch in his belt. Hers would be just one of many names on Lincoln O'Neal's international list of sexual conquests.

Tonight, when it was all over, tonight, when she was alone in the bed where they had shared such splendor, she would cry into the handkerchief he had given her. Until then, she would act as casual as he did. As he had pointed out to her beneath the mesquite tree, she was good at playing roles.

"Surely you've got time for a beer," Cage said.

"All right," Linc agreed. "One beer."

"I'll get it." Jenny pulled herself up by the armrests of her chair. "I've got to go inside to the bathroom anyway."

She took only a few steps toward the front door before she clutched her tummy and exclaimed sharply, "Oh my!"

Cage shot out of his chair. "What is it? Another one of those damn cramps?"

"No."

"Indigestion? I told you to lay off that barbecue. He uses enough cayenne to—"

"No it's not indigestion." Jenny smiled radiantly. "It's the baby."

"The baby?" Cage repeated stupidly.

"The baby. Such as in rock-a-bye baby."

"Oh, Christ. Oh, hell." Cage gripped her arm. "How do you know? Are you in pain? When—" Suddenly his chin snapped up and he peered closely into her face. He even turned her toward the porchlight to see her better. His eyes narrowed suspiciously. "Are you sure?"

Jenny burst out laughing, realizing that he thought she was staging a false alarm to detain Linc. "Yes, I'm sure."

"But it's three weeks early."

"According to the calendar maybe. But Baby thinks otherwise. Now, unless you want me to drop your daughter on her head here on the porch, I think you'd better go upstairs and get my suitcase. It's in the—"

"I know where it is. Oh, hell, it's really the baby. Jenny, will you sit down please!" Cage roared when she took a step toward the door. "Do I call the hospital, the doctor? How far apart are the pains? What can I do?"

"First you can calm down. Then you can go get the suitcase like I asked you to. I'm sure Kerry will call the doctor. His number is posted on the cork board near the phone in the kitchen," she told Kerry calmly. "Linc, would you please check on Trent? I think Lisa just fed him a June bug."

Jenny returned to her chair on the porch and watched with amazement and a great deal of amusement as they all rushed around like headless chickens, bumping clumsily into each other as they raced to do her bidding.

Cage forgot his manners and reverted to using the language he had learned in the oilfields from the roughnecks. Trent was enjoying the crunchy June bug so much that he set up a howl when Linc, who was looking a little green around the gills and moving as though his hands and feet had suddenly grown disproportionately large, fished it out of his mouth.

Of the three, Kerry maintained the most composure. It was her hand that Jenny grasped before the wheel chair rolled her toward the labor room as soon as they arrived en masse at the hospital.

"Everything will turn out fine. I know it." She smiled at Kerry meaningfully as they wheeled her away.

Since Cage was Jenny's birth partner and his participation was required in the labor room, it fell to Kerry and Linc to watch Trent and Lisa and to notify Cage's parents and the Flemings. They were told that for the time being there was nothing they could do and that they might just as well stay at home until further notice.

Cage came to the waiting room to give them periodic reports, which amounted to nothing except that the baby hadn't arrived yet.

"How's Jenny?" Kerry asked him.

"She's beautiful," he said enthusiastically. "God, she's just beautiful."

When he left, both Kerry and Linc were smiling over the man's apparent love for his wife. But when they glanced at each other, their smiles faded. Knowing that her unreciprocated love for him must be transparent, Kerry turned away to check on the two young children. The supply of picture books and Bible stories in the hospital waiting room had been exhausted. Finally Trent and Lisa had fallen asleep on the sofa. Kerry and Linc had, at different times, offered to take the children home, but Cage was insistent that they stay.

"Jenny wants Trent to be here when the baby is born," he told them. "That way he'll feel like he's a part of it."

"Funny how they can sleep through all this hospital commotion," Kerry said now as she ran her fingers through Lisa's dark hair.

"Yeah." Linc's chair was only a few inches from the corner of the sofa where she sat, but it might as well have been miles. "Any prospects on Lisa's adoption?"

Kerry shook her head. "The foundation is working on it."

"I hope Immigration doesn't start hassling you."

Kerry rubbed her hands up and down her arms as though suddenly chilled. "Surely they wouldn't send a child back there." She stared down at the sleeping Lisa, then looked up at him. "Before you leave, I want to thank you again for all you did to get us out."

He shrugged irritably.

"No, please, let me thank you. We wouldn't have made it without you. And before I forget..." She reached for her purse and took out the check she had filled in and signed earlier in the day. She extended it to him.

His eyes dropped from her face to the check. With a sudden movement that startled her, he snatched it from her hand. He read it, noticed that it was drawn on her personal account and that she had a beautiful signature, then viciously ripped it in half.

"What did you do that for?" She had been hoping that by paying her debt, she would feel a sense of finality. As long as she felt obligated to Linc, he was still a part of her life. Until he was extricated completely, she couldn't get on with the business of living without him. "It's untainted. I never touched my father's money. My mother left me an inheritance."

"I don't care where the money came from."

"Then why did you tear up the check?"

"We're even, okay?" he said harshly.

Her lips parted slightly as she sustained another painful blow to her heart. "Oh, I see. You've already been paid for your services." She drew a shuddering breath. "Tell me, Linc, was last night worth fifty thousand dollars?"

Furious, he surged to his feet.

"We've got a girl!"

Cage's sudden appearance startled them. They spun around. He was grinning from ear to ear. "Six pounds, seven ounces. She's beautiful. Perfect. Jenny's fine. No complications. You can see the baby as soon as she's weighed in, foot printed and all that." After he received their hearty congratulations, he knelt down and whispered to his son, "Hey Trent, you've got a new baby sister."

Though Kerry protested, Cage insisted that she go in to see mother and child first. At the end of the corridor, she checked in with a nurse and was led into a postnatal ward. Jenny was the only new mother in there. Her daughter, wrapped in a fuzzy pink blanket and wearing a stocking cap, was cradled in her arms.

"I had almost forgotten how wonderful it is to hold them for the first time," she said serenely as she gazed down into the mottled, wrinkled face that she thought was beautiful.

Kerry was touched by the peaceful expression on her friend's face. Jenny's conversation was liberally sprinkled with Cage's name, and Trent's, and Aimee's, which was the name she had given her daughter.

Kerry left the room, knowing that she'd seen love epitomized. The Hendrens were filled with it. It shone from them. Kerry celebrated their happiness, but also envied it. Jenny's contentment with her husband and children only highlighted the emptiness of her own life.

She had lost her mother prematurely. Her father had died in disgrace. Kerry, hoping to rectify some of the wrongs he had committed, had taken on the responsibility of a whole nation. Oh, she had succeeded in her mission, but what did she have to show for it personally?

In a way, she had been as manipulative as her father. She hadn't resorted to corruption, but she'd been just as fraudulent. People commended her on the tremendous sacrifice she had made. But in her heart she knew that she hadn't made any such sacrifice. What she had done had been for herself, not for the orphans of Montenegro.

She had used them as a cleansing agent to scrub away the stain on her family's reputation. She had endangered nine children, put their lives in peril, so she could feel absolved and guilt free. It was her way of saying, "Look at me. I might bear my father's name, but I'm not like him."

And to whom had she been trying to prove that? To a world who really didn't give a damn? Or to herself?

She returned to the waiting room. Cage was holding his sleepy son on his lap, while in Spanish, he was describing the new baby to Lisa. The little girl was sitting in the crook of Linc's arm. One of her hands was resting on his thigh in an unconscious gesture of trust and affection.

It was then that Kerry knew what she was going to do.

# *Chapter 14*

I wasn't ready for it, were you?'' Cage's question was rhetorical. The passenger riding in his classic Lincoln didn't answer him, but continued to stare out the windshield. ''When Kerry announced that she wanted to adopt Lisa, I nearly dropped my teeth.''

Cage looked across the seat at Linc. He'd been anything but chatty since they'd left for the airport. His rugged features were set and grim. Cage, as usual, was driving too fast, so the scenery was nothing but a blur beyond the windows. The landscape wasn't keeping Linc enthralled and silent. No, his sullenness was the product of something else. Cage had a fairly good idea what it was.

Companionably he went on, ''What do you think made Kerry suddenly decide she wanted to raise a child alone?''

''How the hell should I know?'' The question was explosive, angrily erupting from Linc's chest. ''Why does that woman do anything? She's a wacko.''

Cage chuckled. ''Yeah, that crossed my mind, too.'' He glanced at Linc from the corner of his eye. ''Sure makes for an interesting lady, though, doesn't it? That unpredictability."

Linc made a disagreeable snorting sound, crossed his arms over his chest, and slumped deeper into his seat. "Unpredictability is another word for irrational. I'm telling you she's crazy. Posing as a hooker. Posing as a nun. What the hell kind of rational person goes around pulling dumb stunts like that? She acts now, thinks later." He turned to Cage and pointed a warning index finger at him. "Someday her recklessness is gonna get her into a helluva lot of trouble."

Cage, hiding his smile, thought that Kerry was already in a helluva lot of trouble. Linc O'Neal was "trouble" if he'd ever seen it. Cage liked him better for it. He'd been trouble, too, and had always enjoyed his reputation of being the 'bad' boy in town.

It had been a rough night. It showed on both their faces. Neither had shaved. Their eyes were slightly bloodshot. They were still wearing yesterday's clothes.

But there hadn't been time that morning for them to return to the house before the commuter plane was scheduled to take off. Linc had insisted that he make this plane and not be delayed any longer. He'd also insisted that he could hitchhike to the airport or call the town's only taxi service, so that Cage could stay at the hospital with Jenny. But Cage had been equally as adamant about driving him. Jenny and the new baby were inaccessible during doctors' rounds anyway. After he had dropped Kerry at the house with Trent and Lisa, he and Linc had left for the airport.

The goodbyes Linc and Kerry had exchanged had been brief and polite, with the two of them barely looking at each other. Cage hadn't had the heart to tell Jenny that Linc was leaving. She would be disconsolate when she found out that her matchmaking attempts had apparently failed.

Personally Cage thought that both Kerry and Linc needed a kick in the butt to bring them to their senses, but he couldn't very well lecture Jenny and then go meddling in their affairs himself. Still, it wouldn't hurt to rattle the seemingly unrattleable Mr. O'Neal just a bit.

"I would imagine that Kerry is going to have quite a bit of trouble on her hands. And soon."

Linc's feigned indifference slipped. "What do you mean?"

"First with this adoption thing. She's a single woman. The immigration people specified that the orphans could only be placed with established families so they wouldn't impose an additional burden on the American taxpayers. I'm not sure that they'll consider a single woman an 'established family.'"

"It's no longer all that uncommon for singles to adopt."

"No, but it usually takes longer. And, as you know, there's a time limit on these adoptions."

"They wouldn't send a four-year-old orphan back to Montenegro," Linc said.

"Probably not." Deliberately Cage made his smile too bright and falsely optimistic. "And if they did, knowing how headstrong Kerry is, she'd probably go back with Lisa before she would give her up."

"Back to Montenegro? She'd have to be crazy!"

"I wouldn't put it past her. Once that lady's mind is made up, there's just no changing it. She may look as fragile as a butterfly, but she's as stubborn as a mule. Believe me, Jenny and I found that out."

Linc lit a cigarette with shaking hands. He went through the motions mechanically, and, if his frown were any indication, he derived no pleasure from the tobacco.

"In that respect," Cage continued, "she's a lot like Jenny."

"Jenny doesn't strike me as being stubborn," Linc remarked distractedly.

Cage laughed. "Looks can be deceiving. I didn't think I was ever going to talk her into marrying me. There she was, pregnant and living by herself. I begged her to marry me. She dug her heels in and stubbornly refused."

Linc was staring at him in astonishment. "Jenny was pregnant with Trent before you got married?"

"He's mine," Cage said testily.

Linc held up both hands. "Hey, I wasn't suggesting otherwise. It just seems, I don't know, out of character for Jenny."

"It was. I take full responsibility. Someday when we've got more time, I might tell you the whole sordid story."

Linc settled back into his brooding. "Everything turned out well. That's what's important."

"Yeah, but it was touch and go there for a while." Though the speedometer registered ninety, Cage draped his left wrist over the steering wheel and laid his right arm along the top of the seat.

"I'd been tomcatting for almost twenty years before I slept with Jenny. I'd always taken extra precautions. You know what it's like. I'm sure you never go anywhere without a supply of foil packages in your pocket." Cage grinned a just-between-us-hell-raisers' smile.

Linc smiled back sickly.

"There'd never been an unfortunate accident." Cage smiled wryly. "I was damned lucky. The one time I didn't use anything, I was with the woman I'd always wanted. That first time with Jenny, contraception was the farthest thing from my mind. Who knows," he said, shrugging, "maybe I had a subconscious desire to give her my baby so she'd have to take me in the bargain."

Linc was staring through the windshield again, but he was no longer slumping. His posture was rigid, as though he anticipated being ejected from the seat at any moment. He ran his palms up and down his thighs. He was grinding his jaw.

"Turn the car around," he said abruptly.

"Huh?"

"Stop and turn around. We're going back."

"But your plane leaves in—"

"I don't give a damn about the plane!" Linc barked. "Take me back to the ranch."

Gravel sprayed everywhere when Cage whipped the large, long Lincoln off the highway and onto the shoulder. He executed a flawless U turn and floorboarded the accelerator. He waved to the highway patrolman they passed. The officer only waved back. Catching a bat out of hell was a better bet than catching Cage Hendren when he was in a hurry.

The distance back to the ranch was covered in a third of the time it had taken to get to the turn-around point. To Linc, who was rocking back and forth in his seat while he brutalized the inside of his jaw, it seemed to take forever.

He hadn't even thought of that!

Sure, he'd planned on using something when he left the *cantina* with his "whore." But his supply had gotten left somewhere along the way with the rest of his gear. The morning he'd gone tearing after Kerry in Linc's pickup, he'd been so damned mad that contraception had never even occurred to him.

And, Lord, how many times had there been since then? How many times in that one night of erotic fantasy-come-true had he . . . ? It must have been at least . . . ! He couldn't even count the times.

Cage pulled the car right up to the end of the sidewalk. "If you don't mind, I think I'll go back to the hospital."

"Sure." Linc jerked his bags from the back seat and got out, slamming the car door shut behind him.

"I'll probably be there for the rest of the day. Make yourself at home. If you want to get rid of Trent, call my folks to come pick him up."

Linc was already halfway to the front door. He nodded absently to what Cage was saying to him. Chuckling, Cage put the Lincoln in gear and drove it back down the lane.

In the entry hall of the house, Linc dropped his bags to the floor. The sunlight had been so bright outside that it took a moment for his eyes to adjust to the dimness. Impatient and unwilling to wait, he bumped into several pieces of furniture as he scouted the rooms on the lower story of the house. When they proved to be empty, he took the stairs two at a time.

He pushed open the door to the guest bedroom, but there was no one there. By the time he reached Trent's room, he had worked himself into a froth. *Where the hell was she, for crissake?*

He shoved the door; it went swinging open and banged against the inside wall. Kerry had changed out of the wilted linen dress and had put on a pair of jeans and a cotton camisole. She was barefoot and her hair was hanging loosely down her back. She was sitting on the edge of the twin bed where Lisa lay sleeping. Trent was softly snoring in the other one.

For a moment, they only stared at each other.

Then Kerry bounded to her feet. "You scared me half to death!" She kept her voice down so the children wouldn't wake up, but was as angry as a spitting cat because he had caught her crying. "Why did you come barging in here like that? I thought you were a burglar!"

In three long strides, Linc was beside the bed and gripping her arm. He pulled her off the bed, across the room, and out the door. When they were safely on the other side of it, he thrust his chin out belligerently and said, "No problem. If I'd been a burglar you could have impersonated a karate expert."

"Very funny. And let go of my arm." She wrested herself free of his grasp. "I just got those children to sleep. They were exhausted, but too excited to settle down. Then you come charging through the door like a rampaging bull and— Wait a minute. I thought you'd be on your way to Dallas by now. What are you doing here?"

"Proposing."

Kerry gaped at him. "Proposing? Proposing what?"

"Marriage, of course. What does a man usually propose to a woman?"

"Lots of things. Among them, marriage is usually the last resort."

His face was dark and fearsome with annoyance. "Well that's what I'm proposing. Marriage."

"Why?"

"Because I make good on my obligations, that's why. On the way to the airport, Cage reminded me of something."

"What?"

"That we didn't use anything to keep you from getting pregnant." He bobbed his head firmly, as though he'd just dropped a bomb of startling information. "You didn't think of that, did you?"

Her hesitation was so fleeting that he didn't even notice it. For a fraction of a second, she entertained the thought of letting him go on believing that they'd been careless. But earlier that morning, she had resolved that she would never use people again for her own gain. She couldn't trick Linc that way; it would be unconscionable. By the same token, it enraged her that the only reason he had come back proposing marriage was because he felt obligated to do so.

"As a matter of fact I did."

That served to suck the wind out of his sails. Kerry took a great deal of pleasure in watching his puffed up arrogance fall like a knifed souffle.

"I thought about it over a year ago," she told him triumphantly. "Before I went to Montenegro, when there was a very real possibility that I might be raped by guerrilla soldiers, I started taking birth control pills. So, Mr. O'Neal, you've got nothing to worry about. You're relieved of your 'obligation.' Now, if you'll excuse me, I'm very tired."

She spun on her heel, but took no more than a few steps before he grabbed the seat of her britches and jerked her to a halt. "What now?" she demanded.

"You're forgetting something else," Linc said.

"Well?" Kerry folded her arms over her chest and all but tapped her foot with impatience.

Curbing an urge to strangle her, he said, "Lisa. Do you honestly think they'll let you adopt her?"

"Yes."

In spite of her ready affirmation, Linc saw the chink in Kerry's confidence and, like a mountain climber looking for footholds in the side of a sheer cliff, dug into it. "Well I'm not so sure. And neither are Cage and Jenny. He mentioned it on the way to the airport."

"I'll exhaust every possibility."

"You still might lose."

"Then I'll take her to live someplace outside the United States, to Mexico, anywhere."

"Oh, and that would be just dandy. A terrific life for a kid, having no sense of stability, no country to claim."

"I won't give her up," Kerry cried softly. "I love her."

"So do I!"

The words echoed down the wide hallway. After the reverberation, the resulting silence was filled only with the sound of their breathing.

"You do?" Kerry asked in a soft voice.

He nodded curtly. "It was tearing my guts to shreds to leave her this morning. Did you see the way she clung to my neck, not wanting me to go?"

"She cried when you drove off, even though she had promised you she wouldn't."

Linc was visibly moved. "See? She loves me, too."

Kerry's heart had begun to race, but she wouldn't let herself get too optimistic. She'd been disappointed too often in the past. She looked at the floor. "You could apply to adopt Lisa yourself."

"I'd have the same problems as you. Maybe even more because I'm a man. We'd have a better chance of success if we applied for her as a couple. And it would be best for Lisa. She needs both a mother and a father. I know."

Kerry's heart twisted with love. The basis of Linc's remote nature came from his never having known parental love. She wanted to throw herself against him, to cover his beard-stubbled chin with wildly happy kisses, but she restrained herself.

"That's still not a good reason to marry," she said, playing devil's advocate. "We'd be burdening Lisa with the tremendous responsibility of keeping two adults happy with each other."

"We wouldn't have to depend on her for our happiness."

"Wouldn't we?"

He turned his back to her and moved away. He slid his hands, palms out, into the seat pockets of his jeans. When he turned back to her, he looked more vulnerable than she'd ever seen him. "Lisa's not the only reason I want us to get married."

"No?"

"No. I, uh, I wasn't too hep on the idea of leaving you either. You're a pain in the ass, but I still want you."

"In bed?"

"Yeah."

"I see." Her heart sank like lead.

"And—"

"And?" She lifted her head quickly and looked at him inquiringly.

"And . . . I, uh . . ."

"What?"

He ran his hand through his hair and blew out his breath. He looked supremely irritated. "Cage said you could be damned stubborn. You want to hear me say it, don't you?" Kerry only looked back at him innocently. He swore softly.

Then, flinging his arms out to his sides, he said, "I love you, okay?"

"Okay!"

Kerry launched herself against him. He caught her, closing his arms around her and holding her close. Their mouths searched for and found each other. The kiss they exchanged was torrid and left them gasping for breath.

"I thought you'd never say it."

"I didn't think I ever would either. Not while you were awake anyway."

*"Awake?"*

"It doesn't matter," he said, laughing. "I love you, Kerry. God knows I do."

"I love you, I love you, I love you."

"I'll probably make a terrible husband. I'm mean. Rotten. Crude."

"Wonderful. Talented. Brave."

During another hard kiss, he lifted her up to straddle his lap. She wrapped her legs around his hips and locked her ankles behind his back. He ate at her chin and neck while he fiercely whispered endearments.

When he pulled back, his eyes speared into hers. "I don't have much to offer in the way of worldly goods. I don't have a pot to—"

She pressed her fingers over his lips. "You should have kept that fifty thousand dollars. You'd be that much richer."

"Very cute." He kissed her fingers aside. "I'm serious, Kerry. I've got money. I've been stashing it away for years, but I don't even have a suitable roof to put over our heads."

"I do. I have a lovely house in Charlotte, North Carolina."

"You never told me that."

"You never asked. It's beautiful. I know you and Lisa will like it."

"You've also got a college degree."

"But I don't have a single Pulitzer Prize and you have two."

"You know how I make a living. I'll be away a lot of the time."

"No way, Lincoln," she said, shaking her head. "If you think I'm going to turn you loose on a world full of beautiful women once you're my husband, forget it."

"You can't be suggesting that you come along."

"I certainly am."

"You and Lisa?" he asked incredulously.

"Think what an asset we'll be."

"Name *one*."

"How many languages do you speak?"

"I've almost mastered English."

"Well I speak four and have a working knowledge of three more. With us teaching her English, Lisa will soon be bilingual. Think of all the help we'll be to you."

"Yeah, but in a few years, it'll be time for Lisa to go to school and—"

"I'm a teacher, remember? I'll tutor her."

"But that's not quite the same. She'll need—"

"Linc, are you trying to weasel out of this already?"

"No. I just want you to know what you're letting yourself in for."

"I do." When he still looked skeptical, she said, "Look, we went through hell and came out loving each other. It can only get better from here."

He smiled and then gave a shout of genuine laughter. "You've got a point."

"Everything will work out. We'll make it work. One day at a time, okay?"

"Baby, when I can feel your heat this close, I'd agree to anything." He hitched her up higher. "If we didn't have so many clothes on, do you realize—"

"I've already thought of that."

She squirmed against him and he grimaced with supreme pleasure. Carrying her, he went into the guest bedroom. As soon as her legs slid from around him and her feet touched the floor, they began tearing off their clothes, depositing them on the floor with heedless disregard for tidiness.

They moved into the adjoining bathroom, tacitly agreeing that a shower was in order. Linc reached into the shower stall and adjusted the water taps. He stepped in and drew Kerry in with him.

Beneath the spray, their mouths met as eagerly as their bodies. Their hands were so busy they regretted having to take the time to soap them, but when they did, their pleasure was multiplied a hundred times. They moved against each other with the sleek seduction of sea animals in a mating ritual.

He turned her around, put her back against his chest, and ran his hands over her front, massaging her breasts, rolling her nipples between his soapy fingers. His hard sex probed between her water-slick thighs. That slippery friction was breathtaking. When he slipped his fingers into her, she was as wet and warm as the water that trickled down their bodies.

Their skin was still damp when he laid her on the bed and bent over her. "We'll fight."

"All the time."

"You don't mind?"

She reached for him. "Linc, don't you know by now that you have to go through a little hell . . ."

He gave himself to her and completed the thought. "To get to heaven."

Silhouette Sensation

COMING NEXT MONTH

## NOTHING IN COMMON
Elda Minger

Burt Thomson lived in the San Fernando Valley with his two sons, their enormous sheepdog, Wadsworth, and total chaos. The day that Wadsworth redesigned their neighbour's flower garden — for the third time — Burt knew he had to get help. Sandy Hensley took no time to work her own special brand of magic on the Thomson family and soon proved that she and Burt had a lot in common…

## NIGHT MOVES
Heather Graham Pozzessere

Bryn had to retrieve the photos she'd taken of rock star Lee Condor — her young nephew's life could depend on it. But *why?* And how could she possibly get them back from Lee? She had made an enemy of him precisely because he would be too dangerous as a friend — or a lover!